Jon Cleary is often referred to as one of the statesmen of Australian storytelling. He was born in Erskineville, Sydney, in 1917, and has been a self-supporting professional writer since the 1940s, working in films and television in the United States and Britain.

He is also one of Australia's most versatile writers. His most famous novel, *The Sundowners*, the epic tale of an Australian outback family, has sold more than three million copies, and his work has been translated and published in 14 countries. With his Scobie Malone crime series he was labelled 'the best practitioner of Australian crime fiction' by the *Sydney Morning Herald*. A number of the recent Scobie Malone stories have been optioned for a television series.

Jon Cleary has collected a number of literary prizes, including the coveted Edgar Award, the Australian Literary Society's Church Medal for Best Australian Novel, and the Award for Lifelong Contribution to Crime, Mystery and Detective Genres at the inaugural Ned Kelly Awards.

With *Miss Ambar Regrets* Jon Cleary has again shown his versatility by creating a classic love story.

Miss AMBAR REGRETS

JON CLEARY

HarperCollins*Publishers*

HarperCollins*Publishers*

First published in Australia in 2004
by HarperCollins*Publishers* Pty Limited
ABN 36 009 913 517
A member of the HarperCollins*Publishers* (Australia) Pty Limited Group
www.harpercollins.com.au

HarperCollins*Publishers*
25 Ryde Road, Pymble, Sydney, NSW 2073, Australia
31 View Road, Glenfield, Auckland 10, New Zealand
77–85 Fulham Palace Road, London, W6 8JB, United Kingdom
2 Bloor Street East, 20th floor, Toronto, Ontario M4W 1A8, Canada
10 East 53rd Street, New York NY 10022, USA

National Library of Australia Cataloguing-in-Publication data:

Cleary, Jon, 1917– .
  Miss Ambar regrets.
  ISBN 0 7322 8155 5 (hb).
  ISBN 0 7322 7633 0 (tpb).
  I. Title.
A823.3

Cover design by Christabella Designs
Cover image: photolibrary.com
Typeset in Sabon 11.5/17 Sabon by HarperCollins
Printed and bound in Australia by Griffin Press on 70gsm Bulky Book Ivory

5 4 3 2 1   04 05 06 07

For Isabel, Vanessa and Natascia

Chapter One

1

'Jack,' — Les Dibley had begun work on a country newspaper, had reported the world and now, after forty years' loss of illusions, was news editor at Channel 15 — 'gird your loins and go over and interview Miss Ambar.'

'Who is Miss Ambar and why do I have to gird my loins?'

'Because she's an absolute dish' — Les is fifty-eight years old and occasionally speaks in ancient tongues — 'and we know what your loins are like. She's the second lead or something in a pilot they're shooting, though they say she'd have trouble playing a fencepost.'

Les has six demented kids and a wife who spends her time clouting the kids with one hand and turning the pages of *The Perfumed Garden* with the other. He comes to work to escape all that bedlam and repressed lust. Or so he says. I met Mrs Dibley once and she struck me as a plump happy woman who would turn only the pages of a cookbook and protect Les against the loss of any further illusions.

'You're sending me to interview an *actor*? Am I being demoted?' The usual demotion was to interview a pop star. I was a senior crime and disaster reporter and in those days, at twenty-six, had all the self-esteem that a career in front of a camera encouraged. 'Why me?'

'Mr Entwistle suggested you,' said Les and blessed himself. He was an atheist who had his own God, only so that he could mock him. God was Jared Entwistle, the channel's chief executive. 'He is taking a personal interest in Miss Ambar.'

'If she's such a babe, why don't you interview her?'

'My loins couldn't stand the excitement. Talk to her today and we'll shoot it tomorrow morning. Two minutes max.'

'An actress satisfied with two minutes on camera?'

'Actors are satisfied with a snapshot from a Box Brownie, so long as it's in focus.'

'What's a Box Brownie?'

I left him, went out through the rear of the newsroom and walked across to the single large studio where the channel shot its in-house productions. They were usually not above the level of cheap 'reality' shows with names like *Best Boy* and *Best Girl*, featuring amateurs with no talent and who mistook energy for personality; but somehow such shows got ratings and advertisers and that was all that counted.

Channel 15 was the youngest of Sydney's four commercial networks; doomed, said all the experts, from its outset. But, with a shrewd board and a cost-conscious CEO, concentrating on the 18–35 demographic and with a staff who worked their butts off in the hope of offers from the larger, better-paying channels, it had survived and was always in the black, or one of the darker tones of grey. I had been there for three years and stayed, I told myself, because I liked working for Les Dibley. I had a lazy man's contempt for ambition, content with what I had. A hundred thousand a year, a mum and dad and sister who loved me. And no encumbrances.

I was a loner, but not lonely. I preferred the company of a woman to that of a group of men. Sure, the lure was sex, but it was a better vice than binge drinking and how to make more money. Saturday afternoons I played tennis with three guys; after a couple of beers they went home to their wives and I took a girl to dinner and to bed. Okay, it might seem selfish, but I never thought of it that way. That was the way it was in the summer of 2001.

It was a bright blue sky day, the sort of day when a man — well, a young man — thinks all the girls in the world should smile at him. I was a romantic back then, if on a day-to-day basis. Long-term romance was something to be avoided.

I went into the studio building, into the half-world that is a TV set. Crews were setting up a hospital triage desk; some of them knew me and nodded greetings. A girl in a nurse's uniform went by, gave me a look that indicated triage on me, and passed on. I was News, which meant I wasn't artistic and creative. I called after her, 'Where can I find Adele Ambar?'

'Out the back.'

I walked on through the building, past half a ward, half a kitchen, half a police squad room — the walls of how we live taken down for the cameras. Out in the sunshine again I stopped, looking for Miss Ambar, the dish who couldn't act. I don't wear sunglasses — you can't wear them on camera and I've learned to do without them — so I squinted around, then saw her. She was lying on a sun lounge under a beach umbrella, reading a book. That was a good sign: if she could read a book she might be able to string two or three words together.

'Adele Ambar?'

She looked up, raised her sunglasses. 'Yes?'

'I'm Jack Shakespeare —'

'You're kidding.' She smiled, perfect teeth in a perfect mouth; at least she had a sense of humour.

I pulled up a canvas chair, sat down, the sun behind me.

'I have to interview you, they want to do a small piece on you for tomorrow's news.'

'Have to?' Again the smile.

'It's my pleasure.' Then I, too, smiled; chatting up girls was one of my lesser skills. 'What are you reading?'

She looked down at the book on her lap as if it were no more than a prop, as if it belonged to the character she was playing in whatever show she was in. 'The biography of Edith Evans.'

I nodded. *Who the hell was Edith Evans*? 'Interesting?'

'You haven't a clue who she is? Or was?' Again the perfect smile, but a little twisted this time.

'No.' I had learned in my three years chasing news that fame can be as fleeting as a summer shower.

'A great English actress, last century.' Last century had finished only a few months ago, but already it had the sound of the Middle Ages. 'Some day I'd like to be half as good.'

I'd had time now to take stock of her. She was, as Les Dibley had said, an absolute dish. Black wavy hair that hung loose, dark blue eyes, thick straight brows, straight nose, cheekbones and jawline that looked as if they had been carefully sculpted, lips that sneered at the need for collagen. And a body and legs — she was in shorts — that invited the better adjectives. Sure, I know I sound as if I'm writing a commercial, but I'm also a reporter and a reporter is supposed to tell the truth. Up to a point, that is: libel has many angles.

'Can we mention her in the interview?'

'No.' Even then she had a sort of cool authority, as if she had so many things worked out. Which later made me wonder how she could be so self-deceiving. 'That would make me sound big-headed.'

'Maybe it would just make you sound ambitious? There's no harm in that.'

'Are you ambitious?'

'No.' Suddenly, in my own ears, that sounded smug.

She looked at me, as if for the first time. 'Are you a show business reporter?'

'No, I'm Channel 15's senior crime reporter.' Where had she been?

'Sorry, I only watch the ABC news.' But she smiled again as the dagger went in. The national non-commercial network attracts snobs, we commercials used to say.

So far I was getting nowhere. I took out my tape recorder. 'Maybe we could start with where you come from, how you got into show business?'

'I'm not in show business. I'm in *acting*.' She *was* a snob. Ah well, you couldn't have everything.

She came from out beyond Orange, on the western slopes. Her parents ran a sheep-and-cattle property there; wool and cattle were still selling when she was growing up and she had been sent to a private school in Sydney. Leaving school she had trained for two years at farm management — 'But I had always wanted to act, even at school. So I enrolled in the Bialoguski Academy.'

'In Russia?' That was quite a jump.

'No, in Erskineville.' An inner-city area, not large enough to be a suburb, a planet away from Moscow and St Petersburg. 'They specialise in The Method method.'

'I thought Method acting went out when Marlon Brando got fat.'

'Do they teach you cynicism at Channel 15?'

'No, they teach it at journalism school, you major in it.'

Then a voice called from the back of the studio building. 'Adele, time to go!'

She lifted herself off the sun lounge; I noticed she moved gracefully, as if she might have done some modelling. Or perhaps she was acting. 'I'm sorry,' she said. 'Maybe we can talk later?'

'I can't — I'm due at the courts this afternoon. A guy is to be sentenced for rape, a pretty dirty one.'

She wrinkled the perfect nose, but it wasn't that she was lacking in compassion: 'Is the girl all right?'

'I think so, other than the long-term effect. Look,' I heard myself say, 'are you free tonight? Dinner?'

The sunglasses were back down over her eyes but I

could tell she was measuring me. Then she nodded. 'Why not? I'll be here till seven.'

'It's a date.'

And that was how it all started.

2

The rapist got twelve years and his family, shouting that he was innocent and the girl was a slut, attacked me and my cameraman outside the court. I got a bruise over my eye, a cut lip and a torn shirt; the cameraman had his camera pushed into his face, breaking his nose. The perils of intruding on the guilty. It was what Les Dibley called 'ripe news' as distinct from 'rotten news'.

Back at Channel 15 the first aid girl from the canteen attended to my eye and my lip, kissed me on the cheek and told me I'd live. I got out a clean shirt from my desk, I always keep a spare in my desk, went to the washroom, showered and came out looking reasonably respectable.

'Go home, have a beer and a nice lie-down and I'll see you in the morning,' said Les.

'Can't. I'm taking Miss Adele Ambar to dinner. On expenses.'

'Not on expenses, son, unless it's Pizza Hut. Channel 15 can't afford extracurricular research. Good luck. I was right, right? She's a dish. Gird your loins.'

'Loosely,' I said.

She was waiting for me outside the studio building. Her hair was pulled back in what I think is called a chignon;

she wore a dark blue dress, sleeveless, with four gold buttons down the front. A blue-and-white silk scarf was round her throat (I later found she had a fetish for scarves) and a light blue cardigan was thrown over her shoulders. I stopped thinking of her as an interview and thought of her as a date.

'What happened to you?' She sounded really concerned, took my hand and peered at my face.

'The rapist's family thought he was innocent. Rupe, my cameraman, and I were the nearest targets. The judge and the Crown Prosecutor had skipped out the back door.'

I led her, still holding hands, across to the parking lot, where my MG was. Each year I bought a different car, always second-hand to keep the price down; it was showing off, but nobody sneered at it, not back then. The Olympics had finished only months ago; the IT bubble (though nobody recognised it as a bubble) was still getting bigger; greed and ostentation were virtues. Economic rationalists preached from ivory towers like mullahs from mosque balconies. Though in those smug, innocent days very few knew what a mullah was.

She looked at the car with approval, which made me look at her with more approval. She took the scarf from round her throat and tied it over her head. She slipped her arms into the cardigan and I helped her. It was cashmere, so she wasn't short of a quid. Whatever else she was, she was the product of a private school, her parents ran wool and cattle, she was safe and comfortable. Except, as I was to discover, from the termites of ambition.

I took her to Jasper's in Hunters Hill, a small quiet

restaurant in an area, almost an enclave, where the past lingered like shadows and money spoke to money in quiet tones, unlike in the eastern suburbs across the harbour, where it was loud and brash. I live on the Lower North Shore, as it is called, though, aquatically speaking, it is the real north shore. We like those from across the water to apply for visas when visiting us.

When we walked into the restaurant everyone looked at us; or at her. I had that sudden feeling of possession, no matter how temporary, that men get when the woman they are with is admired. Foolishly, I wished for a larger audience. I should have taken her to a football final.

We were seated at a table that gave us a good view of the room. She glanced around, then said, 'Damn!'

'What's the matter?'

'An ex-boyfriend.'

An ex-boyfriend, not *the*: I sensed a team of them extending into the distance. I glanced sideways and saw two men and a woman at a table on the far side of the not-large room. The younger of the two men was looking at us and I recognised him.

'Tod Maddux?'

'You know him?' She sounded unworried.

'Only by repute or whatever you want to call it.' He had been an international cricketer without ever becoming a star, the sort of player who came and went like a waterboy. Then he had retired and become a sports agent, handling cricketers, footballers and swimmers as commodities. I wondered if he had handled Adele, then put the thought out of my mind before it got out of control.

'Forget him,' she said; she had a way of taking command of a conversation, as if it were a tennis match. 'He's history.'

'We don't talk history? I'm supposed to be interviewing you.'

'Forget that too, or dinner's already over.' But she smiled and I forgave her; as became habit in the future. 'Where do you live?'

'Are we going back to my place after this?'

'No.' Still smiling.

'I live down the river, in Longueville. At home, with my sister. My parents are in New York — my dad's a press officer with the UN.'

'Living with your sister, doesn't that cramp your love life?'

'I only go out with girls who have their own place.' None of this was meant to be taken seriously; it was just snip talk, cutting the barbed wire that is often there on a first date. 'Where do you live?'

'Kirribilli. My parents have a flat there they never use, except when they come to town to shop.'

'Alone?'

'No, I have a flatmate, an actor.'

'An actress?'

'No, an ac*tor*. He has no money and I let him live rent-free to keep the place neat and tidy.'

'And is he? Neat and tidy?'

'If you mean does he make passes at me, no, he doesn't. He's gay.'

Why did I feel relieved? We were only half an hour into our date and I was already trying to get rid of competition.

We slowly got to know each other, living, if you like, a fortunate life. But that was how it was in the summer of 2000–2001. A comfortable existence; no bubbles yet burst; a belief in honesty, at least for chief executives; and terrorism still more a word than a fact. Another country.

We were at the coffee stage when she looked up and said softly, 'Oh shit!'

Maddux was coming towards us, face aglow with a smile like cheap neon. 'Adele!' He sounded as if he always spoke in exclamations, like a fast bowler appealing for acatch behind. I waited for the Nijinsky leap, but there was none. 'What a coincidence! I was going to call you!'

'I wasn't hanging on the line.' She was cool, like an umpire who had said no to the appeal. 'Oh, this is Jack Shakespeare.'

He nodded, with no recognition: another bloody ABC-only viewer.

'Sorry to barge in.' Like hell he was; he'd have barged into a funeral service. 'Del, love, I've got something I'd like to talk to you about!'

'You're a sports star too?' I said to her. I knew I was acting like an idiot, but Maddux had that effect on me. And on others, I'd bet.

'No, she's not,' he said, not looking at me but directly at her. 'It's a photo shoot, Del, two weeks in Italy!'

So he had branched out to a models' agency. I could see the sudden interest in her eyes, but she remained cool. 'Call me tomorrow, I'll be out at Channel 15.'

'You've changed your number —'

'So I have,' she said, as if she had forgotten. She might not know how to act on stage or in front of a camera, but she knew how to play hard to get. 'I'll call you.'

He could take a rebuff, he'd had plenty of practice. 'Do that — tomorrow. I'll tell them to hold the job for you. Well, my friends are waiting for me. Nice seeing you again, Del, you look great! You, too ...' As if he had forgotten my name.

'Shakespeare,' I said. 'Will.'

When he had gone she looked at me and smiled again, something she hadn't done when he had been at the table. 'I'd hate to cross you in an interview on camera. You're like those fascist guys on *Fox and Friends*.'

'I thought you only watched the ABC? I'm sorry, but he just got under my skin. What did you ever see in him?'

'It's none of your business, Jack.' Her voice was still cool, not sharp or offended. 'I'd like some more coffee. And a brandy, please.'

'To steady the nerves,' I said, but managed to smile.

'No,' she said, 'men never make me nervous.'

I took her home to Kirribilli, another enclave, just east of the Harbour Bridge. On the point are the Sydney residences of the Prime Minister and the Governor-General, but no political mist hangs over the area nor is there any genuflection on the part of the local residents. The PM and the G-G go past in their official cars and get no more attention than if they were a passing bus. The bent knee and touching-the-forelock are rare diseases amongst the natives.

We pulled up outside a tall block of flats on the ridge

facing the harbour. It was a warm night and some flats had their balcony doors open; some ancient from another age was playing Peggy Lee, one of my father's favourites, singing 'Alright, Okay, You Win'.

'Peggy Lee,' I said.

'Who?'

'A contemporary of Edith Evans.'

She laughed and hit me, which was a good sign. I went to get out of the car, but she put a hand on my knee. 'No, don't come up.'

'Neat and Tidy is home?'

'Probably. But I'm not a girl who offers encouragement on a first date. I like you, Jack, but we take our time, okay?'

'Alright, okay, you win.'

'Did you get enough tonight for our interview tomorrow?'

'Bits and pieces. But I still have to find out what makes you tick.'

She leaned across and kissed me on the bruise above my eye. 'We'll see.'

'Is that a yes or a no?'

'Whatever.' A code word of that time, meaning everything and nothing.

3

But I didn't get the interview.

'She's been sacked,' said Les Dibley. 'The producer and the director prevailed over Mr Entwistle. The deciding scene, I hear, was one she had with a dog. The dog out-acted her.'

'Why was Entwistle promoting her? Was she one of his girlfriends?'

'Who knows? Mr Entwistle lays them end to end, like dominoes. You look disappointed, Jack, son. I hope you haven't fallen for the lady?'

'No.' But I wondered if I had put a foot off the ledge. 'I just found her . . . *interesting*.'

Les sat back in his chair. He was a short, squat man with a beer belly and a red, mottled face that would never be allowed on camera. There were rumours he had been a ladies' man in his youth, but it must have been in another body and with another face. I sometimes wonder what I'll look like in middle and old age, but never linger on the thought. The future must always look bright and young, not wrinkled and sagging.

'Jack, one in four women are *interesting*. The ratio is worse in men, but don't quote me to our male colleagues. *You're* interesting, Jack, but don't let it go to your head — you still have a long way to go to be *really* interesting. Also don't let it go to your head that Miss Ambar is interesting. Be professional.'

I waited a week, because I didn't want to intrude on her if she was down in the dumps about her sacking; I didn't want to embarrass her, though I learned later that embarrassment was not one of her weaknesses. I covered a drive-by shooting, another rape trial, a domestic murder–suicide. The Olympic spirit of just months before had evaporated, gone when they doused the Games' flame.

I bought a dozen red roses and drove down to Kirribilli. It was another warm night and the balcony doors were open, but tonight it was Eminem or some other yeller. When I pressed the call button on her flat number, a male voice answered: 'Yes?'

'Is Adele there?'

'No. Who's this?' I told him and he said, 'Oh, she's mentioned you. Come on up.'

I hesitated, but when the buzzer sounded on the security door I pushed the door open and went into the lobby and to the lift. When I got out of the lift on the ninth floor Adele's flatmate was standing in an open doorway. He looked at the roses and said, 'Oh, you shouldn't have.' I was glad there was no one standing in the doorway to the other flat on that floor.

But he smiled as he said it and his voice wasn't camp. Why had I expected it to be so? I'm not homophobic, I told myself, but I was still wearing some of the prejudices that had clung to me since my teens.

'Come in. Adele's gone to Italy.'

That almost stopped me, but he looked welcoming enough and I was curious. Not about him, but about her. I was doing due diligence, though I didn't think of it as that.

'I'm Tom Barini.' He was slim and dark and anonymously good-looking, the sort of actor who would always be in supporting roles. He had a good voice, but it sounded sad, as if he lived with disappointment. Which, I guess, is the natural habitat of most actors. 'Shall I take those or do you want to save them?'

I handed him the roses. 'They probably won't last till she gets back. How long's she gone for?'

'Two weeks. I spoke to her an hour ago, she's in Milan.'

'Catwalk stuff?'

'No, it's a *Vogue* model job. Underwear.'

'Do models wear underwear?'

We were fencing, appraising each other; but he was on safer ground than I was. Or more established.

'Like a beer?'

I looked around the flat while he was in the kitchen getting the beers. It was neat and tidy, all right: a place for everything and everything in its place. There was a studio photo of him and another one of her, like business cards at the ready in case a producer or director called. There was a small bookcase, full (at a quick glance) of books on the theatre. The furniture was Ikea, the carpet was wall-to-wall bargain, and on one wall was a good-sized painting of a colonial homestead. The sheep-and-cattle property?

I noticed two bedrooms that opened off the small hallway where I had come in, and I wondered if he made up her bed or she did it herself, tucking in the sheets neat and tidy. Neither my sister, Lynne, nor I had neat bedrooms.

He came back with the beers, in tall glasses, not cans, and led me onto the balcony that looked over the harbour and across to the Opera House and the sequin-starred facade of the city skyline.

'Why do they have so many lights on at night?' he said, and I sensed he was like me, feeling his way.

'It has something to do with the power surge when they turn 'em on and off.'

A long pause, then: 'Adele said you were going to do an interview with her.'

'They called it off.' I sipped my beer, then said, 'How'd she take it when they dropped her?'

'Pretty badly, I think, though she's never been keen on TV work. But she hides her feelings. Or from me anyway.'

Then I said bluntly, like a crime reporter, 'How good is she as an actor?'

He sipped his own beer, looked out at the city skyline as if there might be lights there to tell him what to say. He was reluctant: 'Not good ... I'm a movie buff, I collect books on old movies, rent videos of them. Years ago there was a movie with Gary Cooper and George Raft.'

I had seen old movies with Cooper in them, stiff-faced and awkward, but I'd never heard of George Raft.

'There was a scene between them outside a cigar store. In those days American cigar stores had a large wooden statue of a Red Indian outside their front door. Cooper and Raft played their scene beside the wooden Indian. A critic wrote that the Indian over-acted and should have been cut from the scene.' He took another sip from his beer. 'Adele would make a good bride for the wooden Indian.'

'My grandfather used to say that Hedy Lamarr was the most beautiful non-actress he'd ever seen. You ever see her in late movies? She couldn't open a door, let alone an expression, but doing nothing and saying nothing you couldn't take your eyes off her.' I sipped my beer. 'Have you ever told Adele what you think?'

He looked at me as if I'd asked if he had ever raped her. 'Good God, no! Jesus, I love her too much to say anything like that to her.'

'Love her?' Still the crime reporter.

For a moment he had been stiff and angry; but suddenly he relaxed, gave me his pleasant smile. 'Not like that. She tell you I'm gay?'

'Yes. Sorry I asked that question. Both questions.'

He was silent for a while, then he said, 'What's your interest in her? Aside from wanting to interview her?'

'I'm not sure.'

'You married? Got a partner or a girlfriend?' He sounded like a stern father or a big brother.

'Not at the moment.' There had been three in the past six years, but somehow the relationships had become unravelled, like sweaters worn too long. Though I guess none of them would have liked to think of themselves as knitwear. 'It's not just her looks. It's ... I dunno. Does a guy ever know what attracts him to a woman? I mean, a hundred per cent certain?'

He smiled again and I found myself really liking him. 'Look who you're asking. Jack, tread carefully. I wouldn't want to see her hurt.'

'I'm a long way from doing that to her.'

I left half an hour later and went home to Longueville. The suburb is as old as a bed of lava; house prices wouldn't recognise the word *bargain*. The Shakespeare house was a solid 1920s' blue-brick with a wide porch across half its front. It had a wide lawn bordered by azaleas and camellias, all looked after by a gardener who came in once a fortnight. Along the front was a low blue-brick stone wall, a low parapet against invaders. The whole lot suggested *family*, solid values of the long ago. It gave me comfort, as if occasionally I needed to look back at faded photos where everyone was smiling.

Lynne was in the living room, watching 'Law & Order', a favourite program with both of us. She wore a terry-towelling robe and her head was wrapped in a towel; she was filing her nails while the two New York cops interrogated a suspect. She never went out on Thursday nights; it was repairs night. She was a very ordered person except in her love life. She was good-looking in an unremarkable way: brown hair cut short, blue eyes, a generous mouth. The mouth had been too generous, kissing guys who never stayed. She had left home twice to live with men she thought would make her happy. She was home again now after another lesson in disappointment.

'You're home early. You get a knockback?'

I took off my tie and jacket, kicked off my shoes and slumped down opposite her. The house had been furnished by my mother, not us. The furniture was like the house: solid, a little dull, comfortable. There were two good paintings on the walls, one by Justin O'Brien, the other by Frank Hodgkinson. On the mantelpiece over the 1920s' fireplace was a photo of our mother and father, young and full of optimism before the sepia of cynicism clouded them.

'She's in Milan for two weeks. You know her? Adele Ambar?'

'She did some modelling for our summer catalogue.' Lynne is 2IC in the marketing office of Australia's biggest department store. She believes anything can be sold. Except love, as she has discovered. 'You know how to pick 'em.'

I didn't answer. Lynne and I knew each other too well; there was just two years between us and I never played the older, know-everything brother. She had never told me what broke up her relationships, but I had seen the scars before they had faded.

'She's got one drawback,' she said, eyes on her nails. 'She's in danger of becoming one of those no-talent celebrities that clutter up the Sydney scene. You should warn her.'

'Oh, sure. Why would she listen to me, a guy who's taken her out just the once? I met her flatmate tonight, a guy named Tom Barini. He's gay and I think he's in love with her —' Lynne looked up from her nails. 'Okay, he loves her like a brother.'

'You're sweet,' she said and gave me the sort of smile she had given me when we were kids and fought and she won.

'He told me she's a terrible actress, almost a joke.'

'That's what I mean, a no-talent celebrity. I saw her in a small role at the Ensemble. It was embarrassing, but the guys in the audience drooled over her. Are you drooling over her?'

'Not yet,' I said, and gave her the same sort of smile she had given me.

Then we turned our attention to 'Law & Order'. I had three half-scripts in the closet in my bedroom, all of them half-finished because I couldn't get near the conciseness, the quick establishment of character, that I saw in the Matt Wolf series. The quality was always there in his work, but it wasn't there in my own scripts and I knew it. It wasn't modesty that made me reach that assessment, it was more lack of purpose. Which, as I would come to realise over the coming months, was the difference between me and Miss Ambar.

Chapter Two

1

She came back from Milan a week later. I waited a few days, then I called her.

'I wasn't sure you'd want to do the interview,' she said.

'That's off, I'm afraid.'

She was silent a long moment, then she said, 'I guessed it would be.'

'I was going to ask you to dinner again. No interview.' Why did I sound nervous in my own ears? Was I afraid of being knocked back, of everything, whatever it was, being over before it began?

Again there was the silence. Over the coming months I would realise that she often gave considered answers; she was not impulsive. Yet there was that contradiction, that seemingly never considered opinion of herself as an actor.

Then: 'Tom told me you brought roses.'

'Yeah, I did. From me, not Channel 15.'

Then abruptly: 'Tonight? Pick me up at eight. Are you the punctual sort?'

'Very.' I hated to be kept waiting, as other girls had found; one girl, who told me she hadn't been on time at her own birth and wasn't going to change, walked out on me after two dates. But in the months ahead, with Miss Ambar, I'd do a lot of waiting and be surprised at my own patience.

'I'll be ready.'

She was, came down to meet me as soon as I'd pressed the buzzer. She wore a pink dress with a pink fringed drape or shawl round her shoulders. Her hair had been cut short in a bob or shingle, whatever they call it, with a fringe. She was still a dish.

'Where were you thinking of taking me?'

'Jasper's again.'

'The same people own a restaurant here in Kirribilli — Milsons. I sometimes take Tom there, when he has no money and needs a lift. They know me.'

Indeed they did; it was the Queen of Sheba dining out. But I was introduced and the waitress recognised me. 'Oh, I've seen you on the news. Channel 15?'

I could have kissed her. She took our orders for drinks and went away. The restaurant was larger than Jasper's and noisier, but it wouldn't have mattered if we were in the Olympic stadium. I was just happy to be with her and to be seen with her. Possession is nine-tenths of the male vanity.

'How was Milan?'

'Fabulous! The Italians really have something ...'

Berlusconi and the Mafia and cars that have to be kept at 5000 revs or they splutter out. We're here in Australia, Miss Ambar, I thought, home of the Holden, the meat pie and the sports hero of the moment. None of which I subscribed to ...

'I went to La Scala — I'm not an opera fan, it's too artificial —' She saw my raised eyebrow. 'What's the matter?'

'You're in fashion and you're calling something else *artificial*?'

'Oh, I can see you and I are going to get on well! You're an opera fan?'

'No, I'm like Tom — I'm a movie fan. And the occasional play. I've even been to symphony concerts. *Dragged* along, but I went and enjoyed them. Ballet, no. Books, yes. That's me culturally. Now what about you?'

'So this is an interview, after all.' But she smiled and raised her glass, champagne, to me. 'We'll get along, Jack. Don't rush it.'

So I didn't. I found myself looking beyond her looks. She was a country girl born and bred from several generations of country folk, but the bush had never been meant to hold her. There might be memories of dust between her toes and bindi-eyes stuck in her feet, but she wouldn't treasure the memories.

'Tom comes from the country too, outside Perth. What do you think of him?'

'I like him,' I said.

'You're not a gay basher?'

'No. I don't want to hold hands with them, but I get along with them. He's in love with you, you know.'

'I know,' she said without the slightest hint of false modesty. 'And I love him. But it's brother and sister love. He has a brother back home, but evidently they don't get along. I comfort him when some of his affairs fall apart.'

'What happens when yours fall apart?'

'I'll tell you when we know each other better.'

'I think we're getting to know each other better by the minute.'

'Let's order dessert,' she said and gave her attention to the menu.

Over the next half-hour we'd catch each other looking at each other; nothing was said, but there were questions and answers, or half-answers, in our glances. There is an old proverb, *Four eyes see more than two*, which has nothing to do with wearing glasses. I just wondered if she was seeing what I was, faint and dyslexic as it might be. Love in the distance.

I drove her home through the sort of night that poets invent or that they experience more than the mundane rest of us. When we pulled up outside her block of flats I waited till she said, 'You want to come up?'

There was no music playing, no Peggy Lee nor bang-the-drum, twang-the-guitar rock'n'roll nor anything from artificial opera.

'Is Tom there?' I didn't want to sit around in a threesome and I certainly didn't want to go into her bedroom if he was in the next one. That was, if I was asked into her bedroom and I had the feeling I was going to be.

'No, he's gone bush. They're touring country schools, doing potted versions of Shakespeare.'

'I was always embarrassed being potted.'

'Do you write your own jokes or are they out of some school book?' That was taking us up the garden path to the front door. 'It must have been hell for you at school with your name?'

'Not as bad as another guy, his name was Streisand. He was always being asked to sing.' I could carry a tune, so long as it was light: '*Send in the clown — where is the clown? — don't bother, he's here.*'

'How'd he take it?'

'He's a lawyer now and threatening to take a class action against the whole class.'

That took us up in the lift, where the perfume she was wearing seemed to thicken, which is a good sign, as I have learned. I took her hand and she smiled at me and I was glad Tom Barini was out in the bush potting that other Shakespeare. As her flat door closed behind us I took her in my arms and kissed her, long and deep. I slipped the stole off her shoulders and fumbled at her dress.

Then she said in a strangled whisper, 'Be gentle, Jack. It's been a long time . . .'

I frowned, but said nothing. What did she mean? But now was not the time for conversation. I kissed her again and went on undressing her. Naked she was beautiful all over. Except . . .

'It's called a Brazilian wax, all models do it. I did that lingerie shoot for *Vogue* and the briefs were *very* brief. I'm naturally pretty bushy down there and bits kept peeking out. The photographer said it was distracting him.'

Talk about a bad hair day . . . 'It would have doubled the male subscription to *Vogue*,' I offered.

'So the photographer suggested a Brazilian —'

'The photographer did *that*? Did he get out of focus?'

'Relax, a make-up girl did it. You don't like?'

It looked like Groucho Marx lying on his side and leering; but now was not the time to be a crime reporter. 'It's ... decorative?'

Then she laughed, came into my arms again and put her tongue in my mouth.

Tutored in homage to the clitoris, I was not a bull at a gate. But don't hang around waiting for a sweaty description of the next hour. In my second year at university I read an old novel by Evelyn Waugh. In it he reduced a seduction to its bare essentials, a one-line paragraph: *That night I took formal possession of her.* I remember I fell out of bed laughing; it was the first time I'd encountered the stiff upper lip in sex. Ever since then I'd never been able to read erotic passages without wondering how Old Evelyn would have rendered them. He'd have reduced the *Kama Sutra* and *The Perfumed Garden* to books on etiquette.

So just leave our hour to: *I took informal possession of her.*

When exhaustion finally stopped us, I lay looking at her, marvelling at my luck. Then I heard myself say, 'I'm falling in love with you.'

She looked at me for a long moment, then said gently, 'Not yet, darling. Not yet.'

'Not yet?'

'I've had guys saying to me since I was fourteen that they were falling in love with me.' I stared at her, but it wasn't conceit; she was just stating a fact that worried her. 'I've disappointed all of them.'

'Jeez, how many were there?' I'd never had this sort of pillow-talk before.

She laughed; my hand was on her belly and I could feel the laugh starting down there. 'Jack, that's none of your business.' She turned towards me. 'I haven't done anything with my life so far. I want to act, to be on stage, be someone *else*, show what they're feeling ... Didn't you want to be what you are, a TV reporter? You're successful —'

'Del, it's not something I want to be doing for the rest of my life. Twenty, thirty years down the track, still standing in front of a camera talking about some bastard rapist or a guy who's murdered his wife and kids.'

'What *do* you want then?'

'I'm not sure.' Now was not the time to tell her about the half-finished scripts in the bedroom closet; I wasn't sure that they were stepping-stones to what lay down the track for me. There is a trap in being comfortable too soon. 'I'm taking my time.'

'Well, so am I. With men who want to fall in love with me.'

'You're conceited,' I said, but I didn't believe it.

'No, I'm not. I just know what I was lucky enough to be born with. I've got two very good-looking parents — my mother is beautiful. It's just genetic, nothing to be conceited about. You're not bad-looking — do you stand in front of the mirror sometimes and admire yourself?'

Not *bad*, looking; I'd actually thought I was better than that. 'No, I look at myself on the screen, when I'm on-camera, and think why the hell did I twist my mouth like that or do something wafty with my hands.'

'You *are* conceited,' she said.

I was fondling her breasts, happy as a kid in a playpen full of balloons.

'Careful,' she said. 'They're not basketballs.'

Then she laughed and rolled on top of me.

Later, she got off the bed and went into the bathroom. When she came out she looked down at me and said, 'Goodnight, Jack.'

'I'm not staying?'

'No. That may happen some time in the future, but not tonight. I'm sorry —'

'Miss Ambar regrets?'

'If you like.'

But there was more to it than that. There was something behind her eyes that I couldn't fathom, a look of pain. Questioning people for television, I have learned to look into eyes. But I am still learning.

'Okay.' I got out of bed, put my hand on her shoulder and stroked it, loving the satiny feel of skin and flesh. 'I'll hang around till the Brazilian is fully grown again, okay?'

'I'll let you know,' she said, shadows still behind her eyes.

2

Two mornings later I had just got out of bed when my mobile rang. It was Les Dibley: 'Get out to the helipad, the guys are waiting for you. There's been a terrible pile-up on the Mitchell Highway, just north of Orange, a tourist bus and a semi-trailer. Christ knows how many dead. Call me soon as you get there.'

I can hurry without panicking. I shouted to Lynne that I had to leave in five minutes and when I came into the kitchen she already had some toast buttered for me and instant coffee ready. 'I know I sound like Mum, but you're not going off on an empty stomach.'

'I might have an empty stomach when I get out there,' I said and told her what had happened.

'Bloody disasters — why do they always make the best TV news?'

'Don't blame us. Blame the viewers.'

It is the defence of all journalists, but it is true. Or partly true: both sides of the TV screen are to blame. Notice the difference when we present *good* news, say a kid reunited with his lost dog. Goo runs down the screen like tears.

Channel 15 is up on the Epping Road, which runs north-west out of the city towards middle-class suburbs. It has a nature reserve on one side and is backed by some light industry on the other. Our helicopter can take off from its pad there without complaints from nearby residents. Viewers want the news, but with the sound down, please.

The crew were waiting for me. Rupe Hellinger, broken nose repaired, was already in the chopper. He's in his late forties, short and muscular, a wheeler-dealer, a joke with the rest of us. He once tried to pay his Visa account with his Visa card, to get the bonus points. But business, despite recent jokes in it, has no sense of humour. Rupe was also a Stoic, or so he claimed, though he was always wondering aloud why everything happened to him.

This morning he was not joking. 'I'm not looking forward to this. I covered the Kempsey bus smash.' A horrendous two-bus crash some years earlier. 'Fucking horrible.'

I looked at Jason Tully, our sound man, six months into the job and still starry-eyed at his luck. 'If it gets too much for you, let me know. Don't throw up on my shoes.'

'I'll be okay,' he said, but he sounded doubtful.

'If you blokes are ready?' Joe De Luca, our pilot, was old enough to be my or Justin's father. He had flown in Vietnam but never spoke of it. He had seen and delivered enough horror.

We lifted off and headed west towards the Blue Mountains, climbing quickly into the geography of clouds, white continents that broke into islands as we flew beneath them. I was always surprised at the wilderness still in the valleys of the mountains, not much more than a hundred kilometres from the coast. Then we were moving down over the western slopes and the vast plains lay ahead of us, the outback and the edge of the world. There had been good spring rain and I marvelled, as I always did when I was part of the eye in the sky, at the green peacefulness. Homesteads, solid as rocks, stood amongst clumps of trees; dams were pewter shields laid down in peace; a mob of sheep moved slowly like a cloud shadow on a windless day. We came in over the town of Orange, which also had a peacefulness, from this height, of its own; we picked up the Mitchell Highway and headed north. Then we saw it.

'Holy Christ!' shouted Rupe Hellinger.

There in the huge peaceful painting was the defacement: a glinting, twisted mass of metal in the middle of the long stretch of road, ambulances and fire engines and police cars strung out beside it. As we came down in a paddock I saw that a semi-trailer and the tourist coach had collided head-on and a second semi-trailer had ploughed into the back of the coach, turning it into a silent concertina. I turned my mind away from the thought of what had happened to the people in the coach.

We were not welcomed, we never are, but nobody tried to obstruct us. A local TV crew was already at work, but they too ignored us. It was two hours since the accident, but firemen and others were still trying to cut the dead from the wreckage. I knew enough not to talk to the ambulance medics right now and went looking for a senior police officer. I found him, a grey-haired inspector, standing beside his car, fatigue and shock disfiguring his broad, sunburned face.

'How'd it happen?'

He looked at me as if to tell me to piss off; then he shook his head. From long experience, I guessed, he knew that bad news had to be reported. 'Am I allowed to swear on camera?'

'You can if it helps. It'll just come out as *beep-beep* on tonight's news. Things can be fucking terrible, but not on television.'

He nodded. 'Yeah. One of the drivers, the bus driver or the bloke in the semi-trailer, must of fallen asleep. They hit head-on, like you can see, the other semi-trailer ploughed into the back of the bus.'

'How many were in the bus?'

'Forty-four. There are twenty-two dead, not counting the three drivers, and the rest of the passengers are in a pretty bad way. It's fucking terrible.'

'Thanks, Inspector.'

I followed Rupe Hellinger as he took his camera amongst the carnage. Aid workers, ambulance medics, firemen, cops looked at us with real antagonism, but none of them said anything: we were a necessary evil in today's voyeuristic world. I was surprised at how suddenly sympathetic I was to their point of view.

We moved back to the side of the road, with the mass of twisted metal in the background, and I did my piece. I noticed that Jason was white-faced, but his hand holding the powder-puff mike didn't shake.

When I'd finished I looked along the road and saw a woman standing alone, face buried in her hands, her shoulders shaking as if she were freezing from some cold wind the rest of us couldn't feel. For a moment I was tempted to move towards her, but pulled back. Her grief, shock, whatever it was, was her own. I turned back to Rupe and Jason: 'I'm staying. You guys go back to Sydney.'

'Why?' asked Rupe.

'There's got to be a follow-up to this. The relatives will be arriving soon. The story's only half-over.'

I stepped over a railing fence and retreated into a paddock. I stood in the thick lush grass and called Les Dibley on my mobile, told him I'd stay overnight and interview relatives as they arrived.

'You can't keep your crew there —'

'They're on their way back, Les. I'll hire the local crew, and I'll pay for it out of my own pocket if you're worried about the bean-counters in the main office —'

'Pull your head in, son. You're talking to your immediate boss. I'm not worried about the bean-counters — fuck 'em. I don't want you going to pieces out there amongst all the grief that's gunna happen —'

'I'm holding up, Les. I just don't think we can walk away from this as a single piece on a bloody dreadful accident. I'll be back some time tomorrow.'

There was a silence for a moment, then he said, 'Look after yourself, Jack. Bring me something worthwhile, something to balance the shit about celebrities and the bullshit from politicians.'

I clicked off my mobile and looked around for the weeping woman, but she was gone. I was glad.

Our helicopter took off, taking with it what I knew would be the lead item on tonight's news. If the end of the world doesn't happen in New South Wales, it won't be the lead item on Channel 15. I hung around for another half-hour, managing a word or a few with the medics and the firemen, then I bummed a lift back to town with the police inspector, Gerry Hardman.

'Do you like your work?' he asked.

'Not jobs like this, no. There must be things you don't like about yours.'

He nodded, eyes on the road; he was driving carefully, I thought, as if afraid of what might come down the road straight at him. He had a deep, dry voice that seemed to come up through sand in his throat. 'The next few days, when the relatives come ... some will be here tonight. That why you stayed? Leave it, son. Talk to 'em tomorrow, not tonight.'

I said nothing for a few miles, then I asked, 'You know a family out here, the Ambars?'

He turned his head then, frowning. 'The Ambars? They're an institution out this way. They've been here since Captain bloody Cook. Where'd you hear of 'em?'

'I know their daughter.'

'Adele? She's an actress now, isn't she? Down in Sydney.' He made it sound as if she were in Antarctica.

'Sort of. She models too.'

'Yeah, she'd be good at that. She was a beauty, every young bloke in the district was panting after her.' He let me consider that, then he said, 'You her boyfriend?'

'No,' I said, separating myself from those who were panting after her. 'Just a friend.'

'You want to meet her dad? He'll be in town, he's the shire president. We called him soon's we heard about the ...' For a moment he seemed lost for a word. 'That out there on the highway. He'll be organising accommodation for the relatives when they arrive, getting 'em into hotels. Him and the wife, they're a great team, everyone respects 'em.' Then he looked sideways at me again. 'They miss Adele.'

'I can understand that,' was all I could say.

We were coming into the outskirts of the town. Orange was one of the earliest towns on the western side of the Great Dividing Range, as an early map-maker, given to copy-writing, described it. First settled 175 years ago, the town grew and grew, but it never reached the size some of its earliest promoters predicted — 'one of the great cities of the continent'. Gold was discovered close by 150 years ago and the small city had been in the money, one way or another, ever since. It had wide streets, a beautiful city park, and the solid, almost smug air of a town safe from the insecurities of those equally smug centres on the coast.

The police station had been built in the 1950s or 1960s, a product of government architects of those days who thought in terms of package design rather than architecture. It was designed not to fall down, the main requirement of the politics of the day. Any aesthetic-minded crim, being led into it, would have been depressed.

Luke Ambar was at the station, just about to leave. I was introduced to him and at once he said, 'From Channel 15? Well, what d'you know! Adele has told us about you.' He was the strong, garrulous type; words exploded from him: 'You're staying on? Interviewing the relatives? Good idea! Where're you staying? Not booked in? Come out and stay with us, my wife'll be delighted to see you. So how is it out there, Gerry?'

'Fucking terrible,' said Hardman; then grinned wearily at me. '*Beep-beep.*'

Ten minutes later Luke Ambar was driving me out to Bulinga Creek, the family property. I sat beside him in the Range Rover, saying little, not able to say much because of him. He could talk under a flood with or against the flow. He was of medium height, broad and compact, dressed in blue work shirt, moleskins and a broad-brimmed hat, the archetype man from the bush. And he was handsome, no doubt about it. It's genetic, Adele had said, and I could see what she meant.

We turned off the main highway just short of the accident scene. He glanced towards it in the distance, the sun glinting on the twisted wreckage as if it had to be highlighted, shook his head but made no comment. I waited, still not saying very much, to see what Mrs Ambar would be like.

'You're not very talkative for a TV commentator,' Ambar said, then turned his head and grinned at me. 'Adele and my wife are always at me to shut up. But I was born talking, so my mother said. My dad was the same and his dad before him. It's genetic.'

Half an hour's drive out of town we turned off the road into a gateway between two fieldstone posts and drove up a long avenue of poplar trees, still full of summer like tall green bottles of perfume.

'My grandmother planted those. She went to France when she was young and fell in love with French roads, always lined with poplars. She was a gay old bird, had more boyfriends than our prize ewe.'

Granny Ambar sounded a bit like her great-granddaughter.

We came out of the avenue of poplars, swung round a circular gravel drive in the middle of the well-kept lawns and gardens, and pulled up outside a wide-fronted solid house that could have been a vice-regal residence. The Ambars, it was plain, were Old Money, with a capital O and a capital M and lots of capital to back it. This was the house in the painting in Adele's flat.

Luke Ambar was still talking: 'My great-great-grandfather built this. He came out here from Sydney in 1848, walking all the way, took him a month or more. He came to Ophir during the first gold strike. He was one of the lucky ones, he struck it rich and held on to it. He never went back to Sydney. He bought land around here, 40,000 acres originally, when it was cheap. We have 6000 now, around 3000 hectares as they like to call it these days.' He sounded a trifle sad, as if through some fault, maybe his, the Ambar world had diminished. He said, almost as if I was not there, 'It's in my blood.'

I had never learned what my great-great or even my great-grandfathers had ever done. My maternal grandfather had been a postman, never struck gold or won even a small lottery, just delivered such notices to the lucky ones. My paternal grandfather had been a gardener working for Frank Packer and he had told the newspaper mogul that my father, while still at school, wanted to be a newspaperman. And Sir Frank, who had soft spots in a flinty heart, got my father started as a copy boy on the old *Daily Telegraph*. If my family had any old money it was just coins forgotten in a bottom drawer.

I got out of the Range Rover and there, standing on the wide verandah at the front of the sprawling house, was Adele twenty years down the track. The resemblance was uncanny, even the smile was the same. And, as Adele had said, her mother was beautiful.

'Look who I've brought home, Kate — Del told us about him. From Channel 15 — Fred Shakespeare.'

'Jack,' I said and shook Kate Ambar's hand.

'You're covering that dreadful smash down the highway?' Even the voice was familiar.

'Yes, I'll have to be getting back to town after lunch.' I had decided I couldn't wait till this evening or tomorrow, as Gerry Hardman had advised, to interview the arriving relatives. Les Dibley wouldn't appreciate my spending an evening with a girlfriend's family. 'They'll want something from me on the late news.'

They showed me through the house and I saw what Adele had left behind: comfort, security, love. The house was a museum that was still alive: Victorian furniture, a painting by Rupert Bunny of the poplar-loving grandmother, woodwork that shone under a century or more of polish. Adele had left all this for — what?

'She hankered to be an actress from when she was about twelve,' said her father. 'Have you seen her act?'

'No. Have you?' I put the question as tentatively as I might put questions later to the grieving relatives arriving in town.

'Just the once,' said her mother and closed the subject as if clamping a lid on it. 'Shall we have lunch? It's ready.'

It was cold chicken, salad, cake and white wine. Kate Ambar brought it to the table in the huge kitchen and I noted there didn't seem to be any help in this big house. As if reading my thoughts Mrs Ambar said, 'Luke's grandmother had four servants in her day, even his mother had two. Today, I have a woman who comes in three times a week. The good old days have gone forever.'

I looked at and listened to these people who, I began to realise, were coming to terms with losing their daughter.

And I noticed the occasional quietness in him, of spirit, when he would suddenly stop talking. One hundred and fifty years of heritage would be sold to strangers because Adele would never come home.

'Are you one of her boyfriends?' he asked abruptly.

I've been to bed with her. But his question was wider than that. 'No. Just a couple of dinner dates, that's all.'

He was suddenly ... sad? I wasn't sure, but he was certainly less talkative, as if, though I was only a dinner date, I had brought Adele back here.

Kate Ambar looked along the table at him, then abruptly she stood up, spoke to me. 'I have to go into town, I'll drive you back.'

The atmosphere had changed. I wasn't made to feel unwelcome. Luke Ambar was suddenly talkative again, telling me how they hoped they might see me again, either here or down in Sydney. But I had brought Adele back home, only as a ghost.

We left Bulinga Creek in Kate Ambar's Volvo, sliding down the long avenue of poplars as down a chute, then out onto the road back to town. She drove fast, but kept her eyes on the road. I looked at her, at her profile, and said, 'You're so like Adele.'

'No, I'm not. The looks, yes, but other than that ... I knew what I wanted when I was eighteen and I settled for it. It was my husband. I saw Luke and knew I wanted to spend the rest of my life with him. Our disappointment was that I couldn't have any more children after Adele — Luke would have loved a son. He loves Adele, adores her — Why am I telling you all this?'

'Because you think I may have some influence with her?' I shook my head. 'I haven't.'

'Are you in love with her?'

I had known other girls' mothers, but none of them had been as direct as this. It was almost mid-Victorian: are your intentions, sir, honourable? 'I'm not sure. I'm taking my time.'

'Why? What are you taking your time for?'

'Because I'm not sure of her. Not like you were with your husband.'

She took her eyes off the road for a moment, looked at me, then concentrated on her driving again. We rode in silence for a mile or two, the countryside stretching away on either side of us in green peacefulness, as if there were no troubles in the world.

Then she said, 'She can't act, you know.'

I hesitated, then said, 'So I'm told.'

'She'll improve, but she is never going to be the great actress she dreams of being. She'll finish up one of those middle-aged actresses you see in soap operas and second-rate films, competent and that's all. And she'll be sad eventually, because she'll realise it all too late.'

Then suddenly she took her foot off the accelerator, let the car coast to a stop. Still gripping, and I mean *gripping*, the steering wheel, she closed her eyes and I saw the tears at the corner of them. Half a mile down the highway was the crushed beer-can wreckage of the bus smash, but it was not the sight of that that had brought on the tears. I put my hand on her arm. Like most men, particularly Australian men, I was awkward with women. But I was learning.

'Kate —'

She blinked, took out a handkerchief and wiped her eyes. 'Sorry ... There are painters who will never be artists ...'

'Writers the same.' Maybe this one. 'There was a poet, a man named McGonigle, the world's worst, who always thought he was as good as Keats and Shelley —'

'I've heard of him.' She started up the car again, drove on, slower this time. 'I'd hate Adele to be the McGonigle of the theatre.'

Then we were pulling up outside the hospital on the edge of town. She switched off the engine and looked at me. 'Did she mention Peter to you?'

'Peter? Peter who?'

Resting her hands on the wheel, she looked straight ahead for maybe half a minute. Then she looked back at me. 'Treat her gently, Jack.'

'Why?' That was what *she* had said. *It's been a long time.*

'Peter was a local boy, he was in love with her, had been since she was about thirteen or fourteen. She liked him, but she was never in love with him. He committed suicide eighteen months ago.'

'She's never said a word about him.'

'It shattered her. Everyone — his parents, Luke and me. Peter wasn't ... he wasn't *unstable*, but he was — I guess the word is highly strung. He took everything much more seriously — he was born here, raised here, but in some ways he was never a country boy. Adele took off right after his funeral, went to Sydney ... I don't know if ambition is her way of trying to forget ...'

'I'm glad you told me, Kate. I'll tread carefully.'

'Don't say I mentioned Peter. Let her tell you in her own time . . .' She started up the engine, nodded at the hospital. 'This is the best place for you to start your interviewing. Or the worst.'

'I never enjoy it,' I said. 'Thanks. For everything.'

'I hope we meet again soon.'

She drove away and I went looking for the cameraman and the soundman from the local station. I hired them and we did four interviews, with me trying to be as gentle as I could. I arranged for the interviews to be beamed back to Channel 15, thanked the guys for their cooperation and said they would be paid, and got a lift out to the airport.

I flew back to Sydney on the evening plane. As we banked out of the airport I looked north, but Bulinga Creek was lost in the dying of the day. I wondered where or how Peter whoever-he-was had committed suicide over a girl who didn't love him. But that was a story I never wanted to cover.

3

Two days later Miss Ambar rang me: 'I hear you met my parents.'

'Yes. Nice people.'

'What did they say about me?'

'They love you like a daughter.'

'None of your TV wit. My mother likes *you* . . . What are you doing tonight? I have two tickets for —' She named a theatre in the northern suburbs that put on solid, comfortable plays. '*The Cherry Orchard*. Do you know Chekhov?'

'Not personally . . .'

'Oh shit! What have you got there, a book of jokes?'

But she was laughing and I laughed with her. Laughter is a sort of glue, but it is unreliable. 'I'll pick you up. Adele . . .'

'Yes?'

'I'm falling in love.'

She stopped laughing. 'Forget it. Pick me up at seven.'

I clicked off my mobile, sat back in my chair and looked up to see Hilary Reingold, our PR girl, seating herself on my desk and crossing her very attractive and lissom legs. I have taken her out a few times between girlfriends and have been between those lissom legs. Viagra-on-the-hoof, it was she who taught me the clitoris has more nerve-ends than the CIA. In another age and another country she would have been a courtesan, ideal training for public relations. She is blonde, pretty rather than beautiful, intelligent, and some time down the track there will be heartache. She loves her job, she says, more than she can ever love a man. I sometimes wonder how much she believes it.

'You've taken Adele Ambar to dinner. How'd it go?'

'Where do you get your information?'

'Publicity is like the CIA — we have our sources. And we're more reliable.' She is anti-American, but *sotto voce*, as she likes to say. Channel 15 buys all its overseas shows from the US. It has heard of the BBC, but only vaguely.

'Why are you interested in Miss Ambar? She was fired.'

'Because dear Mr Entwistle is up the wall about it.'

'About me taking her out to dinner?'

'About her being fired. He and the director of the pilot aren't talking to each other. Jared wants her back.'

Jared was Mr Entwistle. 'I think there's Buckley's chance of that. She has her pride.' I wasn't sure that she had, but I didn't want her coming back to Channel 15 on Entwistle's say-so. I didn't realise it then, but I was trying to build a stockade round her, a post at a time. It would be a long construction job. 'Am I being roped into something?'

'I'm not sure. He wants to see you.' She looked at me shrewdly, a cousin who knew a little too much about me. 'You haven't got a thing for her, have you?'

'I like her,' I said. 'I've taken her out to dinner twice. Not to interview her.'

'Why do guys confide in me?' she asked the almost empty room.

'Because you ask intimate questions.' I wasn't going to confide too much. 'There's nothing going between us, Hil. She's a looker, I like her and that's all there is to it. But I'm not going to talk about her with Entwistle.'

'Tell him that.' She slid off my desk, kissed me on the forehead. 'He's waiting to see you now.'

I walked across to the administration building and into the large reception area. The walls featured huge blow-ups of the channel's stars, some almost as big as the egos, that flashed their smiles at unsuspecting visitors as they entered. I wondered how Charlene, the receptionist, managed to survive the day amidst the gallery of huge faces. 'Don't they get you down?'

She was young and pert and impregnable and thought The Beatles and The Rolling Stones were cavemen groups. 'Only when they appear in person. But don't quote me. Mr Entwistle is expecting you.'

He was, indeed; he was on his feet as I came in the door to his big office. He was what I think is called floridly handsome, big, beefy and with his thinning hair on top camouflaged by the thick hair along his temples. He wore a blue shirt, white collar and cuffs, and his trousers were held up by bright blue braces. He was heartily affable, but I knew that was something he could put on with the cuffs and braces. He was a bean-counter, the most ruthless sect since the Assassins.

His office was a temple of vulgar extravagance. Three of the walls, one with a picture window in it, were papered with green woven wallpaper; the fourth wall was Japanese goldleaf paper at, it was rumoured, a thousand dollars a roll. The walls also held photos of Entwistle with celebrities, real ones, not the Sunday social pages ones. Entwistle with Steve Waugh, Cathy Freeman, Ian Thorpe; with John Travolta, President Clinton and Nelson Mandela. No one could remember his ever having met Mandela and it had been suggested (by Les Dibley) that it was an old black piano player from a revived jazz trio. On a sideboard there was a metre-long model of his ocean-going yacht (half-owned by Channel 15). At the staff Christmas party each year it had become the custom (suggested by some anonymous idiot) to present Entwistle with a small gift for the shelves of his office. They were all there: paperweights that looked like cannonballs, ancient maps, a gold-embossed *Encyclopedia of Television*. Les Dibley had once suggested we give a can of borers for the model yacht, but that had been overruled by the few crawlers and brown-noses on the staff. Entwistle seemed oblivious of the fact that the whole company mocked him.

'Coffee? Beer? Something stronger?' The corporate-box treatment. I wasn't to be ticked off.

Entwistle was a corporate-box regular at all sporting functions, his second home. He and his wife and two children lived under the same roof in Bellevue Hill in the eastern suburbs, an ingot's throw from the estate of the nation's richest man; but husband and wife went their separate ways. Hilary Reingold, who had a satellite eye, had told me all about them. Mrs Entwistle was famous for her bosom, revealed night after night at social gatherings as canyon-like cleavage. During the day, summer and winter, she displayed it in cashmere; her floormops were also said to be cashmere. Their two girls went to an exclusive Catholic school and, Hilary said, had been disappointed to learn that the Virgin Mary, despite her connections, had had no social ambition. They were the family from Bellevue Hell.

'No, I'm fine, thanks, Jared.' He liked to be called by his first name, except when he was firing you.

He went round behind his desk, as if to remember to establish the pecking order. 'I liked those interviews you did out at Orange. They gave a sort of ... dignity to the Late Night News. Beautiful.'

'Thanks, Jared. One does one's best.' A stiff-necked politician had once said that to me in an interview.

'Of course, of course. I try for the same.' He sat back suddenly in his chair, stared at me, then said, 'You did an interview with Adele Ambar.'

'It never got to that,' I said cautiously. 'I took her to dinner, but she never opened up.' An unfortunate phrase and I wished I hadn't used it.

But he took it up. 'She didn't open up about that unfortunate sacking from our pilot?'

'She didn't mention it at all.'

'She was ideal for it. She has that touch of class it needed.'

I had only a vague idea of what the pilot and the series were about; it was another of the flood of police series on TV. There were more cops on TV than cooks, which was saying something.

'We need class on TV and she has it. I told her that —' Then he stopped, clamped his thick lips together as if chiding them for being too loose.

'I hear you took her out a second time,' he said, opening the lips again.

I wanted to ask where he got his information, but you didn't ask an Assassin where he got his knife. 'Yes. But still no interview.'

'She's a lovely girl, isn't she?'

The bugger's keen on her, maybe infatuated. How much encouragement had she given him? Had he got her into bed? Jealousy spread over me like a rash. But I remained cool, if not calm. 'I think everyone would agree on that. Even the director who fired her.'

'He wants her back.' I could see the gun held at the director's head.

I took a risk: 'Jared, am I being asked to do something?'

He said nothing for a moment, then he nodded. 'She won't speak to any of us. I've called her, he's called her, so has Hilary. She just hangs up on us. You're our last resort, Jack.'

'Jared, I've got no influence with her at all. We never even discussed the series —'

'Try, Jack. Ask her to come in and see us. The part is still there for her —'

'You haven't filled it yet?'

'Well, yes, there's a girl in it. But we haven't signed her yet — she's on trial.'

I'd heard it before: actors are just cattle. And I was being asked to persuade the prime — cow? ewe? — to come back to the market.

'Well, I'll see what I can do . . .'

'That's all I'm asking, Jack,' he said, in a voice that meant that was all he was *telling* me. 'Use the technique you used on those relatives out at Orange. Subtle.'

Tasteless as an Assassin. 'I'll do my best, Jared.'

But as I left I wondered how much influence I would have with Adele.

Chapter Three

1

None, as it turned out. I brought up the subject while we were driving to the theatre. 'Jared Entwistle had me in his office —'

'Forget it, Jack. I wouldn't go back there if they offered me the *lead* in the series — I was only going to be decoration anyway. Mr Entwistle is not one of my favourite characters.'

'He's got a crush on you.' I looked at her sideways while we waited at a traffic light. She was in pale blue tonight, a dark blue scarf holding her hair in place in the open car. I wondered what she had worn when she went out with Jared. Talk about borers in his model yacht; they were nothing to the borers of jealousy. 'I think he's a dirty middle-aged man.'

She looked sideways at me and smiled. 'You're wondering, aren't you? No, he never got me into bed. He tried his luck and I used my knee. I almost gelded him.'

The light turned green and I shot the car away on a surge of relief.

The theatre was in a quiet tree-lined street, surrounded by one or two small shops and solid houses. This was a long way from the bright lights of Broadway or the West

End or whatever she aspired to. She took off the scarf, did her hair, then turned to me. 'How's that?'

'Beautiful.'

She took it for granted, clutched my hand and led me into the theatre. It could not have had more than five or six hundred seats at the most and every one was filled. These were solid North Shore middle-class burghers and their wives, sure of themselves and their surroundings and their neighbours. Maybe only half-realising it, the country was developing its own castes.

As we settled into our seats people looked at her, but it was not with any sign of recognition: it was her looks, not her identity, that attracted attention. She seemed oblivious of it, but I wasn't. She was mine — for tonight. Again I got that feeling of possession, no matter how fragile.

'I love the proscenium stage, don't you?' she whispered. 'I hate theatre-in-the-round. You're acting in the audience's lap.'

'I remember sitting under Lady Macbeth once —'

The curtain went up on Chekhov. I'm no drama critic, but the production struck me as competent, no more. The actress playing Madame Ranevsky, a soap opera star taking a holiday, was competent. That was the operative word, but Adele sat leaning forward all through the performance, eyes shining, lips silently mouthing the words. It was as if she were drugged.

After the curtain went down we went to a coffee lounge on the Pacific Highway. She had come out of her trance, but it was almost as if she needed the coffee to break it.

'Didn't you *love* it?'

'I can take or leave Chekhov. I prefer something meatier, Mamet or one of Williamson's better plays. Chekhov, whether he meant it or not, was writing about a society that was dying.'

She seemed surprised that I had any sort of appreciation of the Russian, but my mother hadn't neglected my education in the arts. Though to be honest, this was the first time it had come to the surface with a girl on whom I had non-theatrical designs.

'But that's the point! He saw the sadness —'

I took a risk. 'There's some sadness out the other side of Orange. Something's dying there.'

She stared at her coffee, stirring it more than it needed. Then she lifted her gaze and I saw the sudden pain in her eyes. 'Don't you think I know it?'

'Yes, I think you do. But heritage shouldn't be allowed to die.' I found it hard to believe what I was saying. When had I suddenly been converted?

'What do you know about it? What are you protecting?' She was almost harshly defensive.

I didn't want to spoil the evening with an argument and I was kicking myself for having brought up the subject. 'Nothing, but that's the way it is. Haven't you noticed, 95 per cent of wilderness defenders live in cities? It's the same with heritage defenders.'

She relaxed, smiled wanly. 'I could never go back, Jack. Not to live the rest of my life there. Try to understand that.'

I'm trying to understand more than that about you.

When we got outside again to my car I said, 'Is Tom back from potting my namesake?'

'He wasn't when we left. But you're not staying the night.'

'I'll keep trying.'

We drove back to Kirribilli, pulled up outside her block of flats. I got out, helped her out and held her to me. 'Why do you have to look so bloody beautiful?'

'Blame the heritage,' she said and kissed me.

We walked up the slope of the driveway and found Tom Barini and a slim blond guy having an argument outside the front door.

'I haven't come all the fucking way over here to be brushed off now!'

Tom, looking over the guy's shoulder, was relieved and embarrassed at the same time. Adele said in a quiet, level voice, 'Having trouble, Tom?'

'Mind your own fucking business,' said the stranger.

I stepped in front of Adele. I was half a head taller and at least ten kilos heavier. He was slim and good-looking, with a gold ring in his right ear and blond hair done in the style just coming in, standing straight up on his head as if the hairdresser had misdirected the hot tongs and shoved them up his anus.

I'm not a natural-born fighter; Anthony Mundine could knock me out just talking at me. But at university I played rugby and as a TV reporter I've been attacked twice by peace demonstrators. I have learned how to use the knee and the boot even though I wouldn't know the Marquis of Queensberry if I knocked him down.

'I think you'd better beat it, mate,' I said, trying not to sound like Bruce Willis. 'You're outnumbered.'

He stared at the three of us, then abruptly he pushed past me and went off down the driveway. Adele reached for Tom's hand: 'Oh darling! Another bad choice?'

He nodded, then leaned forward and she took him in her arms. Over his shoulder she said, 'Call me tomorrow, Jack.'

Unlike a lot of reporters, especially young 'uns like myself, I've learned when to exit. I leaned forward and kissed the back of her head. Anyone coming up the driveway would have wondered at the three of us at that moment, a tableau of some sort of love.

I drove home to Longueville. Lynne was getting out of a 4WD as I pulled the MG into our driveway. With her was a guy about her own height, built like a bullock, plain-faced as the back end of a bus. Lynne can sometimes really pick 'em, as if, blindfolded, she has put her hand in a lottery bin.

'Oh!' She sounded surprised. 'I thought you weren't coming home tonight . . . Oh, this is Nick Klavos.'

Now I recognised him. He played front row for Northern Suburbs, his natural habitat down there in the sweat, with the gouging and necks as wide as shoulders. He was in the State's Super 12 team, but always on the bench, one of the men sitting there waiting for someone to be clobbered and carried off so that they run on to the cheers of the crowd, or at least their relatives. I had never seen Nick Klavos get off the bench.

He grinned, a pleasant flash in his plain face, shook my hand and said, 'I was just seeing her to the front door.'

I went inside and left them. Ten minutes later Lynne came in, hair awry and mouth spread like a crushed strawberry. 'You got another brush-off?'

'No, something came up. Where'd you pick him up? You going in for boneheads now?'

'He's doing his Master's in Philosophy —'

'In the front row?'

We always went on like that and each of us knew it was out of the protective instinct. 'You want some tea?' she said and went out to the kitchen.

I followed, told her why I was home earlier than expected. 'She's this guy, Tom Barini's, guardian angel.'

'Is she the mothering type?' She put out cups, saucers and biscuits. She mothers me. 'That can be a trap.'

I studied her, trying to see her as a stranger. Why wasn't she happily married, as our parents were? Why wasn't there a dependable man in her life, maybe a child or two? Suddenly I wanted to hold her in my arms as Adele had held Tom Barini. But you didn't do that with your sister, not till the tears called for it.

'How far into the future do you look?'

She poured hot water into the teapot; we never had teabags in our house, always loose tea. Our mother looked at teabags as if they were used condoms.

'You and your girl must have had an interesting evening. That what you talked about?'

'Only indirectly. I'm asking *you*.'

'Jack . . .' She sat down opposite me at the kitchen table. The couch for talks about the future, the kitchen table. 'I think about it a lot. Every time after I'd had a bust-up —'

For a moment I thought she was going to cry and I was ready to put my arms round her.

But she went on: 'It's not easy for women these days. Men are, I dunno, more ... *cagey*. Dad was only twenty-three and Mum twenty-one when they married. That doesn't happen that often now, not unless the girl's pregnant.'

'They marry young out there in the western suburbs.' Another country.

'We're not talking about the guys out there. They don't earn the money I'm talking about, they're not as selfish. They don't earn as much as you, for instance. I've never heard you talk about marriage ...' She bit into a biscuit, then looked hard at me. 'How many times have you even *thought* of marriage?'

Not once. I hadn't even thought about it with Adele.

'You see?' she said, reading my thoughts; she was good at that. 'I'm not thinking of marrying Nick Klavos. But he's a nice guy and he understands women.'

'The things they learn in the front row of a scrum.'

'Don't be a dickhead,' she said, and I guessed she was right. 'Sometimes I could clout you.'

Then the phone on the kitchen wall rang. I got up: late-night calls were, too frequently, from Les Dibley. But I hoped this one might be from Adele asking for help. Instead, it was our mother calling from New York: 'It's not too late, is it? I always forget to check your time.'

'No, Lynne and I have just come in.'

'You've been out together?'

'No, Mum, we're not reduced to going out together. Lynne's been out with a Greek philosopher and I've been out with an actress.'

'What interesting lives you two lead.' Our mother's sarcasm is gentle, never meant to hurt, just to remind you that she has been around longer than you.

'How's Dad?'

'He's down in Brazil at the moment with the Secretary-General. The UN is looking into string bikinis.' She has been around almost as long as the UN too, I think. Or has got her thinking straighter. I should ring my father and ask him about Brazilian pubic cuts. 'I'll put Lynne on.'

'Your actress? Is she nice?'

'Very nice, Mum.'

I handed over the phone to Lynne and went to bed. And, for the first time in my life, wondered what it would be like to be married.

2

I reconstructed this from what Adele told me.

She took him up in the lift, her arm still round him. 'Tom, darling — rough trade again? You *promised* me ...'

'I was just so damned lonely, Del. I've been a fortnight on my own —'

'You were with that company —'

'Seven of us, four guys and three girls. The others were all straight. They paired off the first night and from then on I was on my own. Pick-ups are few and far between in country towns. That guy tonight — I knew it was a mistake halfway home —'

'Darling, you've got to *promise* me. I don't want any rough trade brought back here, understand?'

He had nodded, then kissed her. 'I promise ... I'm thinking of going home —'

'To Perth?'

'Mum and Dad keep asking me to come back. Dad says he's accepted what I am.'

His father, evidently, had kicked him out when he had come out.

'What's for you back there?' Adele asked. 'You'll never get any work in TV there. Or the theatre.'

Perth, for her, like most easterners, was Ultima Thule. No wonder the West Australians, back in 1933, voted to secede from the nation, but the Constitution, written mostly by easterners, wouldn't let them go. In so many countries there is something about being born in the east that breeds a certain arrogance, as if they are the ones who let the sun come up.

Where was I? Oh, back with Adele and her story ...

'There's Vern,' said Tom, 'the guy I walked out on. He's the one I'm ... I'm *comfortable* with, Del. I'll get a job — a teacher or something. I've got my Arts degree, for what it's worth these days.'

'You'll give up acting? All your ambition?'

'Del, I never had as much ambition as you've got —'

(It must have hurt her to tell me that.)

'— I'll go home, I may be a bit unhappy for a while, but ... I miss my mum and dad and my brother. I was very happy with them till ... till I found out what I was. And I was happy with Vern — he's been asking me to come back. Over there in the west there's some theatre — maybe I can do a bit, part-time. And I won't need any rough trade —'

She had kissed him then.

He just didn't leave for the west soon enough.

3

'No,' I said.

'You mean she refused point-blank to come back for the series?' said Entwistle.

'Point-blank.'

He sat back in his chair. He was in a pink shirt today, white cuffs, pink *flowered* braces. On the shelf behind him the yacht looked somehow off-course, as if a strong nor-easter, or a cleaner, had hit it abeam or wherever yachts are hit.

'We've had another idea,' he said. *We* meant *I*. 'We want to try her out as a news presenter. She's got the looks and the voice.'

He was determined to rope her back in somehow. I looked at him with the superiority of someone who had — well, been to bed with her. It's a hell of a scale and no compliment to the girl, but men write their own standards. As any woman will tell you, with or without invitation.

'Reading the weekend news, Saturdays and Sundays.'

One of the current women presenters had been a protégée of his, a good-looking girl who had been to elocution classes and enunciated not only every word but every syllable. She made the news sound like a reading class for newly arrived immigrants.

'How d'you think she'd go?'

'I think she could do it,' I said, sure that she wouldn't. 'You want me to put it to her?'

'You mind? I hate this, Jack, using you as our runner . . .'

'No problem, Jared.'

Bullshit was running down the walls, spoiling the Japanese gold leaf.

'Do your best, Jack. That was a nice piece on the bushfires.'

There had been a major fire in the Blue Mountains and we had covered it. 'Bushfires always look good,' I said.

'Pity they do so much damage.'

'That's the way it is, Jared, the bad with the good.'

I escaped before the big room began to smell.

Our State political reporter had called in with a bad throat and I was sent to Macquarie Street to do a piece on a preliminary report on the success of the Olympics. You would have thought the senior ministers, and not Cathy Freeman, had won the 400-metres track final. There was not a hint of the in-fighting and back-biting that had gone on before the Games; bullshit flowed again, this time on camera. Because I was not the regular State man and didn't have to protect my patch, I asked the question: 'What happens now, Minister, to the Olympic complex?'

Les Dibley had told me about the debt left by Montreal, still paying off *its* Games twenty-five years after they had been held, and Barcelona. There was a hush as I asked the question, as if I had queried the Pope on the viability of the Vatican.

I couldn't dent the euphoria. 'People will flock to it as they did to the Games —'

Then the news conference was over and I heard the Minister ask a minder: 'Who's that bastard?'

'Another one from Channel 15, Minister. They're worse than the bloody ABC sometimes. Christ knows where they dig 'em up.'

Two nights later I took Adele to dinner again, once more to Jasper's. She was in yellow; she seemed to have a wardrobe that ran through the spectrum. She was fortunate in that she had the sort of colouring that went with any shade. In the car on the way to Hunters Hill she told me about Tom Barini and what had happened the other night.

'It'll probably be for the best, his going home. But I hope he doesn't spend the rest of his life regretting he gave up his ambition.'

'Del, we don't all have *your* ambition. Most of us settle for less.'

'Never.' She shook her head. Then she said, 'I've got another part. I went up to the theatre where we were the other night and did a reading for them. They're doing another Chekhov, *The Three Sisters*. I've got the part of Masha.'

I had never seen the play nor read it. 'Is it a good part?'

'Wonderful!'

Her eyes were shining, you'd have thought she had just won an Oscar. At times there was almost a schoolgirl's enthusiasm in her. I had seen it in Lynne, when she had wanted to be a designer, Sydney's latterday Coco Chanel. Chanel, actually, was the designer she chose as her model rather than the more outlandish ones that have come along since. Then the light had died as she realised her talent was no more than ordinary and she had turned to marketing. I wondered how long it would take for the light to die for Adele.

'The three sisters dream of Moscow —'

'Masha or whatever her name is, she's a dreamer?'

But by then we were in Hunters Hill and I was looking for a parking space; come Judgement Day people will be looking for parking spaces. When we got out of the car I waited while she took the scarf from her head and arranged her hair. She looked at me and I said, 'Thank God for genetics.'

She took my hand and I knew that, for the moment, she was in love with me. But I knew, too, it was seasonal; short seasons.

Though I was the semi-regular, when we walked into the small restaurant it was Adele who got the attention.

My dad, when he was still in newspapers, had once gone to London to cover a conference of some sort with Prime Minister Bob Hawke. While there the London office had asked him to do an interview with Marcello Mastroianni, one of Dad's favourite actors. During it he had asked Mastroianni what it was like to escort Sophia Loren, another of Dad's favourites, into a restaurant. Mastroianni, a man with a true sense of values and Italian to boot, had replied, 'As if I owned the world.' I knew what he meant that night at Jasper's.

Over the first course I told Adele what Entwistle wanted. 'He sees you eventually as the female Brian Henderson. He hopes male viewers will increase by fifty per cent, slobbering over you while you read the casualty list in some disaster.'

'You don't want me to take the job, do you?'

I was shocked; the avocado-and-prawn savarin turned sour in my mouth. 'For Crissakes, you don't *want* it, do you?'

'Relax, Jack. I wouldn't say yes to Mr Entwistle if he offered me the whole of Channel 15. I'm an actress, darling, not a news reader.'

I said very cautiously, 'You'll want to go a long way further than the —' I named the suburban theatre.

'Of course I do!' But she wasn't angry at me; she had missed the implied criticism or warning, whatever you want to call it. I was still amazed at her myopia. But then I had been looking at myopia for the past three years while fronting a TV camera. Politicians, corporate executives, union bosses, relatives of rapists: you name 'em, myopia has a bigger spread than AIDS, cancer or any other affliction you care to name.

'Some day I'll phone you and ask you to come to London or New York,' she challenged me. 'Will you come?'

'If Mr Entwistle permits —'

'Stuff Mr Entwistle.' She raised her glass; she always started dinner with a glass of champagne. I wondered what the Three Sisters drank, pining for Moscow. 'To us, Jack.'

'Lovers?'

'Friends. I told you, don't rush it.'

I raised my own glass, a light beer. I might change to champagne if and when the relationship became more permanent.

When we had finished dinner she excused herself and went to the toilet. One of the co-owners of the restaurant, a man tall enough to be a basketballer, brought me the bill. 'I've seen Miss Ambar before. Is she an actress?'

'Sort of. And a part-time model.' I hoped he hadn't seen her in any lingerie commercials. You can be proudly possessive, but exposure should be limited.

'We'll always be happy to see her here.' Then he added with a smile, 'You too, Mr Shakespeare.'

'You got that out just in time, Mark.'

As he went away he passed Adele coming back to our table. He said something to her and she gave him a smile that should have had twenty per cent, plus goods and services tax, deducted from the bill.

When we got outside the evening had turned a little chilly. I got a rug out from beneath the small tonneau and wrapped it round her. 'Got to keep you warm.'

'Forget it, Jack. No bed tonight. Tom is home.'

Tom, the unwitting protector of virtue.

'And all this week I'm studying. I like to read the script right through, just before I go to sleep. That way I take it into my subconscious. Sarah Bernhardt used to do it.'

Bernhardt, Edith Evans: all her exemplars appeared to be dead. I wondered when she would get around to Mrs Siddons or even Nell Gwynne. Well, probably not her.

Nell had been an actress who had known a good bed when she was laid in it.

We drove back to Kirribilli, got out of the car and walked up to the front door of the flats. We stood there under the light, in the same spot where Tom Barini and his rough trade had had their argument. But there was no argument between us. I took her in my arms and she didn't resist. There is something about the pliability of a woman's body that even Adam must have appreciated before he found out it was sinful.

'Will you come and see me in *The Three Sisters*?'

'I'll bring my sister. The four of you can swap dreams.'

She looked at me as if making up her mind about something. Then she kissed me passionately and was gone, leaving me with the sudden feeling that, somehow, I was taking on the shape of an anchor.

4

I don't jog, on the advice of a senior orthopaedic surgeon. I went to see him after I'd wrenched my knee getting out of the Channel 15 chopper. He claimed that when he and two other surgeons had got out of college they had looked around for a specialty and invented jogging. They looked down the track, the road, the footpath, and saw the jarred ankles, squashed cartilages and grinding hipbones of the future and rubbed their hands for future diagnoses. The invention had paid off for him in spades, hearts, clubs and diamonds, especially the latter. His wife was seen at charity functions gleaming like an old-time Indian ranee.

They had a mansion on the North Shore and a beach house at Palm Beach. Every year they went off on a six-week world trip, ostensibly to orthopaedic conferences where the ailments of the world's suckers were discussed with glee. I disagreed with none of his perceptions.

I don't jog, but I walk. Five kilometres every morning, except when I'm called out on an early job. I play squash twice a week and tennis once a week, careful of the ankles and the knee-joints. I don't play golf, believing it as boring as going for a walk while reading Hansard. I gave up cricket and rugby because I was too often on call for a job. I don't smoke, drink just a little and kid myself I'm as fit as the next man, so long as he's not a gym crank.

I'm a practising Catholic; I have to practise, otherwise I'd be hopeless at it. I haven't been to Confession since I was sixteen, when I took my first girl to bed (actually, it was the back seat of her father's car) and discovered sin was not the joyless thing old Father Finnegan had said it was. I have to hide a smile when I interview sportsmen who bless themselves and thank the Lord Jesus Christ when they score a century or sink an eagle putt or knock an opponent stone-cold unconscious. I've checked the Bible and there is not the slightest evidence that Christ was ever interested in sport, that He played marbles as a kid or kicked a ball when He was an adult. St Paul never mentions sport in the innumerable letters he wrote to the Ephesians and the Corinthians and all other places where letters were delivered in those days. Even if he were using today's e-mail, I doubt if he'd mention sport.

I'm a smart dresser, but only because the camera demands it; when did you ever see a daggy presenter, except on the ABC?

I think fashion designers are the greatest bunch of con artists since the lot who fashioned the Great South Sea Bubble; but the suckers of the world unite and bow down in worship and the billions flow in. But don't quote me, not till I've retired.

I'm tight with money and never squander it. I always have a nice sum left over at the end of the tax year and I've invested it in solid stocks. I saw the IT boom for the bubble that it proved to be, but my colleagues looked on me as someone who kept his money under his bed in a jam jar. The jam jar is full of National Australia Bank and other bank stocks.

I mention all this only because I had, almost involuntarily, begun to think of marriage. I had never discussed any of these things with Adele. I had no idea how she kept fit; what religion, if any, she had; what she thought of fashion, even though she was a part-time model; and how she spent, or saved, her money. I figured that with the latter she didn't have to worry too much. Out there in the heritage there had looked to be plenty of the necessary.

I didn't see her for another week, though I called her every day and she sounded glad to hear from me. Then on the Sunday I took her to lunch up at Palm Beach. This is not like Palm Beach, Florida, though it has pretensions of wealth. Expensive houses cling to the hill above the beach, but there are no grand estates. Once upon a time it was the domain of Old Money, but today New Money, as everywhere else in the country, has bought its way in. Les Dibley once suggested we do a satirical piece on Palm Beach and its summer population, but the board of directors, all New Money, vetoed *that*. Satire, George S Kaufman once said, is what dies on Saturday night. It dies at lunchtime amongst New Money.

As we walked into the café-restaurant she got the looks again even from the women. I felt like Marcello Mastroianni, owner of the world.

She started with the usual glass of champagne. Point taken: money was no object, I'd have to keep working. Now all that was to be discussed were fitness, religion, fashion. 'How's it going? The rehearsals?'

'Oh, it's wonderful! The director can sometimes be a bit hard to please' — On her? But I didn't ask — 'but I love the characters. Chekhov understood women so well.'

I waited, then she smiled and put her hand across the table and on mine. 'I think you're learning, darling. It's a pity you're not Russian.'

'I've heard of a few Russians who didn't try to understand women. Peter the Great, Stalin, Yeltsin —'

Across the road, on the beach, were the big bronzed Aussies who, I'm sure she'd tell me, didn't understand women. And all I had, apparently, were learner-plates.

'What religion are you?'

She looked at me, curious. 'Why?'

'Just asking. I'm Catholic, sort of. The Vatican doesn't rely on me.'

'I'm C of E, sort of. I haven't been to church since I left boarding school. I believe if you smile on God, He'll smile on you.'

'Lucky Him.'

I decided to leave the fashion and money questions till a later date. After lunch we went for a walk along the road above the beach. There was an armoured brigade of 4WDs, all with bullbars, to repel any raiders from the sea. The sea itself looked inviting, but I hadn't brought my trunks nor she her swimsuit. All at once I was glad. I was fiercely possessive again, this time not wanting her perved at by other fellers, and she would be in a swimsuit. Jealousy is inborn in woman's heart, said Euripides, a natural-born misogynist. He should have looked into the hearts of some of the guys around him.

'What are you thinking about?'

'Politics. Are you Liberal, Labor, Green or what?'

'Whatever part I'm playing at the time . . .'

I shouldn't have asked.

I took her back to Kirribilli, the day still bright and shining. 'Is Tom home?'

'No, he won't be back till tonight. Come on up, I need relaxing.'

I hadn't heard it called that before, but I've never quarrelled with relaxing, in bed or out of it. We spent almost an hour in strenuous relaxing. I was totally in love now and not just because I was in her. My namesake had a score of ways of describing it, but I couldn't think of a single phrase, other than to gasp:

'I love you!'

She was on top of me, exhausted. She stared at me as if I had hurt her, then she bent down and kissed me very tenderly. 'Don't, darling. Not yet.'

'Not yet? You think it's something I can turn on and off like a spigot?' Like a spigot: Shakespearean language.

She giggled, fell off me and lay on her back. 'When did the Water Board come between us?'

I felt rebuffed, even hurt. Yet there had been promise when she had said 'not yet'.

I mechanically stroked the Brazilian cut; it was like trying to seduce a thin hairbrush. I tried for a lighter note, but humour in bed is pretty low: 'I'm head over crotch in love with you —'

She kissed me again, said, 'Put some ice on it,' and got out of bed. 'What would you like for supper? I can't cook, but I'm very good on the microwave.'

How come a country-bred girl couldn't cook? But I didn't ask. We showered, dressed and had a pizza and coffee. Then Tom Barini came home, looking a little worn and exhausted, and I wondered if he had been out with rough trade again. I felt sorry for him and, somehow, protective. Like a brother.

'Adele tells me you're going back to Perth?'

'No,' he said and looked her. 'I had lunch today with George Betts.' I knew he was a well-known director, gay and well regarded. 'He wants me to play Tom in *The Glass Menagerie*. They're doing it at The Wharf.'

Adele jumped up and hugged him. I'd learn as time went on that she was never jealous or envious of anyone else's good luck in the theatre. 'Oh darling, I'm so thrilled for you!' She sat down again and looked at me. 'Do you know Tennessee Williams? And I don't mean personally.'

'We did him at university. I remember some of Tom's lines. *The play is memory. Our father was a telephone man who fell in love with long distances.*' I remembered them because in my early struggles at writing they were the sort of lines I'd aimed at. 'It's a good part, Tom. Congratulations.'

He had looked on edge when he came in, but now he was relaxing. Well, not in the way we had been a short while ago. 'I start rehearsing tomorrow. It opens in two weeks. We've been pushed into a slot that suddenly happened. It runs only a week.'

'Oh damn! I shan't be able to come and see you — we'll still be running. But Jack will come and tell me all about it —'

'I'll be the Gentleman Caller.' She looked puzzled and I said, 'He's in the play.'

'I know, I know!'

But it struck me then that she had never read the play nor seen it. It also occurred to me that, for all his fame, Williams was rarely seen on the local stage these days. Maybe he had become old hat, or whatever the term was that they used in the theatre.

Tom seemed to give me new respect, as if he had thought all I knew about were TV sitcoms. 'If it goes well, they've promised me other parts.'

Adele kissed him. She was genuinely glad for him, but I wondered what doubts lay in her own mind. But even as I wondered, I knew there was none. Some day, she dreamed, she and Tom would star in a play together. Chekhov, of course.

I rose, kissed Adele on the back of her neck. 'Time I was going. Good luck, Tom. It's a sad play, as I remember it. I'll bring tissues.'

He grinned, happier than I had seen him before. 'I'll look for you in the audience and direct the last speech at you, okay?'

I couldn't remember the last speech. 'Sure, I'll look forward to it.'

At the front door Adele kissed me. 'You're sweet, Jack.'

'That's what all my other girls tell me.'

She smiled, kneed me in the crotch and shut the door.

I went home, dug out my old university books from the trunk on the back verandah. Tom's last speech to the audience was a long one and sad. *For nowadays the world is lit by lightning! Blow out your candles, Laura — and so goodbye . . .*

I wondered if Adele would ever blow out her candles.

Chapter Four

1

I took Lynne to the opening night of *The Three Sisters*. We went in her car, a Honda Civic, which she drove with her foot through the floorboards and somewhere between the front wheels. Somehow she had never been picked up for speeding and her driving record was unblemished; even speed cameras seemed to turn a blind eye to her. She had never had an accident and the No Claim bonus on her insurance policy was 100 per cent. Some people drive in a vacuum.

The theatre was full. Chekhov was popular up here on the North Shore, although I couldn't imagine the burghers pining for Moscow, not even in the Tsar's day. We had good seats and I settled into mine with some trepidation, as if I might be too close to the disaster on stage.

Adele was not disastrous. She fitted into the ensemble playing, but only just. She said her lines clearly in that very good voice of hers; she had learned to project, which so many of our actors, brought up on microphones, have never learned. But she missed entirely the wryness that should have been in her character. I've come to know, since, that apathy floats through Chekhov like a faint fog and his characters are aware of it and fight it, though almost apathetically. Adele was unaware of it; or if she was, she failed to show any recognition. But she didn't disrupt the play and the curtain went down to strong applause.

Lynne and I waited in our seats till almost everyone had gone. Then I said apprehensively, 'What did you think?'

'There were just two sisters in the play,' she said. 'Your girlfriend was a distant cousin.'

'I can't tell her that.'

'You'd be a bloody idiot if you did.'

We went out, waited by the stage door till Adele came out. I introduced Lynne and Adele said, 'Did you like it?'

'It was great,' I said, avoiding the personal and hoping she wouldn't notice.

'I loved it,' said Lynne, sounding sincere; you learn that in marketing. 'The three of you really fitted like sisters.'

Lies, I guess, are as complimentary as roses.

Lynne drove us back to Kirribilli, with me in the back seat and Adele up front. She and Lynne got on like — well, like sisters. Or cousins. When we pulled up Lynne looked out at the street. 'I lived here once, down the street there. With Bernie, remember?'

'Dimly,' I said. Bernie Hoxcroft, as I remembered him, had been a bastard and I had been glad when Lynne had come back home.

'One should never come back to old territory,' Lynne said and smiled at Adele. 'You agree?'

'I try avoiding it all the time,' she said and smiled in return.

'You want me to get out and go for a walk while you two sort out your old love lives?' I asked.

'He can be a pain sometimes,' said Lynne. 'Take her to the door and I'll wait. Night, Adele, I did enjoy the show.'

I took Adele to the front door of the flats, kissed her. 'I'll call for you tomorrow night, in the MG.'

'You really thought I was okay?'

Okay, just, was the word. 'I really thought you were. Chekhov understood women.'

'Do you?' But with a smile.

'I'm trying.' I kissed her again. 'I love you.'

'You can, for tonight,' she said and kissed me back.

Going home to Longueville at eighty ks an hour, running amber lights, just beating the red, Lynne said, 'She's in love with you.'

'I don't think so. Halfway, maybe. She's in love with long distances.'

'What's that supposed to mean?'

'New York and London. I'm paraphrasing Tennessee Williams.'

'Who's he?' Going through a red light.

'Bloke I went to uni with.'

Next morning the *Herald* critic ran his piece in the late edition. He was complimentary of the play and the production, mentioning the director and the players. Of Adele he said: 'Miss Ambar misses Chekhov's subtleties, but she looks so beautiful and moves so gracefully that one forgives her as one forgives the Venus de Milo for being armless. Let Chekhov take care of his own subtleties.'

It was cruel and I was glad I was able to escape it. Les Dibley rang me at 7.30 and forty-five minutes later I was on the helicopter, bound for the Hunter Valley and a strike and lock-out at a coal mine. I was there for two days, in that lovely shallow valley of contrasts where coal is mined and grapes are grown. The ugly black hills of coal and, in the distance, the green rows of vines: two of the country's biggest money earners. God must have had some laughs when he was building the world.

Sitting on the sidelines I wondered what Chekhov would have made of the strike. There was apathy here; but anger beneath it. There was danger below the ground, down there beneath the roots of the vines. There was the grim realisation that times were changing, that the unions were losing their hold. It would go on for weeks, but after two days Channel 15 called us home. Other dramas had to be covered, viewers had short attention spans, they had troubles of their own.

On the fourth night of the play's run I picked up Adele at the theatre. She was friendly but subdued and I suspected she thought I might have read the *Herald* review. But I dodged it, asked how the show was going and whether she had settled into it. I was becoming diplomatic, not a trade taught at journalism schools.

'The audience seem to like it. Will you go and see Tom in his play?'

'Of course. How's he fitting into it?'

'He's loving it. I don't think he'll go home now, not to Perth. He's hoping this will lead to other parts. Did you know Tennessee Williams was gay?'

'Yes. Maybe that was why he wrote such good parts for women, he understood them better than us ignorant heteros.' She just gave me another of her smiles on that one. 'Is Tom home tonight? They don't rehearse at night, do they?'

She looked sideways at me. 'I'm not sure — that he's at home, I mean. Whether he is or not, it's not on tonight, Jack.'

I said nothing for a mile or two, then: 'When your play finishes, can we go away for a few days? I'm due for some leave. Maybe to Noosa or somewhere?'

There was a long pause, then she said, 'That would be nice.'

I squeezed her thigh and almost went through a red light.

As soon as I turned into her street in Kirribilli I saw the flashing red-and-blue lights halfway down. Four police cars, an ambulance and a small crowd filled the roadway. The blocks of flats lining both sides of the street were lit up as if there was another fireworks display on the harbour.

'Oh God, that's outside my place!'

Adele went to scramble out of the car, but I held her in, swung up the driveway and parked on the footpath. I held her hand as we went hurriedly down to her flats. Crime scene tapes were round the whole of the front lawn and a uniformed cop blocked our way: 'Sorry, you can't go in —'

'But I live here! What's happened?'

'Just a minute, miss. Stay here, please.' He went away, came back in a minute or two with a detective I recognised, Sergeant Killick. 'This lady says she lives here.'

'You are?'

'Adele Ambar. I live on the eighth floor.'

Killick lifted the tapes and we ducked under them. He said nothing as he led us across the front lawn to the ambulance officers who were zipping up a body-bag. 'I'm sorry to ask you to do this — but do you know this man?'

I knew before the bag was unzipped who it was; and so did Adele. Some people can look at a dead body and be unmoved; not because of callousness, but just because they can't comprehend that this is someone who will no longer move nor talk nor think. But Adele reacted as if she had been physically punched; she fell back against me. I looked past her and down at the smashed face of Tom Barini. Adele couldn't speak and I said, 'His name is Tom Barini.'

Only then did Killick seem to recognise me; his attention all the time had been on Adele. 'Jack, can you take Miss — Ambar? — up to her flat? Rainone is up there and I'll be up in a minute or two.'

'What happened?' I asked.

'He evidently fell from his balcony.' Adele had her face buried in my shoulder and he shook his head: *don't ask any more questions.* 'Take Miss Ambar upstairs.'

We went up in the lift, she still numb and dumb except for an occasional faint moan like an animal that had been hurt. The front door of the flat was open and there was a crime scene tape strung across it. Detective Sergeant Rainone, another man I knew, was in the narrow hallway, taking his mobile away from his ear. 'Hullo, Jack — Phil said you were on your way up.'

A forensic crew were at work in the flat. Rainone led me and Adele out to the kitchen and closed the door. He introduced himself to Adele as I sat her down on a chair; she nodded, but seemed only half aware of him. I felt helpless, but looked around for a kettle or electric jug.

'I'll make some tea,' I said and began to do just that. The mundane, the everyday: anchors in whirlwinds of emotion.

'North Sydney police called us in —' Rainone was a slender, dark-haired man in his forties, the years of service stamped there in his thin face. He and Killick were with Crime Agency and he was the sort of cop that was disappearing from the service as younger, better-educated men came into it.

Then Phil Killick came into the kitchen; he was the senior of the two of them. I knew him, too, as well as I knew Rainone. He was good-looking in a nondescript way, bulky, a bit overweight. He had a relaxed air about him that put you at ease; even criminals, I'd bet. If Adele had to be interviewed by cops, I'd choose these two.

'You making tea, Jack? Not teabags, I hope?'

I'd looked in the cupboard. 'Afraid so ... What happened?'

Killick sat down opposite Adele. 'Miss Ambar ...'

She had been staring at her clasped hands on the table, but now she raised her eyes, blinked and tried to take the blankness out of them. 'Tom fell from the balcony? Was he drunk or something?'

'I'm afraid it wasn't like that.' He took a breath, though you couldn't hear the intake: 'There was a fight — someone threw him off the balcony —'

'*Threw* him?' She put her hand to her mouth, a theatrical gesture; but she wasn't acting, not now. For a moment she looked as if she was about to be sick. Then she drew herself together; it was a physical movement, one could see it. 'Someone *murdered* him?'

'It looks that way,' said Rainone and sat down at the table. The kitchen was a fair size for a flat and though the table was small there was room for four people to sit at it. 'People in the flat next door heard an argument — the living room is a bit knocked about —'

I was getting out cups and saucers, trying to be useful; or not useless. I had seen plenty of evidence of murder, but from the outside; this was from the *inside*, or almost. 'Nobody saw who was here with him?'

Killick hesitated, then said, 'I'm sorry about the details, Miss Ambar ... Mr Barini screamed as he fell from the balcony. That prompted the woman in the next flat —'

'Mrs Lucasta,' said Rainone.

'She opened her front door and saw a man getting into the lift. She didn't get a look at his face, just saw that he was blond.' He hesitated again, looked at me, then back at Adele. 'What was your relationship with Mr Barini?

I answered for her as I switched off the electric jug: 'They were flatmates. Tom was gay.' I poured the hot water into the pot, on top of the teabags. Trying to keep things normal. 'I'm Adele's boyfriend, if that's what you're asking.'

She looked up at me at that and for a moment I thought she was going to contradict me; but she didn't. She said, her voice small, very flat, 'Tom occasionally brought strangers back here, when I wouldn't be here —'

'Rough trade,' I said and poured the tea into the cups. 'We got rid of a guy a couple of weeks ago. A blond guy —'

'You know who he was?' asked Rainone.

'No.' I'd found some Tim-Tams in the cupboard and put those on the table. Rainone reached for one and munched on it as if I'd provided his favourite biscuit. It suddenly struck me, as it had not on those other occasions of murder, that this was everyday business for them. 'He was someone Tom picked up, either at the Cross or on Oxford Street. Somewhere. He got nasty and I offered to take him on.' I sat down on the fourth chair, pushed a cup of tea in front of Adele. 'Drink that, Del.'

She was recovering; she managed a small smile, not of humour but as if trying to see if her face was working. She pulled the cup towards her, looked at Killick and Rainone and said, 'He's very protective.'

'The best sort of boyfriend,' said Killick. Then he looked at me: 'Can you describe this feller?'

'Yes.' The general public, as the police well know, is notoriously unreliable for giving descriptions. But, as an interviewer, I had learned to read faces, to tell the liar from the truth-teller, the real emotion from the fake. I closed my eyes and he was there on the screen of my lids. 'He was half a head shorter than me, slim. He had blond hair, almost white, standing straight up on his head — you know, the latest fashion, as if someone just scared the shit out of him. An earring in his left ear. He had a thin face . . .'

'Eyes?' said Rainone. 'What colour?'

'I can't remember.' What man can remember another man's eyes? A woman's, yes.

'Brown,' said Adele. 'Very dark. I remember the contrast with his hair.'

'You know where Mr Barini hung out up at the Cross or in Oxford Street?' Killick was old-fashioned enough to say *in* and not *on* Oxford Street. 'He ever mention a particular pub or club?'

'No.' Adele was almost composed again. 'He kept that part of his life private.'

'Does he have family?'

I looked at Adele. 'We'd better call them. Have you ever spoken to them?' She shook her head. I turned back to Killick and Rainone. 'They live somewhere outside Perth. I'll call them —'

'The number's in the diary beside the phone,' said Adele.

'Just say he's dead,' said Killick and I caught his warning look. 'No details. We'll get in touch with their local police and have them do it. Not over the phone.'

I went out to the living room. The forensic team were just finishing, working unhurriedly, efficiently; homicide is a business. I looked up the number, a country one, and dialled it. I looked at my watch: midnight. It would be ten o'clock in West Australia, the Barinis would still be up, maybe watching 'Homicide on the Streets', safe from all the danger there on the screen. I put the thought out of my mind as I heard the ringing phone.

Then: ''Allo? Who's calling?'

It was a woman's voice, accented. It had not occurred to me that, despite Tom's surname, he might come from an immigrant family; or anyway, that he was a first-generation Australian.

'My name is Jack Shakespeare, I'm a friend of Tom's —'

'Something's happened to him!' It was not a question, it was a declaration, her voice rising to a shriek. 'What is it? What happened?'

'Mrs Barini —'

There was a sobbing moan, then a man's voice, flat Australian, came on the line: 'What's going on? This is Paul Barini — is it something to do with my brother?'

I gave my name again, then said, having difficulty with the message, 'Tom is dead, Mr Barini —'

'How?' There was a catch in his voice.

'A fall from his balcony. I can't tell you any more than that.' Trying not to make it sound like the lie it was. 'The New South Wales police will be contacting your local police. They'll come to see you —'

'Tom had a flatmate — Miss Ambar?'

'She's okay. She was not involved.'

'There's something you're not telling me —'

'Mr Barini, wait for the police to come. Please ... I'm sorry I had to speak to your mother first. How is she?'

There was a moment; then: 'She's Italian. We believe in premonitions. Thanks, Mr ...?'

'Shakespeare.' And, as sometimes happened, thought my name bloody ridiculous. *Though it be honest, it is never good/To bring bad news ...*

I hung up and Rainone was standing beside me. 'You handled that well.' He held out a hand; in it was a letter. 'We found this in his room. It has his parents' address —' He named a town I had never heard of. 'I'll call Perth headquarters and have them put me through to the locals.

The family should be told tonight, not wait till the morning.'

'It's a bugger of a job.'

He nodded. 'I've been knocking on doors since I was twenty years old and first came into the force. It never gets any easier.'

I left him and went back into the kitchen. Killick was still sitting opposite Adele, relaxed and sympathetic. He looked like a father with his daughter and I wondered if he had kids.

'I've advised Miss Ambar not to stay here tonight.'

'We should call your family,' I said to her.

But she shook her head adamantly. 'No, I'm not going to get them out in the middle of the night — the morning will do, I'll call them early —'

'Get some night things,' I said. 'I'm taking you home to Longueville. I'll ring Lynne and tell her we're coming. She's my sister,' I explained to Killick.

'Good idea. We need a woman standing by.' He stood up, looked suddenly weary. 'Thanks, Jack. You've been a help. Take care, both of you.'

Then he went out of the kitchen and I sat down opposite Adele. 'Darling heart . . .' I had never called a girl that before, never ever.

She smiled tiredly, put her hand on mine. 'I love you.'

I had been waiting for that for weeks, but I knew it was only of the moment. 'Get your things. We're going home.'

The police were still there when we left, but the crowd had drifted away and most of the lights in the adjoining flats were out now. There were no TV vans nor radio cars and I was glad of that. Tom should die privately.

We rode home in silence through a silent night but for the slurring sound of passing cars. Out on the upper reaches of the harbour a lone ferry was just a moving bank of lights, piggy-backed on its own reflection. I looked at Adele once or twice, but she was miles away; or locked in her head, doors shut against the thought of how Tom had died. I said nothing as I pulled the car into our driveway and helped her out.

Lynne, in a dressing-gown, opened the front door as we came up onto the verandah. She opened her arms and Adele, without hesitation, moved into them. I left them like that, moved past them into the house, carrying Adele's small overnight bag. I'm not too skilful at handling women's emotions.

I went through to our kitchen and made another pot of tea: the opiate for all situations; but loose tea, not teabags. I was standing there beside the sink, sipping the tea, when Lynne came in.

I pointed to the teapot. 'Shall I take her in a cup?'

'No. I've made up Mum and Dad's bed, put her in there. Get into your pyjamas, tie the cord very tight, button up the fly and go in and go to bed with her. No sex. She needs comfort, not that.'

I put down the cup, kissed her on the cheek and went into my bedroom and undressed. I got into my pyjamas, tied the cord tight, didn't check the fly, and went into my parents' bedroom. Adele lay on one side of the bed, my mother's side, the bed lamp still on.

'Lynne says I'm to keep you company —'

'I asked her to send you in.'

She flipped back the sheet and I got in beside her. I turned out the lamp and took her in my arms. There was no movement in the crotch and we went to sleep, like an old married couple.

2

She was still asleep next morning when I slid out of bed. I showered, dressed, had breakfast with Lynne, then went back into the main bedroom. She was sitting up in bed, mobile to her ear.

'All right, I'll see you this afternoon. No, I'm fine — Jack has looked after me.' She clicked off the phone and looked at me. 'Mum and Dad — they're coming down for a couple of days.'

'You're going back to the flat?'

'Yes. I'll be okay, with Mum and Dad there. The longer I put it off, the harder it will be to go back.' Her hair was tousled, she wore no make-up, but she was still beautiful. Especially when she put out her hand and smiled at me: 'Thanks, darling. For last night.'

'That's what I'm here for. Comfort . . . I have to go now, we have a staff meeting at 8.30. You'll be okay?'

Her face had suddenly clouded, as if for the first time since waking she had thought of Tom Barini. 'I'm a jinx.'

I said nothing, just sat waiting.

'Tom . . . There was another boy — he's dead, too . . .'

I played dumb, always a good role to play. *The J Shakespeare Manual of Acting ...*

'I had known him since I was, I dunno, thirteen or so. He was always in love with me ...'

I've had guys saying they were in love with me ... What had happened to the others, the ones who hadn't committed suicide?

'He was — he was very *intense*. He would quote poetry to me and I loved it. Dylan Thomas was a favourite ... *Through throats where many rivers meet, the curlews cry ...* I was romantic and I loved it — but I didn't love him. I made a mistake — I went to bed with him — it was, I dunno —'

'An act of charity?' *Jesus, the misuses of love!*

'I don't know. Maybe. But then it was getting deadly serious — he was *owning* me — and I had to put a stop to it. I remember the last night — he was crying like a child. Then he went home and hanged himself.' Her hand was holding mine, her nails suddenly digging into me. 'I'm a jinx —'

'No, you're not. Tom didn't die because of what he felt for you — he was just unlucky. Bloody unlucky. The other guy —'

'I shouldn't have told you —'

'No, I'm glad you did. It's out of the way now ...' I stood up. 'I've got to go. Can I see you tonight?'

'Mum and Dad are coming to the theatre to see me.' I waited for her to say, The show must go on. But she was too down-to-earth for that, another of her contradictions. 'Come to the flat afterwards.'

I leaned forward and kissed her. Is there any better perfume for the male animal than that of a woman just woken from sleep? 'I could crawl back into bed —'

'Another time.'

When I went out to the kitchen Lynne was putting the breakfast things in the dishwasher. 'I've called the office — I'll go in later. I'll take Adele back to her flat, if that's what she wants.'

'Thanks.'

She nodded. 'You've still got your problems.'

It was my turn to nod. 'We'll just have to see.'

When I went out the front door it was raining heavily. I had pulled a cover over the MG last night, but now I had to struggle in the rain to put the hood up. Jim Gainsford, our next-door neighbour, backed his BMW out of its garage, wave derisively at me through his rolled-up windows and drove off to his dry, air-conditioned office in a merchant bank. The elements never hit him the way they did a roving TV reporter in an open sports car. Of course landslides of falling stock prices and other financial catastrophes might hit him, but he always looked dry, unbedraggled and kempt.

The heavy rain continued as I drove up to Channel 15. Trucks and buses swept by, throwing off waves like destroyers in high seas; bus passengers sneered at me and some laughed as if they had seen the joke of the year. I passed two accidents, had to slow down to a crawl; went by a queue at a bus stop, standing there like refugees without hope. Thunder crashed and swords of lightning turned the rain to silver lace. Suddenly, for no reason, I was glad that Tom Barini had not died in the rain, lying there on the front lawn, his body sodden as well as broken.

My assignment from the morning conference was a clash of gangs at a school out in the far western suburbs. The rain had stopped, the thunder had gone out to sea to scare the gulls, the lightning had gone back into its scabbards. Rupe Hellinger and Jason Tully and I drove out to the school in the channel's van, through air washed as clean as the distant sea. The school was a mix of two solid brick buildings and half a dozen metal structures in large grounds as flat and treeless as a gravel plain. This was a State public school and you could see where the money ran out, at least till the next election campaign.

We were not welcome. Two teachers, a thin grey-haired man and a young stout woman, met us at the gates, as if they had been on the lookout for us. 'You're not to interview any of the students —'

'All we want to know is what happened,' I said. 'It's news —'

'Stuff the news,' said the woman. She was plain as a bag of cement, but you could see the strength in her. She would battle for the kids, gang members or not; the school was her world. 'Leave the kids alone. We'll sort it out. Don't point that camera at me,' she snarled at Rupe, 'or I'll sort you out!'

'She will too,' said the grey-haired man and a smile worked its way out of his wrinkled face. '*Please.* Leave before the classes come out for recess. If the kids see you, you know what they'll be like. Please do us a favour and leave.'

'Sure. Just to protect us with our boss, have any other crews been out here?'

'No,' snapped the woman. 'Just you.'

'You win. I'll tell our boss it was a false alarm.'

'I wish it were,' said the grey-haired man and looked like a man who had been losing battles all his life. 'But thanks. We'll handle it.'

'Bloody oath we will!' said the woman, but the look on the man's face held no hope.

Going home Rupe Hellinger said, 'You don't have any kids, do you, Jack?'

'None that I know of. Come on, Rupe, you know I'm not married.'

Jason, grinning, said, 'He's getting old.'

'That's my point, I think,' said Rupe. 'When I was at school, back last century' — there it was again: last century, receding into history — 'there were no *gangs*. There were cliques, but no gangs. You had a fight, it was one on one, down the back of the dunnies —'

'The Boer War,' I said to Jason. 'They never stop reminiscing.'

'They were better times, I tell you,' said Rupe and he sounded like an echo of my dad. 'Another country.'

Les Dibley accepted our excuse that there was no story of gang warfare at the school; he was of the old journalistic belief that accepted that no news was not good news, just news that had been suppressed. Sub-editors know more secrets than ASIO or the CIA will ever know.

'I did hear, though, that you witnessed some news last

night and didn't report it. Something about a bloke being tossed off a balcony.'

'It was a friend of a friend. Miss Adele Ambar, actually.'

'I'd heard that too. Is she your new girl?'

'Almost.'

He looked at me shrewdly. 'Tread carefully, son. In the meantime, our boss —' He blessed himself again. 'He wants to see you. He's heard the news on your almost girlfriend.'

I went across to the executive building, up to the office with its expensive walls and the yacht, which seemed to be headed in a different direction from when I had last seen it. The cleaner was either a frustrated mariner or a careless duster.

Entwistle was in a dark grey shirt with white collar and cuffs and white braces and an off-white tie. He looked, sartorially, a bloody joke. 'Jack! Great piece yesterday on that smash-and-grab. It had *immediacy*!'

You can't miss immediacy when you interview a jeweller thirty seconds after he's been whacked with an iron bar. We were driving back from another job, when the smash-and-grab gang burst out of a jeweller's shop, jumped into their car and shot out in front of us, jerking us to a stop. We'd missed the actual crime by only a few seconds.

'Thanks, Jared. You wanted to see me?'

'Ah yes.' Behind his desk, leaning back, man to man. Sometimes his oiliness took unction to the extreme. 'I heard our Miss Ambar was in an incident last night. It's in this morning's papers.'

Our Miss Ambar. 'Only incidentally, Jared. I'd picked her up at her theatre, she's in a play —'

'I read the review.'

'Yeah. Well, when we got back to her flat, the incident had happened. The police were there ... I wasn't going to interview her, Jared, get her feelings about what had happened. He was her flatmate —'

'She was living with him?' His voice sharpened.

'Separate rooms. He was gay ... You don't want me to interview her, do you?'

'No, no. Did you ask her about reading the news for us?'

'Yes. She said no, not at the moment. She feels her acting career is just taking off.'

'Is it?' He looked at me cynically, man to man; I wished the white collar would choke him.

'I think it might, Jared. The audiences seem to like her, if the critics don't.' That was a lie; or anyway, a half-lie. 'I think we have to be patient.'

'We can't hold the job open forever. Well ...' He sat up, pulled papers towards him; we were no longer man to man, the discussion was over. 'Let me know if she changes her mind.'

I was going down the stairs, past all the smiling, look-at-me photos of the channel's stars, when I met Mrs Entwistle coming up. She stopped and smiled, as automatic as a traffic light. 'Jack ... Dickens, isn't it?'

'Shakespeare,' I said. 'People are always getting us mixed up.'

She had a sense of humour, something I hadn't suspected. 'I was kidding, Jack.'

She was in a brown skirt and yellow cashmere, the famous breasts exhibiting themselves; Dolly Parton could have written a song of envy about them. I had met her a few times at channel functions, but her recognition of me had been no more personal than if I had been the channel's logo. I didn't live in the eastern suburbs and I was one of her husband's *employees*. Catherine the Great couldn't have held me in less regard.

But now, suddenly, I seemed to have been raised in status. 'I should know more about you, Jack. My husband is always singing your praises.'

Singing them flat, I'd bet. I gave her the old politician's lie: 'One does one's best.'

She smiled again. 'As one always should. You must come to dinner. Bring your girlfriend — I'm sure you have one?'

I sensed something behind the smile: *she knows about Jared's interest in Adele*. 'She's in a play at the moment —'

'Oh, she's an actress?' She was all innocence there above the sinful bosom. 'Would I know her?'

'Adele Ambar.'

She frowned, as if I'd mentioned Lilian Gish. 'I've — would I have read a review of something she's in?' She had, every line of it. 'Well, when her show closes, do bring her. I'll mention it to Jared. 'Bye. Do one's best, Jack.'

She went on up the stairs, arse weaving like blancmange in an earth tremor. I went on down the stairs and at the reception desk Charlene gave me a smirk. 'You'll get on, sucking up to the boss's wife.'

'One has to do what one has to do.'

* * *

I went home that evening to an empty house; Lynne was out, presumably with Nick Klavos. I cooked a microwave dinner, watched 'Becker' and his irascible approach to life, wondering why the idiot didn't climb into bed with Reggie, the owner of the diner; then switched over to 'The Bill' and watched that, wondering why all the cops on TV were so angst-ridden and so few of them laughed. Then an idea struck me and I got out the scripts from the bottom drawer and started looking at them. I jotted down some ideas and then it was time to get out the car and drive down to Kirribilli. I was a mixture of emotion, because all day, there at the back of my mind, like a ghost in a closet, had been the thought: how would last night affect Adele? Would she be looking for someone, me, to move into the flat with her? To take the place of the ghost of Tom?

She and her parents and I all arrived outside the flat at the same time.

Adele kissed me on the cheek and exclaimed, 'They loved the play!'

'I wonder what Chekhov would have made of Australian country folk?' said Luke Ambar.

'The serfs or us?' asked Kate Ambar and shook my hand. 'Nice to see you again, Jack. Adele has told us what a tower of strength you were for her last night.'

'Yeah, thanks,' said Luke and he too shook my hand, his grip very firm; for once, he wasn't garrulous, whatever thanks he felt was there in his hand. 'It must have been pretty bloody for both of you.'

Kate looked at him on the *bloody*, but said nothing. There had been no blood, not in the flat, and that had been something to be thankful for.

We went up in the lift in a solemn bond. As soon as we stepped into the flat Adele checked her answer-phone. There was a message from Paul Barini, introducing himself to her. He was staying at The Radisson, in Sydney to take Tom's body back home. He would like to come to the flat tomorrow to pick up Tom's things.

'I'll call him in the morning,' she said and looked at me. 'Do you want to meet him?'

I thought about it, then said, 'No.'

'I think,' said Kate, 'it will be enough if just Adele and I are here. He's going to be upset, so the fewer the better.'

'Good thinking,' I said, but I knew I had squibbed it. I was dodging the tangle of other people's emotions, especially a stranger's. It was hard enough as a reporter to stay outside them.

We were now in the living room of the flat. I was surprised at how neat and tidy it was; as if Tom had come back from the dead to put everything in place. I learned later it was Kate who had done just that.

Adele saw me looking around and pressed my hand, sadly, I thought. 'Neat and tidy.'

'Tom was like that,' I explained to her parents.

'Are you?' Kate's question was direct.

'I hang up my clothes when I take them off.'

'Not always,' said Adele. 'Does that answer your question, Mum?'

Kate just smiled and went into the kitchen; Adele followed her. Luke and I went out on the balcony. He looked down, then drew back.

'I don't know why we bought this flat. I hate heights, I'm a ground-level man. Who was the bastard who tossed him off here?'

I had called Detective Sergeant Killick during the day, but all he could tell me was that they were 'conducting enquiries'. I hadn't pressed it, but I knew he and Sergeant Rainone would tell me when they had something definite.

'There's a suspect, Luke, but they haven't yet picked him up yet. Adele and I will have to give evidence if he proves to be the guy and he's charged. Can she handle that?'

'She's strong, Jack. You'll find that out, if things are as I think they are between you.'

'There's still some way to go. She's more in love with the theatre than she is with me, right now.' I'd never before talked like this with a girl's father; but then I'd never got to a point where I'd had to. 'How long are you going to stay down here with her?'

'I'll be here a coupla days, her mum will probably stay a bit longer. I'm down here on business as well as —' He gestured into the flat. 'I'm talking with an investment adviser. What do you know about the bush, Jack?'

'Not much, just that it's there.'

'It may be dying — like that time in that play tonight. I run Murray Grey cattle and merino sheep. That's what the family has run for years, though the Greys came a long time after the merinos. My dad and his dad were right up there with the Faulkners and the McMasters when it came to wool quality. Wool's holding up at the moment, but it's up and down. Meat —' He shrugged. 'Since the mad cow scare in the UK, the Japs, our main market, have been wary about beef. We're due for another drought in a year or so — it comes and goes. I watch the El Niño effect the way my dad used to watch the local weather reports — my granddad would've laughed at the idea that our weather might come from South America.' He sipped the beer he had brought out onto the balcony. 'I want to put money into something that doesn't fluctuate, doesn't depend on the bloody weather. I dunno what, that's why I'm seeing this investment bloke tomorrow. Are you careful with money?'

'Pretty careful.' Adele had come to the door onto the balcony. 'I've noticed when he pays a restaurant bill he tips eight per cent, deducting for the GST charge.'

'You can read bills upside down?' I asked.

'Country women can,' said Luke. 'It's in their mother's milk.'

I might have been tight with restaurant tips, but I had city-bred optimism. Who could live with the thought that droughts came and went with and like the seasons? I wondered if Adele thought like that — accepted that drought came and went in the theatre? I doubted it: the rains, and the roles, would always come.

I felt at home with Kate and Luke Ambar; I had the feeling that I was more than accepted, I was welcomed. When I left, Adele took me to the door, stepped outside it and partly closed it. She put her arms around me and said, 'They're going to push you and me together.'

'I hope so.'

She kissed me, passionately, then slipped back inside and closed the door. I wasn't sure whether it was some sort of sign, but the kiss hadn't been a farewell one.

3

Next morning Lynne asked, 'How's Adele?'

'Bearing up. Her parents are down from Orange, I saw them last night.'

'What are they like?'

'They approve of me, if that's what you're asking. They're on my side against Chekhov, Ibsen and that other Shakespeare.'

'I wouldn't bet on you.'

'How's the front row philosopher?'

'Reliable. That's better than you've got.'

Maybe. I thought about it all day while we stood outside the Central Criminal courts waiting for the verdict on a particularly brutal murder of a man by his wife and her lover. The murderers got life and the dead man's parents came out and faced the cameras and said how pleased they were at the verdict and justice had been done. But the words were stilted, as if they had been advised what to say, and you knew they would go home and no amount of justice would bring their son back and that, in the end, was all that counted.

I looked at Rupe and Jason. 'Let's say we missed them?'

'Good idea,' said Rupe, and Jason nodded. 'Let's find a kindergarten and interview some kids about politics.'

Instead, we went back to Channel 15, where Les Dibley roasted me for wasting the day. But his heart wasn't in it.

'Jack, the public *likes* looking at misery. We've got a clip in from CNN about a train wreck in South Carolina, North Carolina, one of 'em, and they'll watch that tonight over their takeaways and thank Christ they're safe and not on some railway line in South Carolina or whatever. It's the survival instinct, Jack. We need it, we'd go out of our fucking heads if all we saw was Father Christmas handing out goodies.'

'What made you so cynical, Les?'

'Ask your dad, look around you. Biting the hand that feeds you adds to the flavour, that's why cannibals do it. The corporate world, here and everywhere, is full of cannibals, Jack. This country has lost its values, mark my words. The fucking world has.'

'Values have nothing to do with watching good or bad news on TV.'

'Maybe, maybe not. But door-stop sound bytes, twenty seconds on camera, you think that sums up true feelings? What people really believe? We show 'em five, ten seconds on film or tape and they think that's the truth of it all? Men like your dad and me, we live in the past, Jack. The good old days. Some day you'll think of these times as the good old days. Because the world is getting worse.'

'You should read more history, Les.'

'I did, Jack. And the best of times were the Dark Ages, about which we know fuck all.'

'You depress me, Les,' I said and went home.

At six I rang Kirribilli and Kate Ambar answered the phone. 'Adele has already left for the theatre. And Luke has gone home. Our foreman has broken his leg, he fell off the tractor.'

'Can I take you to dinner then?'

'I thought you'd never ask.' Her chuckle was an echo of Adele's. 'I'll be ready at 7.30. I have to wait till Luke calls.'

At 7.30, on time as usual, I picked her up and took her to Jasper's. She was beautifully dressed, though I can't remember what she wore except that it was beige, and she wore a scarf over her head in the open car.

'I was a dolly bird when I was young.'

'What's a dolly bird?'

'Girls who rode around in open sports cars. English girls invented them, they took their corsets off in the sixties. Before my time, but some of us carried on in style.'

'Was Adele ever a dolly bird?'

'Ask her yourself. A mother shouldn't paint her daughter's character.'

'I wish I'd known you when you were young.'

'You wouldn't have stood a chance. I was Luke's dolly bird right from the start.' But she smiled and, for a moment, I fell in love with an older woman. Only for a moment, though.

When we walked into the restaurant, the owner, poker-faced, welcomed us. 'A pleasure to see you again, Mr Shakespeare.'

'This is Miss Ambar's mother.' Then to Kate: 'He thinks I'm graduating to older women.'

When he had shown us to our table, then gone away, she said, 'You bring a lot of women here? Young ones?'

'I used to. Dolly birds. Now just the one — Adele.'

'Jack ...' She put her hand on mine; even the gestures were the same. 'I hope she's not going to disappoint you.'

I shrugged; disappointed lovers could swing an election vote in any country, we're myriad. 'Some day she'll wake up. She'll read the reviews.'

'She never does, you know.'

I had guessed that. Criticism was water off a swan's back; she floated above it, neck arched, eyes shut. 'How does Luke feel?'

'As disappointed as you may be. For different reasons. He's become a worrier, something he never was. That's why he's down here now talking to an investment adviser.'

'What's he going to invest in?' Thinking of my bank stocks in the jar under my bed.

'I have no idea. Like Adele, I'm light-headed when it comes to money. So Luke thinks.'

'I don't believe that. That you're light-headed about anything.'

She pressed my hand again, gave me the family smile. 'I can see why our girl likes you.'

She told me about Paul Barini coming to the flat: 'He seemed a very nice man. And sad. He stayed a while, had a coffee with us, told us how the family had regretted they had sent Tom away. They realised now all he ever really wanted was to be with his partner. But his father couldn't accept what he was and so he came here to Sydney ...'

'What do the family do?'

'They have a vineyard, they grow grapes for the wineries on the Margaret River. They don't bottle their own wine; he said they never had the capital. They're a very sad family right now. They lost Tom because they didn't understand him. Not till it was too late.'

I wanted to ask how well she and Luke understood Adele and her ambition. I didn't, because I felt they were like me. Not that we didn't understand the ambition, but that we didn't understand her non-recognition of her lack of real talent. But we would never drive her away from us.

It was a very pleasant evening. Older women — *some* older women — have an assurance about them with men; I felt entirely at ease with her. I took her home, kissed her on the cheek and said, 'Tell Adele I'll call her tomorrow. When are you going back home?'

'Tomorrow. I think she'll be okay now. Over what's happened, I mean. She's pretty strong, she doesn't fold easily. Have you heard anything from the police?'

'I talked to the sergeant at Homicide today. Nothing so far. Adele will probably have to go to the inquest. And then, if they catch the guy who did it, she'll be a witness. Me too, if it's the guy we think it was.'

'Nothing is ever final, is it?' She kissed me on the cheek. 'What's that perfume?'

'Arpege. It's Del's favourite too. We smell expensively.'

As I turned back to the lift she said, 'Come out to the property some time with Del.'

'I'd like that.'

Next morning I got out of the MG in the parking lot

and passed Entwistle as he was getting out of his Merc 500 in the executives' parking area. Today was one of his sartorial dull days: he was all in blue, no white collar, white cuffs. He looked almost anonymous.

I paused, couldn't help myself, said, 'I met Mrs Entwistle on the stairs the other day. She suggested I bring Miss Ambar to dinner some time.'

You'd have thought it had been suggested I should bring a female gorilla to dinner; for a moment there was sheer terror in his face. 'Oh, I don't know that would be a good idea, not at the moment —'

'Oh, no rush.' The sword was in almost up to the hilt. 'Your wife said any time.'

'She — she's on a shopping spree at the moment. She has a credit card for a brain, you know how it is . . .' Man to man, though I couldn't see what a shopping spree had to do with an invitation to dinner. He was panicking. 'The kids too. You ever been married, Jack?'

'Not that I know of.' The same gag, twice in two days. 'Close, a coupla times.' That was a lie, but I still had the sword in him. 'I can imagine —'

'Yeah.' Then, as if not wanting to ask the question: 'You're not that far with Miss Ambar, are you? Thinking of marrying?'

'Not yet.' I took the sword out, wiped the blood from it. 'Give my regards to Mrs Entwistle. Nice lady.'

I went on into the newsroom, sheathing the sword. I felt like D'Artagnan: I would have to tell the Lady Adele tonight. The mood dissolved when Les Dibley sent us out on a story of two teenage girls who were missing. I interviewed the two mothers (there didn't appear to be any fathers) and knew at once why the two girls had gone missing. Some people, men and women, should never become parents. One of the mothers looked as if she had just got off a weekend of drugs; the other smelled of cheap wine, her mouth slipping from side to side between a grimace and a grin. Each had a youngster clinging to her skirt and I looked at them, four or five years old at the most, and wondered when *they* would go missing. I also wondered what Chekhov would have though of it all, but couldn't remember if he had ever written about the dregs.

I went to the theatre that night, sat through *The Three Sisters*, saw a certain sentimentality that I hadn't seen before. Adele had improved, but only just; she was like an artist who had learned to varnish a painting, but that was all. But the audience seemed to like her, if most of the applause at the curtain was heavy-handed, that of men.

Going home she was quiet.

'Tired?'

'I've been working hard.' She looked sideways at me. 'You notice any improvement tonight?'

I drove cautiously, the MG and myself. 'You're more settled. It all went very smoothly.'

It was enough; she pressed my knee. 'Thanks.'

We went up to the flat, went to bed as naturally — well, as naturally as a young, not old, married couple. Then she rolled off me, but lay with her leg over me and her hand stroking my chest.

'I'm going to miss all this.'

'Why? You giving it up for Lent or something? Lent's over.'

'No.' A long pause; then: 'I'm going to New York.'

I was suddenly cold: truly. I almost croaked, 'Why?'

'I'm going to Actors' Centre.'

'Actors' Studio? Where Brando and those others studied?'

'No, Actors' *Centre*. It's a small school that's associated with the Bialoguski. They have a reciprocal arrangement. I'm going to New York for six months and one of their students is coming out here. I even get a green card, if I can find work over there.'

I was suddenly angry; but somehow managed not to show it. She was slipping away from me and I felt this rage against stupid ambition and blind confidence. I managed to say, almost casually, 'You're taking a risk.'

'Haven't you ever taken risks?'

I'd never been asked that. You coast through your life, meeting obstacles but none of them insurmountable, and one day you are out there on the broad stream, holding your own, smug in what you think you've achieved, even if achievement had never actually been your pursuit. I'd been born lucky. Parents happy with each other and with me and Lynne; a father with a reputation as a journalist and who had connections; my own good marks at university, the almost effortless slide into TV journalism. Come to think of it, the only risks I had taken had been with girls. With this one . . .

'No.'

That seemed to silence her. She propped herself on one elbow and looked at me as if seeing me for the first time. We were both as naked as could be, the sheet thrown back, but she was looking at me as if I had suddenly cloaked myself, nothing showing that she recognised.

'Jack —' She shook her head; hair fell down over one eye, the way I liked to see it. 'Jack — you're smug and — and careless!'

'I'm not careless about you. I couldn't care more for you.'

'I know that, damn you!' She was angry now. She sat up, swung her legs over the side of the bed, turned back to glare at me. 'Why can't you understand what I want?'

'I'm trying.' But she knew — it was in my voice, that I'd never understand. Love is blind, in too many ways, because it is selective.

She was silent a long moment, then she got up and went to the bathroom. I lay there, waiting for her to come back. But she didn't and after some hesitation I rolled out of bed and went to the bathroom. She was sitting on the toilet, with the lid down, weeping. Christ, I thought, what a ridiculous place for me to surrender!

'I'm sorry.' I knelt down.

Then, God forgive me, I started to giggle.

'What's the matter?'

'You're my queen on the throne — I'm —'

She stared at me, then suddenly she too started to laugh. She fell on the floor, grabbed my head and kissed me till I felt my lips would bleed. But there, on the bathroom floor, naked, I knew I had lost possession of her, formal or informal. It was over.

4

She had known for a week that she was to go to New York, but had put off telling me. That, I suppose, was some sort of admission that she loved me, just as a bruising punch often is.

Her parents came down from Orange to take her to the airport. I drove out in the MG, a sports hearse on its way to a funeral. Luke and Kate left us alone for a few minutes and we stood there, holding hands, trying to be private amongst a cast of thousands, as the old movie posters used to say.

'E-mail me,' she said.

'Never. E-mail wasn't meant for love letters. You'll get hand-written *billet-doux*, not even typed.'

'Oh darling!' she said and wrapped her arms round my neck and kissed me to the applause of a rugby team heading for New Zealand. That turned a hundred-deep queue around and the applause increased. It must have been music to an actress's ears, I thought meanly; but held her tight. I was ready to weep, knowing how much I was going to miss her in the — months ahead? Years?

Then she was gone through the gates and the Ambars and I were walking out to the parking lot. 'She'll be back,' said Luke. 'Three months at the outside.'

'No,' said Kate. 'It'll be longer than that. I'm sorry, Jack.'

'I'll give her three months, then go over and see her.'

Kate looked at me, almost with motherly concern: as if she were *my* mother, not Adele's. 'Good luck. Come up and spend a weekend with us.'

'Yeah, do that,' said Luke and there was no doubt I'd be welcome.

'How'd the investment advice go?'

'Great! I think I'm really into something.' He was by the door of the Range Rover; Kate was already in it, at the wheel. 'Information technology, it's all the go in the States. Your crowd, Channel 15, are one of the main partners.'

There had been talk about it around the office, but I hadn't taken much notice. 'Tonetel, that it?'

'Yeah, that's it. Your boss — Pennywhistle? He's one of the directors —'

Pennywhistle? He'd love that. 'Entwistle.'

'Yeah. I thought you might be in it —'

'Not my cup of tea.' I wouldn't have been a partner of Entwistle's in national bonds. 'I'll give you a call and come up some weekend.'

I went round to the other side of the Range Rover, pressed Kate's hand as she held it out the window. She said softly, 'Bear up and pray, Jack.'

Chapter Five

1

A month later I went up to Bulinga Creek and spent a very pleasant weekend with the Ambars. Neighbours came in on the Saturday night, a dozen or so of them, all of them graziers whose families had been on the land almost as long as the Ambars. They were a fading class, history growing fainter on the page, but there was none of the languid apathy of Chekhov's characters. Bone was still there in their backs, white flags were not their banners.

'You see why Luke wishes we'd had a son?' said Kate, as if she had read my thoughts.

'Would he settle for a grandson?'

'You haven't given up hope? Don't, Jack, keep hoping.'

It was four months before I got to New York. Four months and no sex; Father Finnigan would have been proud of me. There was masturbation, always with her in mind, but that is no longer a sin; as the Vatican joke had it, it was okay so long as it didn't get out of hand. I took out a couple of old girlfriends and was tempted, but then I saw Adele being tempted by some stranger in New York and I drew back. It was a dishonest way of being faithful, but honesty and faithfulness are uncomfortable bedmates, like crotch and conscience.

I took Hilary Reingold to dinner several times, took her back to her flat in Elizabeth Bay, but always kissed her at her door and went home.

'I can't tempt you?' she said, leaning against the doorjamb like a K-Mart hooker. 'I know ze treeks —'

'Cut it out. You know I'm sworn to celibacy.'

'What ees zat? Like ze herpes?' But she grinned and kissed me again. 'Some day, honey, I hope I find a guy like you. When I'm forty and over the hill.'

'Hilary, you'll never be over the hill. You'll be seducing fellers till you're seventy.'

'Ooh, I can't wait!'

She kissed me again, gave me the pelvic howdy-do, and went inside. There are reminders that a celibate man can enjoy.

Small history, as it does, happened in headlines and minute-and-forty seconds vision. I covered criminal trials, bushfires, accidents, missing children: everyday history. I also worked on a television script. About a private investigation firm (what an original idea!), one partner gay, the other straight. Halfway through it I found I was writing Tom Barini and myself and that made it easier. I tried to put humour into it, something you rarely find in cop dramas. The guys in my script actually laughed and joked the way people do in real life. But maybe that was because they were private eyes; though, come to think of it, I can't remember too many laughs in Sam Spade's life.

Lynne worried about me. 'You never go out!'

'I'm *okay*, okay? I talk to Adele once a week —'

'How's she doing? She got any work yet?'

'No-o.'

'Did you give her Mum and Dad's number?'

'Yes, but I don't think she's called them yet. I think she's finding it tougher there than she imagined.'

'It figures. Why wouldn't she? There must be a million aspiring actresses in the States . . . I shan't be home tonight.'

I didn't ask why; not directly. 'How's it going with the philosopher?'

She hesitated, then said, 'He's proposed.'

I stood up, put my arms round her and kissed the top of her head. She leaned against me and it was a moment or two before I realised she was weeping. 'Come on! What's the matter?'

'Oh Jack, I wish you could be as happy as I am.'

'Some day —' But I couldn't go any further. I pushed her away, found a handkerchief and wiped her cheeks. 'Tell Nick I couldn't be happier for the two of you. Have you told Mum and Dad yet?'

'No, it only happened last night. I'll call them from work, when Dad should be home with Mum.' She wiped her eyes, looked at me almost appealingly: 'You're really pleased for me?'

'Lynne — I really am. I joke about Nick, but he's nice and solid and he's nuts about you. And he won't always be in the front row —'

She thumped me, playfully, and said, 'Give my love to Adele,' and went off to work. I had a free day and I went back to *Bing and Riley*, my private eyes.

The police were getting nowhere in their search for Tom Barini's killer. I rang Sergeant Killick and he said, 'We're still looking Jack. That feller you described, the blond bloke, we've checked him. He had an alibi we couldn't break. That night he was with — well, never mind who he was with. He's someone you'd know, everyone would. We don't want any sleaze, do we, Jack? Your friend's name would come into it —'

'No, Phil, we don't want that, neither I nor my girlfriend.' It struck me, almost irrelevantly, that it was the first time I'd called her that. 'I shouldn't say this, but I was hoping it was that blond bastard —'

'I didn't hear you say that, Jack. They've kept putting back the inquest, but it's on next week. You'll be called. What about Miss Ambar?'

'She's in New York, she's there for six months.'

'A good place to be. Inquests are no fun. Look after yourself, Jack.'

I attended the inquest, spoke my piece and the verdict was murder by person or persons unknown. I didn't tell Adele, though she enquired a couple of times if the police were close to finding Tom's murderer. After a while she stopped asking and we buried Tom in our memories, which is the safest place when things have to be hidden.

Two months and I had finished the script. I sent it to an agent Hilary had recommended and a month later she called to tell me she wanted to see me. She had good news, she said.

'I've placed it as the pilot for a series with Channel 15 —'

'Oh Christ, not *them*!'

'Why not?' Her name was Chiffon Brown. She was a robust lady with more dimples than a nursery of babies; she looked cuddly, in a large dose, but she was tough. 'They're *looking* for a series, after the last one they tried collapsed.'

The one Adele had been sacked from. Irony is whetstone, it sharpens satisfaction; yet I felt a certain embarrassment. I would never tell Adele how and why my script had been accepted. 'Whom do I talk to?'

'Whom?'

'My dad has old-time standards. He sub-edits me, even from a distance.'

'Well, whom is Jared Entwistle —'

Oh shit. Irony had turned into a hammer, right there at the back of my skull. 'Have you talked terms with them?'

'Yes.' She gave them to me: not a fortune, but good enough for the time I had worked on the script. 'Keep writing, Mr Shakespeare. I think you have promise.'

'That's what Kit Marlowe said.'

'Who?'

Entwistle couldn't have been more flattering: 'Jack, it's great! Fantastic! It's got the most fantastic conceptualisation! I'll prioritise our aims and at the end of the day, basically, it'll stabilise our ratings.'

'You can say that again,' I said and hoped he wouldn't. Behind him the yacht was bucking a gale, or so it seemed.

'I never knew you had that sort of talent.' He went on like that for a minute or two more; the yacht looked headed for the rocks. Then: 'You heard from Miss Ambar?'

'Occasionally. She's studying very hard —'

'We should have found some role for her. She's got looks, talent — well, you'd know. If the pilot clicks and we go ahead with the series, can you write her into it?'

Chekhov and a couple of private eyes? 'I could try. Let's see how the pilot goes.'

There were rewrites; I found that was par for the course:

'The humour in it holds up the narrative dynamic —'

'But people do joke in real life —'

'Sure, but real life is haphazard, it doesn't allow for the dynamics —'

I gave up. They were all film school graduates and knew all about the dynamics. I wondered how many helpers and advisers Chekhov had had; or the other Shakespeare. I didn't complain, because I was already blocking out a feature film script. *And* still reporting murders, bank robberies and other calamities that didn't allow for the dynamics.

I wrote Adele my *billet-doux*, as promised, feeling rather like someone from the twentieth, no, the nineteenth century as the pen (well, a biro) slid over the paper. I phoned her once a week. She missed me, dreadfully, she said, but there was always something else there in her voice: 'I'm learning so much, Jack! They're teaching me a whole new approach to acting —'

How about teaching you a retreat from it? But I didn't voice that, not at 10,000 miles. 'I have a month's leave coming in September —'

'Oh darling, can you come over? I *need* you —'

'I've already booked. I want to see my mum and dad as well. Have you got in touch with them?'

'Not yet.' There was a hint of embarrassment. 'I've been so busy —'

'Well, it can wait. I'd rather be there to introduce you.'

But jealousy bit at me. How many other guys were hanging around her? *I've been so busy* ... Then I told her about the pilot script: 'If it takes off and it goes into a series, they want me to write you into it.'

'Who does?'

Don't mention Entwistle. 'The producer.'

'Oh darling, that would be nice, but I don't want to be trapped in TV.'

It is very difficult to love a snob; but one does one's best. 'I'll write a play —'

'Oh, that would be wonderful!' Since landing in New York she had, it seemed, become theatrical. Actors' Centre had a lot to answer for. 'Together in lights!'

She was starting to annoy me; she had to be rescued. 'Stay away from other men till I get there —'

Her voice softened, was the one I remembered: 'You don't have to worry there, darling. Are you staying away from other women?'

'Celibate as the Pope.'

'Don't go too far.' Her voice softened even further: 'I do love you, Jack.'

But: that was there in her voice too, unspoken.

'I love you too.'

It was that way till I left for the States in September.

Just before I went, Les Dibley said, though he must have known for weeks, 'I hear you've become a *writer*.'

He made it sound as if I'd become a pedophile. 'Guys do, Les, it's an honourable profession. There was one named Shakespeare.'

'Cut out the bullshit. You thinking of giving up working for me?'

'So long as you keep paying me, no. It's a dodgy career, writing, and I like the regular paycheck.' Which was true, so maybe I'd never be a *real* writer. 'Relax, Les. It's just a sideline.'

'How's that — what was her name? Miss Ambar?'

'You're as subtle as a whack in the head, Les. She's okay and yes, I took up writing to get my mind off whatever she's doing in New York.'

'And what's she doing there?' Though I was sure he knew.

'Acting. Or learning to.'

'Good luck, Jack. Give my regards to George Dubya. If the Yanks had our system of compulsory voting, he wouldn't be President.'

'I'll tell him.'

2

Lynne drove me to the airport, gave me a sisterly kiss, hug and advice: 'Be firm, Jack. That's what women want.'

'What do I do? Knock her out cold and bring her back over my shoulder?'

'If needs be.'

'If Nick knocked you cold and slung you over his shoulder, what would you do?'

'Give him back his ring.' She kissed me again. 'Good luck. Give Mum and Dad a big hug and kiss for me.'

'Not Dad, not a hug and a kiss. He's still back in the 1950s. I'll shake hands for you.'

I travelled Qantas, business class, and the hostess who showed me to my seat knew me, or of me. 'Welcome aboard, Mr Shakespeare. I've seen you on Channel 10.'

'Channel 15, actually.'

'Yes. I knew it wasn't the ABC.' Other than that, she treated me beautifully all the way to Los Angeles.

I had been there before, but it was a city in which I would never feel at home. From the air it is a map scribbled on by some kid with white chalk. Those freeways connect the various boroughs, but only with traffic; they are separate communities, held together only by the generic name. There are cities within the city: Beverly Hills, Culver, Burbank. There are communities within the community. I felt that I would always feel footloose in LA.

I stopped over for two days to see an agent Chiffon Brown had recommended. She had sent him the first draft of my film script, telling him it had everything. It was about a homespun Sydney boy who wanted to be a pitcher in American major leagues and his girlfriend, a school teacher, who wanted him to stay home and have kids with her. It was about ambition and, Chiffon said, it had everything: hearts-and-flowers, humour and narrative dynamics.

Moss Dahl was a Jewish cherub, all pink cheeks and smiles, who said he had been in Hollywood since Charlie Chaplin's day: last century. But he seemed genuinely interested in me and liked my script.

'Of course, Jack, they'll rewrite it, seven or eight of 'em. But who cares? You get paid, get a credit and you're on to your next one. It's the way things go now in pictures. Back when they really made movies here — you ever see any of Preston Sturges' movies? Billy Wilder's? The good old days, Jack. Nowadays, all that's in movies is money. So you grab it and run. You going on to New York, you say? Why?'

'I have a girl there. And my parents.'

'Three good reasons. I'll talk to you on your way back. Don't invest any money in New York. I been hearing some nasty tales about some of them bastards on Wall Street. Out here we're all honest bastards. We just take the money and run, nobody gets hurt. In the meantime . . .'

'I'll say a Hail Mary.'

'Mary who?'

I flew across the States, a great land even before the North Americans got there. God might once have been an Englishman, but in His travels He had stopped off and blessed this river-ridden land beneath me. I thought of the brown plains and unreliable rivers and stony deserts I had flown over back home and wondered if God had ever though of doing a job down our way. Of course, in the States as everywhere else, He had let loose human evil, but then He has always juggled balls.

Mum, Dad and Adele were waiting for me at La Guardia. They were standing apart, because they still hadn't met, and when I walked out of the gates they converged on me like rival pamphleteers on a voter. We four met in a confusion of welcome.

I distributed kisses like votes to Mum and Adele, and

clapped Dad on the shoulder. Then, putting my arm around Adele, I introduced her to my parents. The look on their faces, especially Dad's, was full of approval.

'Welcome,' said my mother and it was meant for both Adele and me.

Adele had come out to the airport by cab, so we all rode back to Manhattan in Dad's car, a Volvo. Adele and I sat in the back, holding hands, and I could feel the sap rising in both of us like hot water in a bath. There, how's that for a romantic allusion? Move over, Will.

My parents had an apartment in the East Sixties. Dad was now a senior press man at the UN and he was, accordingly, well looked after. The UN looks after the poor of the world, but there are no poor at UN headquarters. That is my cynicism, not my father's; like a good newspaperman, he never passed an opinion on his employers. At least not till he left them.

'Where do you live, Adele?' asked my mother as we rode up in the elevator.

'Down below Canal Street, on the edge of Chinatown. I have one room and share a bathroom with another girl.'

'She's a struggling actress,' I said.

'Why is it that only artists struggle?' said Dad, but he was smiling. 'Never struggling street cleaners or bus drivers?'

My parents were a good-looking couple, with the majority of the looks on my mother. She was not beautiful, not as Adele was, but she attracted attention; she had that indescribable attractiveness that has nothing to do with sculptured features. She still had her figure, a little full, but she moved nicely, if not quite with Adele's gracefulness.

Dad, on the other hand, had an anonymous look, an asset, he used to say, for a journalist. You could ask a probing question of a visiting president or prime minister and, a week later at another press conference, ask another probing question and the target would never be quite sure where, or if, he had seen you before. Dad was slightly shorter than I, broader, and had an easy charm that, I'm sure, made him as welcome in Namibia and Nigeria as it did in New York. He was perfect for the UN, something, he once told me, that made him uneasy. He was that awkward mix: a cynic with principles.

While Dad mixed drinks and talked with Adele, I followed Mum out to the kitchen. The apartment was larger than I had expected; it was comfortably, just short of luxuriously, furnished. 'The last time I was over here, you were out on Long Island.'

Mum could hear unasked questions; she was a human radar system. 'We're not splurging the family fortune. This is paid for by the UN. Dad's still with the press office, but he's now a sort of unofficial troubleshooter, because of the contacts he's built up. We entertain here, informally, have delegates come in and take their shoes off. The office pays for a chef to come in, he prepares dinner or lunch, he goes and I serve it without help and the delegates think how resourceful and what wonderful cooks Aussie wives are ... How serious is it with you and her?'

'I'm surprised it took you so long to ask. Serious with me. With her, ye-e-es, up to a point. She wants to be the Edith Evans of the twenty-first century. You ever heard of Edith Evans?'

'I saw her in London on our honeymoon. She was a *grande dame*. Will your dame ever be a *grande dame*?'

'I doubt it. And don't call her my dame. You've been in New York too long.'

'Don't I know it. How's Longueville?'

'Smug and comfortable. You want to come home?'

'They say there are no native New Yorkers, they all come from somewhere else. I could never be one. It's been interesting, but it's time to go home. Dad, I think, feels the same way.' She switched on the oven. 'I had the chef come in this morning, told him the Prime Minister of Australia was coming to dinner.'

'Was he impressed?'

'He didn't know we had one. He thought we still belonged to the British Empire. He's from Brazil.'

'How did Dad enjoy that trip to Brazil?'

'He said the girls were very impressive. They wear nothing coming and going.'

'Yeah, so I've heard.'

Mum smiled; there was nothing she ever missed. 'You staying here tonight?'

'I'll take a key, just in case.'

Dinner was pleasant and easy. I played spectator, watching the match between the two teams. But there was no conflict. When it was time to go I said to Dad, 'I'll see you in the morning.'

He looked at Adele: 'He used to be a heavy sleeper, we could never wake him in the morning.'

She fluttered her eyelashes, as innocent as Jennifer Lopez. 'I wouldn't know.'

There is promise when your parents and your girlfriend part on a laugh. I took her home in a cab, she snuggled into my arm all the way. 'I've missed you, Jack.'

'We'll make up for it. Almost five months —'

Her one room, with shared bathroom, was part of an old, narrow, ugly building that had somehow survived the developers. I made no comment, nor did she, but it was a long way from the Kirribilli flat with its harbour views and the ancestral homestead with its avenue of poplars. She was slumming, though I didn't ask what the rent was.

The room was neat and tidy, up to a point. Women comment on how men live, but never the reverse. As soon as the door closed behind us we were at each other like animals, no other word for it. Absence makes the heart grow fonder; it also has an effect on other organs. When I looked at myself later in the bathroom mirror I was covered in welts and scratches, as if I had been pulled through a Brazilian bramble bush.

It took us some time to exhaust ourselves. Then, at last, we were looking at each other with love, not sex. 'I missed you. Not just that, but *you*.'

She kissed me, tenderly, which was all the answer I needed.

Later, lying in each other's arms, I told her about my screenplay. 'If it's taken, I'll be coming to Los Angeles. Would you come out there?'

She took her time: 'I hope you do sell it, darling. But . . .' A long pause. 'No, I don't want to go out there. I'm thinking of moving on to London.'

I let go of her, propped myself up on my elbow. 'Why?'

'I'm getting nowhere here. I played a corpse in "Law & Order" —'

'Was it a good part?'

She hit me, went on, 'I've had one small part onstage, half a dozen lines in an Off-Off-Broadway play.'

Off-Off-Broadway: how far out was that? New Jersey? Ohio? 'But why London? It'll be just as tough there.'

'I know that. But it's more my style — I'm not a Method actor, I've found out.'

The self-delusion was still there; I had to be patient. 'Are you thinking Shakespeare? Stratford?'

She nodded, but smiled, stroked my face. 'How would that be? If I became a Shakespearean actor and married you?'

'If you marry me, you can become whatever you like. A Japanese actress in those, whatdotheycall'em, *kabuki* plays.'

'In *kabuki* plays all the female parts are played by men. Relax, darling, I'll never marry anyone but you.'

'You could try alternatives while I'm waiting . . .' Why does the tongue sometimes speak while the mind is changing gears?

She rolled away from me, sat on the edge of the bed, said without looking back at me, 'You can be bloody cruel sometimes.'

I stroked her back. 'I'm sorry. That slipped out.'

'You've been thinking it, haven't you? That I might have been crawling into bed with someone else.'

'Didn't you think it about me?'

She hesitated, then nodded, without looking back at me. 'I know what guys are like ... I won't say I haven't been tempted. Not because I liked some guy, but because — well, *because*. You'd understand. You don't exactly need Viagra.'

I took her by the shoulders, pulled her back on the bed, looked down at her. 'With you, never ...'

She stared up at me, then put her arms round my neck. 'Oh Jack, never, never let us fight!'

'No fighting.' Then: 'I'm glad you let the Brazilian go back to South America. I like you bouffant — is that the word?'

'Not for down there.'

A while later, just before she turned out the light, she said, 'You can sleep in tomorrow ...'

'I'm pretty worn out. The flight and then this ...' I sleepily patted her belly.

'I have to get up early. I work down at Starbucks in the World Trade Center. I do the breakfast shift. I start at seven.'

'A waitress-actress? That's a cliché, isn't it? Couldn't you get something that paid more? Some modelling?'

'Actors' Centre won't take models, they think it's degrading for an actress.'

'Are they left-wing or something?'

'Very. They're big on Bertolt Brecht.'

Just the school for Dame Edith Evans's successor. But I didn't say that. All I said was, 'I'll come down to Starbucks and you can serve me breakfast.'

She kissed me and turned out the light.

3

In my sleep I heard the sound of the fire sirens. I had come awake when Adele got out of bed, was half-awake when she kissed me and left, and was back asleep when the sirens sounded. But I ignored them; I'd been following sirens, fire and police and ambulance, for the past three years; they were in my ear, almost like tinnitus. I slept on till the phone, the sound I can't ignore, woke me.

It was my mother. 'I looked up Adele's number — is she there?'

'No, she's gone to work —'

'Jack, there's a story for you. A plane has crashed into one of the World Trade Center buildings —'

'Oh Christ!'

She caught the sudden panic in my voice. 'What's the matter?'

'She works down there — in a Starbucks —' I was scrambling out of bed. 'I'll call you back, Mum.'

The bathroom was next door to Adele's room; fortunately, no one was in it. I splashed water in my face, gulped a glass of water, emptied the bladder and was back in the room within two minutes. Five minutes later, dressed, I was out on the street and running west towards Church Street.

There was no panic in the streets then. I found out later that, at that time, people though the plane into the south building was no more than a dreadful accident. I pushed through the crowd standing on the corner and kept running down Broadway. I was perhaps half a mile from the two tall buildings; I could see the smoke pouring out of the upper side of one of them. Distance on Manhattan is foreshortened by the height and size of the buildings flanking it.

Police cars and fire engines were racing towards the disaster; people were standing on the sidewalks, heads all turned south, spectators at a game they didn't understand. I was running along the gutter, glad I was in fair condition, but my heart was pumping and every nerve in my body was at work, tearing at me.

Then the second plane, appearing out of nowhere, slammed into the north building of the Center. I had no idea how much time had passed since the first plane had hit. The two towers were there in narrow focus, framed by the buildings on either side of Church Street, placed exactly so that the gathering crowds on both sides of the street could see it. Even over the pumping in my ears, I heard the gasp of the crowd; then it was gone as another fire engine roared by. And I kept running.

A cop on the other side of the street yelled at me to stop. I slowed, snatched my Sydney press card from my pocket, yelled, 'Press!' As if that overruled all restrictions; but I didn't stop to debate it with him. I ran on. People were coming towards me out of the smoke, some running, some staggering, some no more than walking slowly, all of them with the glazed look on their smoke-grimed, dust-clouded faces that said they were still in shock. You have seen it all on your screens since then: reality TV. Except this was unbelievable *real*.

I was running into the smoke and dust when I saw her

coming towards me, hurrying but not running in panic. She was dressed in what I guessed was the Starbucks uniform, but she was covered in dust, so that she looked like something out of a cheap horror film. I stepped in front of her and she ran into my arms without recognising me. I held her to me, felt the trembling racking her; she sagged and I had to hold her up. I was trembling myself, with relief, and I had to push my legs apart to brace myself.

'Darling —'

Only then did she recognise me. She clung to me as if the ground beneath us was going to turn to water and we were about to drown. She didn't ask where I had come from, how I happened to be there. I *was* there. I could see the look of relief and thankfulness in her face.

I carried her to the sidewalk, found ourselves in front of the open door of a small delicatessen. I carried her in there ahead of the deli owner; he found a chair and I lowered her onto it. She looked up at me out of a death mask.

'It's okay — you made it —'

'Oh Jack ...' She put her arms round my hips and hugged me.

Then the deli owner's wife brought a glass of water and a wet cloth. That day Good Samaritans were in their hundreds in Lower Manhattan. You've read stories of them: they were all true.

The wife waited till we had parted, then she moved in. She was a short, plump woman who looked as if she spent the day tasting samples of what they sold; her husband was built on the same lines. When I went back the next day to thank them, I learned they were Czechs from

Bratislava, who had come to America looking for a new life. What they saw that morning they had never seen in downtown Bratislava.

'I'll take you upstairs, dust you down properly —'

'Like furniture?' The mask cracked in the grotesque smile.

'No,' said Mrs Safarik, 'not like furniture.'

At that I wanted to weep; but didn't. I went out onto the sidewalk, where Mr Safarik was standing, staring down at the unbelievable scene that seemed to have got closer. People were still running, stumbling towards us, going by with that same stunned look on their dust-disfigured faces. We could see police and firemen, but they seemed overwhelmed by what lay in front of them. It was another twenty-four hours before I learned how many of them had died in the rescue efforts.

I was born a journalist. Here was the biggest story of my life and I had no camera crew to record it. Later, that night, Les Dibley would ask me what I'd got and all I'd be able to tell him was memories, which are not news.

'Who would do that?' I asked aloud.

Mr Safarik shrugged angrily. 'Who knows? The North Koreans? The Ayrabs? Them people bombed that place in Oklahoma City? The government never tells us nothing. They are all the same, governments.'

Then it happened. The towers started to collapse, folding like black sandcastles, specks of sand, people, flying out of the windows. Smoke and dust billowed up like a storm I had never seen; it came whirling, boiling up the street, people running before it in terror. The whole block below us, street, buildings, cars and trucks, people, disappeared beneath it.

Mr Safarik grabbed my arm and pulled me back into his store. He slammed the door shut, grabbed papers, cloths, stuffed them beneath the door. He did it with desperate haste, as if he had done it before, though, even when I went back the next day, I didn't ask him when or where.

Adele, still streaked with dust but with her face clean, and Mrs Safarik had come downstairs again. The four of us stood there in the small shop, amongst the hams and sausages and jars of pickles and bowls of relish, and watched the peace of the world roll by, dark as death.

Mrs Safarik blessed herself and her husband put his arm round her and stared out at the blackness that now surrounded us. He muttered something and I had to lean forward to catch it: 'Who? Why?'

We would learn soon enough, but there in that small shop, standing close to strangers who were no longer strangers, we were just ignorant and stunned.

It was another half-hour before the air had cleared enough for us to venture out into it. I thanked Mr and Mrs Safarik, and Adele and I left the store and walked up Broadway, handkerchiefs over our faces against the smoke and grit still in the air. People were going by heading uptown; some still stood on the sidewalks staring downtown. Nobody spoke to us, some didn't even look at us. We could have been refugees, coming out of a desolate country into a community that had suddenly found itself desolate. It wasn't that those we passed were heartless, it was just that they still couldn't believe that what they were seeing was real.

We hailed a cab that, miraculously, appeared out of nowhere. The driver skidded it to a stop. 'Jesus, is the lady okay? You come from *down there?*'

Down there: hell. 'Yeah, she's okay.' I gave him my parents' address. 'Just take it easy, mate. We're a bit fragile.'

'Christ, who wouldn't be?' When we pulled up outside the apartments where my parents lived, he said, 'It's on me. Mate? Where you from?'

'Sydney. Australia.'

'Jesus, and you come all the way for *this?*'

Our legs were unsteady as we crossed the sidewalk to the front doors. The concierge, a stout, bald man, opened the doors and his face was suddenly a folding balloon as he stared at us. I said, 'We're okay. Tell my mother, Mrs Shakespeare, we're on our way up.'

We went up in the gilded elevator, arms round each other, looking at ourselves in the mirror, strangers whom we knew.

4

'It's an outfit called al-Qaeda, run by a bloke named Osama bin Laden,' said my father. 'I thought you'd have heard of him back home.'

'Dad, we're at the arse-end of the world, as one of our prime ministers said.'

'Paul Keating. A most perceptive man, except about his own faults.' Dad, like his father before him, was an old

Labor man, wearing his vote on his sleeve. Except in those days, very short, when he had worked for Rupert Murdoch.

'Maybe the Intelligence guys knew, but they kept it to themselves.' Maybe some newspaper guys knew it too; TV reporters don't get as many leaks as those on newspapers. It is difficult to develop a leak into something worthwhile from a forty-second door-stop. 'But from now on —'

'From now on he's going to be Public Enemy Number One. You'd better get used to pronouncing Muslim names.'

We were at dinner, prepared by my mother, the sort she used to cook for us when Lynne and I were teenagers. Steak, three veg, apple pie (homemade) and cream. She had said, 'We were going to take you to dinner tonight at our favourite restaurant, but I don't think tonight's a night for dining out.'

'You're right, Mrs Shakespeare,' Adele had said.

'Anne,' said my mother. 'Don't laugh. I'm just glad my maiden name wasn't Hathaway. When Jack came along, Ron wanted to call him Othello —'

'You're kidding?' That was the first time I'd heard that.

'Yes. Then he thought Bruce or Clarrie would be better.'

'Clarrie Shakespeare,' said Dad. 'I'd always liked that.'

Mum had welcomed Adele into the apartment as if she were her mother. She put her arms round her and led her into the living room. 'The first thing you need is a drink, then a warm bath. What does she drink, Jack?'

'Champagne,' I said without thinking.

'That wasn't what I had in mind. But maybe ...' She looked at Adele, who had subsided into a deep chair.

'Nothing,' said Adele. 'Just a warm bath.'

'Run a bath, Jack. And you have a shower — you look as if you've been on a weekend drunk.'

'I think she should call her parents — they'll be worried if it's already on the news.' Satellites had made history instantaneous.

'When she's got herself together,' said Mum. 'They will be worried stiff if she breaks down on the phone ... You won't will you? For their sake?'

'No, Anne.' Adele was regaining her strength. 'I understand.'

Mum nodded. 'I'm a mother too.'

There are wavelengths between women that men can only guess at.

Adele rang home at four o'clock New York time and caught her parents at breakfast as they were watching reruns of the awful event. She told them she was okay; no, she hadn't been at work; they were not to worry. I could imagine them not worrying, not much. They would hang up the phone and wonder why she wouldn't come home to the safety, a century and a half of it, of Bulinga Creek.

At six o'clock I called Les Dibley, knowing he would be at work. He was at work at once, on me: 'You get anything for us?'

'Les, where would I get a crew? Every cameraman and soundman is at work here —'

'Where were you when it happened?'

I was going to say I was uptown at my parents' apartment, but I couldn't lie to him. 'I was with my girlfriend, Miss Ambar —'

'Close to the action?'

'Les, for Crissakes, stop talking like a ghoul. Yes, I saw the whole thing — Adele was working in a Starbucks in one of the towers —'

That was a mistake. 'Jesus, there's your story! Local girl on the scene!' His blood pressure goes up and down like petrol prices; only his cynicism prevents it from exploding. 'Get her in front a camera, interview her —'

'No, Les.' I didn't think I'd ever managed to sound so adamant.

He said nothing for quite a while; more than 10,000 miles separated us. Then: 'I could fire you, Jack —'

'I don't care, Les. I'm not going to put Adele through anything like that. She was lucky she got out of it.'

Another long pause; then: 'Okay, I see your point.'

'Do you, Les?'

'Yes! For Crissakes, yes! I'm not fucking heartless!' Then he took another pause and calmed down: 'Get on to CNN, tell 'em we subscribe to them, ask if you can use one of their crews for a four or five-minute spiel on what you saw, on what's happening now.'

'First thing tomorrow morning —'

'Why not right *now*?'

'Les, it's over, it's *happened*. From now on everything is going to be a review. I go down there tonight, everything will be dark but for floodlights and crews working on the wreckage, looking for bodies. Nobody's going to talk to me. Tomorrow morning there might be some take on it all. Nobody knows how many dead there are —'

'Seven thousand, but that's guesswork. What about the plane that went into the Pentagon? And the one that came down — where was it? Pennsylvania? — that was supposed to be on its way to land on the White House?'

'Les, take CNN on that. I've got enough to think about here at the World Trade Center — everything's bloody confusion. And my girl . . .'

Les Dibley took his time again. 'Call me tomorrow morning, your time, we'll be working round the clock and past it. Get me something on camera, you in front of the site.' Another pause, then: 'Give my regards to your girl, Jack. I'm glad she's okay.'

I hung up, went into the dining room, kissed the top of Adele's head and sat down.

She said, 'Everything okay?' She was dressed in one of my mother's skirts and blouses; the blouse fitted, but the skirt had been pinned tighter. She was still pale and calm, but quiet. 'They're not pressuring you?'

'No, everything's okay. I start work tomorrow morning.'

It was then that Dad told us about Osama bin Laden and al-Qaeda, names that became almost passwords in the months to come.

'Americans,' Dad said, 'are already asking why do people hate them. But you can't tell 'em, because it's not their fault. It wasn't their fault that United Fruit got Washington to send the Marines into Nicaragua back in 1927 — that's ancient history to Americans and they're not interested in ancient history. Or in Kermit Roosevelt and the way he engineered getting rid of Mossadeq in

Iran, back in the 1950s — more ancient history. The list is as long as your arm. The Brits did exactly the same back when they had an empire, and the French. But they, the Brits and the French, never cared two hoots what the rest of the world thought of them. We'd be the same if ever Australia got big ideas.'

'Our own little empire? New Zealand, the Solomons, New Guinea?'

'That'd be the extent of it. But the Kiwis would give us the finger every chance they got, especially in the rugby season.'

'Are you going to tell the Americans at UN why the rest of the world hates them?'

He grinned, the sort of grin a newspaperman acquires after thirty-five years in the game. 'I'm an unofficial trouble-shooter, but I don't go looking for trouble ... You like the champagne, Adele? It's French, but don't tell the winegrowers back home.'

At 9.30 Adele rose. 'I'd better be getting back —'

'No,' said Mum. 'Stay here. You'll wake up in the middle of the night and you'll be wanting company. Jack can comfort you.'

If Mum's parents had suggested Dad should sleep with her before they were married, she, Dad and the Pope would have had heart attacks. But now what she suggested was not just — well, *modern*, but natural.

Adele looked at my mother, then suddenly the calmness was gone. She broke down and wept, the day punching her. Mum put her arms round her and led her to one of the bedrooms.

Dad said, 'You've got a good one there. Take care of her.'

'It's not easy. I was telling Mum — she's ambitious, she wants to be an actress. Not *just* an actress, but a drama one, on the stage, not TV or the movies.'

'Will she be?'

I shook my head. 'Never. But I can't tell her that. Did Mum have any ambition before you married her?'

'She wanted to be a politician.'

'*Mum?*'

'She was a red-ragger at university, in every demo they put on —'

'*Mum?*'

It struck me only then that children are often presented with blank periods in their parents' lives. We learn, bit by bit, what they were like when *they* were children, but the formative years are so often like pages stuck together in an autobiography. Mum had studied Arts at Sydney, gone to London on graduation, met Dad, then in the *Sydney Morning Herald*'s office in Fleet Street, married a month later and, it seemed, closed a door on her college days.

'She'd have been a good politician,' said Dad. 'She has the politician's knack of being a friend to strangers. She just doesn't do it for votes.'

'Would you have married her if she had been a politician?'

'I'd have married her if she'd been a gangster.'

Before I went to bed I rang the New York bureau of CNN. A gruff voice came on the line, a behind-the-scenes voice, one you would never hear on camera. I explained who I was and he said, 'Yeah, Channel 15 have already called us from Sydney. A guy named Dribbley or Piddly —'

'Dibley. Les Dibley, he's my boss.'

'Yeah. Yeah, we can help you out. We got two crews down there, around the clock, I'll tell 'em you're coming. The morning? Sure. You write your own stuff?'

No, my mother does. 'Every word. Thanks, mate. I'll be down there first thing in the morning.'

Adele didn't wake during the night. Once or twice I felt her flinch in her sleep, the terror of the day at work, but in the morning she woke and seemed, if not recovered, at least not gripped by yesterday. I kissed her and got out of bed. She reached for my hand, held it tightly.

'Darling ...' She looked as if she was about to say something else; but then she just squeezed my hand. At that moment I think she was on the edge of giving up her dream and coming home with me. If that was it, I missed it.

When I came out of the shower, Mum had brought breakfast in for Adele and was sitting on the side of the bed. 'Adele can't go back to her flat, be there on her own all day. She's going to stay with me, we'll do some shopping.'

The end of the world, perhaps, had started and Mum was taking my girlfriend shopping. She knew how to keep her feet on the ground, shaking though it was.

'You and Dad can go and find out why yesterday happened.'

'That okay with you?' I asked Adele.

She nodded. 'Can you lend me some money?'

It was just like being married; all three of us grinned. That morning I felt as warm and comfortable as I think I've ever been, despite the awful event that brought it about.

It may seem strange, but I never enquired if Adele had made friends in New York; I just didn't want to know. I presumed if she had any, she phoned them during the day to find out how they had fared. I guessed she did the same with those she worked with. If any of them, friends or workmates, had died or been injured in the disaster, she made no mention of them. Nor did I ask: she was safe and that was all that mattered. Selfishness is the other side of the coin to generosity; a cliché, but we can't help its being there. We suffered for all those who had died or been injured or left bereft, but there was always the secret relief that we had survived. Maybe it was being young. Maybe I'll only know when I'm old.

Dad took me downtown in his car, driving carefully as if suddenly the streets had become more dangerous than before.

'What are you going to say in your piece? Avoid platitudes and the obvious. That's a fault with you TV blokes.'

'You're prejudiced.' He was still an old-style newspaperman.

'Not any more. Just disillusioned.'

'With the UN? There was a rumour that the United States wants to get out of it —'

'Rumour is butterflyshit, as distinct from bullshit. It floats around the UN every day ... No, I'm disillusioned with the whole bloody world. Politics, business, the lot. There are still some idealists in the UN, but they're either still wet behind the ears or so old they live in the past. But I try ... There was an American writer ages ago, Hervey

Allen. I came across a line in one of his books. *Always, somewhere, it is morning.*'

I considered that for a moment; then: 'There's a counterpoint to that. Always, somewhere, there is night.'

'Sure, and you takes your pick. The sun rises and there is hope. I look for it.'

'One does one's best?'

He looked sideways at me, grinned. I had always liked his grin, even when I was very small. It was never a wide-open smile, never hey-I'm-everybody's-friend; it was a small smile, one I'd always trusted. 'You've met politicians too?'

'One does. Ten seconds at a time, on doorsteps, platitudes at the ready.'

There were barricades on Lower Broadway. He dropped me at Canal Street and I walked down towards what had been the World Trade Center. There was a great gaping hole in the end of the street, a visual shock. Part of the structure of one of the buildings stuck up like an altar-piece above the still-buried dead. Dust still hung in the air as bulldozers moved in as carefully as tiptoeing rhinos. There were rescue workers everywhere, the yellow uniforms of some of them the only colour in the grey havoc. But you have all seen it: no event in history has ever got the instant and repeated viewing that the WTC tragedy did. It was a propaganda coup, horrible as it was.

I found the CNN crew and spoke to their supervisor. He was a man as old as Les Dibley, even looked like him; he thought he had seen everything till he saw what lay around him today. He knew I was coming and welcomed me.

'You get what you want to say, let me know and we'll shoot it.' Then he looked around him. 'What can you say?'

It took me half an hour to get my impressions together and to get down on paper something that wasn't going to sound banal and bloody obvious. I stepped in front of the camera and said my piece and when I had finished the cameraman and the soundman nodded appreciatively.

'No bullshit,' said the cameraman. 'Thanks, Jack.'

What I said, standing against the terrible destruction behind me, was different, quieter, than what I had said months ago standing against the background of the bus smash on the Mitchell Highway. That morning in New York nobody knew how many had died, how many were buried in the city battlefield; over the coming days the figures would be revised and revised again. It didn't matter: one or one thousand dead in a violent manner tempers your voice. I tried not to sound sepulchrally obvious, in effect to let the background speak for itself.

I spent the rest of the day getting more facts, trying to find out how many Australians might have died; nationality in news makes it local. At five o'clock I went before the camera again, did a wrap-up on the slow recovery of bodies, praised the police and the firemen and other rescue crews, and went home to the safety and comfort and, yes, luxury of the East Sixties.

I rang Les Dibley and he congratulated me on the morning piece. 'Stick around, Jack. The ratings are great —'

I was disappointed in him. 'Les, you're starting to sound like Entwistle.'

There was silence a moment, then his voice was less gruff, softer: 'Sorry. I've been here too long . . . Send us more, Jack.'

I went back downtown the next day, spent an exhausting five hours, did another piece with the CNN crew, went back to my parents' apartment and called Les again.

'Les, I can't do any more. I'm running into banalities, terrible bloody ones, and they're giving me earache, hearing myself say them —'

'We can't have that, our viewers wouldn't know a banality if it bit them in the bum.'

'Cut out the sarcasm, Les. You know what I'm getting at. I stand there in front of all those heaps of wreckage and all I'm doing is stating the bloody obvious. Havoc, after a second or third look, becomes obvious. The story from now on is to find this guy bin Laden —'

'Leave that to the generals, Jack. Okay, go on with your holiday. We'll take the CNN stuff. How's your girl?'

'Recovering.'

'She would've been a great story —'

'No, she wouldn't have. Goodnight, Les. Give the back of my hand to Mr Entwistle.'

'He's listening in on an extension —' I could hear Les laughing as he hung up.

The next few days we lived in an unreal world that had become, devastatingly, *too* real. Adele insisted on going back to her room: 'No, Jack, you need to spend more time with your parents. Though they're playing it pretty cool, what's happened has affected them as much as everyone else. Everything is, I dunno, no longer *certain*. Stay the nights with me, but spend the days with them.'

I did that, but it was no holiday. Dad was hardly home and Mum talked of 'going home'. We were having a light lunch in a café-restaurant on Madison Avenue; outside, life passed by, but it seemed at a slower pace, as if the next corner held — what? There was a certain wariness on the faces, yet at the same time it was not the unfriendly wariness of yesterday's New York faces; the city had come together. One hoped it would last.

'Dad can retire,' said Mum, picking at a typical American salad, half the size of Mt McKinley. Restaurateurs were not going to let the population go hungry. 'We won't be short of money. I want to get back to gardening — I've forgotten what it's like to stand in the middle of your own lawn.' That had always been one of her pleasures. 'And you might be able to persuade Adele to come back.'

'Have you talked to her?'

'Not along those lines. That's your territory. But, if as you say, she has no real future —'

'Mum, have you ever tried to analyse ambition? All the wise guys have their interpretations of it, how high one must jump, how long one must run to make the jump — none of 'em ever queries the ambitious one's eyesight. That's Adele's problem — she looks in a mirror and sees Edith Evans.'

Mum looked at me with a quizzical smile. 'You're developing into a philosopher.'

'Never on TV, not with Channel 15. They'd sack me for frightening the viewers ... I can't talk her out of going to London, trying for Stratford and *The Merry Wives of*

Windsor or whatever. I just have to wait till she sees herself in the mirror.'

'Good luck. What's Lynne's Nick like?'

'Good front row material. Head down, arse up, solid as a rock. You and Dad will like him. Lynne's going to be very happy.'

'I hope you are too.'

Chapter Six

1

A week later Adele and I left for London. My parents drove us to the airport, which was like an antbed that had been warned hot water was to be poured on it. The atmosphere trembled with nerves; farewells were exaggerated to the point of burlesque. Security had been heightened but not planned; it ranged from the farcically stringent to the ridiculously lax. Travel by air had suddenly become the most dangerous way of getting about. Or so it seemed.

'You scared?' Dad asked me.

We were standing apart from Adele and Mum for the moment. Close by a family of four were clinging together as if making up their minds whether to go ahead with their flight. I had read that fear is contagious, but this was the first time I had seen evidence of it.

'A little. That's why I chose BA and not one of the American airlines.'

'They're all going to be vulnerable, even the European ones.'

'Qantas?' I would be going home from London on Qantas.

'I don't think al-Qaeda knows we exist, not so far. Over the next twelve months the bottom's going to fall out of the airline industry. We're going to have to get used to a whole new book.'

'You trying to talk me out of flying?'

The small smile. 'No. I've always worked on the principle that the day you go was written the day you were born. If you don't take risks, you're standing still on the spot where you were born.'

I looked across at Adele and my mother. 'Was it like that with Mum, marrying her a month after you met?'

'All the way. And I'm still flying safely.'

We had never talked like this before, it was as if the possibility of danger had drawn us closer together.

'When will you be coming home?'

'I dunno. I've been thinking about it, but now I think I'd better stay on here. The UN has its faults and nobody criticises it like the politicians from around the world. But what parliament anywhere in the world is perfect? They ignore that. When the US gets itself together after last week — and it's going to be over-organised and hastily planned as usual, it's Washington's way — it's going to go looking for the terrorists, this al-Qaeda crowd. The UN's going to have to hold itself together when that happens. The word is it'll be Afghanistan where the action will start. I can't go home now. Will you go home or stay in London with Adele?'

'I'll go home. I don't think I could get a job in London that pays as well as the one I've got. And if I stayed in

London with her, Adele might be trying for years to be the actress she's never going to be.'

'Good luck.' He shook my hand, pressed my shoulder. No hug: he was born in 1950 and, when it came to a show of affection, he was still back there. Men didn't *hug*; they shook hands. But it was no less genuine. 'It's going to be a different world from now on. Everywhere.'

That remark would be a cliché repeated time and time again. But, like most clichés, still true.

When it came time to kiss Mum goodbye I could see she was having difficulty holding back tears. 'Tell Lynne to get married soon, so we'll have an excuse to come home early. How about you and Adele?'

I looked across at Adele, giving Dad a hug that had other middle-aged men looking on with envy. 'It's a long way down the track, Mum. As she would describe it, we're only in the first act. But I'm trying . . .'

'Do that. She's a lovely girl — and I don't mean just to look at. Some of those others you used to bring home —'

'I was young then, Mum, just a boy.' I kissed her, hugged her. 'Do you still go to Mass?'

'Every Sunday, but it's just between me and God. I've eliminated the Church.'

'When you and He are having your conversation, put in a word for me.'

Adele kissed Mum and Dad; she was part of the family. Temporarily. Then we went through the gates and my parents, New York, Actors' Center and the ruins of the World Trade Center were behind us. But of course they weren't. Memory knows no boundaries, travels without passport.

2

As the plane took off Adele took hold of my hand; not fearfully but lovingly. 'I've never before felt we're so *together*.'

I raised her hand and kissed her knuckles. It was the only answer I could muster at the moment.

We flew business class and Adele seemed to accept it as a matter of course, as if she had never known cattle class. Yet I had the feeling she had little money to spare, that the remittances from home, if any, were small. Back in Kirribilli she had lived rent-free and had picked up income doing part-time modelling and what work she could get in the theatre and in TV. But now she was a long long way from home and, perhaps for the first time in her life, having to pay her own way. I said nothing, asking no questions, selfishly and caddishly thinking that maybe, eventually, penury would drive her back home to me. Love has two sides, selfishness and sacrifice.

I had booked us into a hotel in Knightsbridge for a week, before she was to move into shared accommodation somewhere in West London, with another actress with whom she had worked in Sydney. Against the grain of my character, I hadn't bothered to check the prices; the hotel had been recommended by Hilary Reingold, a girl who could stretch a credit card to poster-size. We booked in and went upstairs and I lay down for an hour with a fit of the vapours when I saw the tariffs. Over the next week I was dazed by London prices; my pocket was white-knuckled all the time I was there. The only consolation was that I was spending it on my love. The libido knows no expense.

We went to the theatre every night; she took it in like a drug. We never mentioned September Eleven, even though it was featured in the papers every day and television showed pictures of the cleaning-up.

There was tension, of course, in London; but the Brits are more accustomed to terrorism than the Americans. Or Australians. The IRA bombings had stopped, but echoes could still be heard. There were scares: mystery packages on Underground stations, on the rear decks of buses; but that was all they proved to be, just scares. The British did not see themselves as the enemy. They sympathised with ordinary Americans, but, some said and not so silently, Washington had itself to blame. But I wasn't interested in politics or, for the moment, terrorism. I was intent only on my girl.

We were busy, in bed as well as outside; we were at it like rabbits that had been warned of a long drought. One afternoon, after we had got our breath back and the blood was settling down, she rolled over on her side and looked at me for a long moment without saying anything.

Then: 'When I succeed here, when my name's up there above the title of the play, will you come back, marry me and we'll settle here?'

It was the first time marriage had been mentioned; it was as if we had avoided it like some incurable disease. I knew that in my generation, in certain circles, marriage was a delicate subject, like homosexuality had once been. I was caught off-guard, even though I had been seeing us together for the rest of our lives.

'What would I do if I came here to live?'

'What you do now.'

'Darling ...' I stroked her shoulder, the flesh smooth as oil under my palm. 'It's a tough game to break into, as tough as the theatre. Okay, I'd come with credentials, but I haven't half the experience most of the reporters here have had. I know nothing about the UK, nothing about Europe or who runs it — why would they be interested in me? I'm not Kylie Minogue.'

'*I* wouldn't be interested in you if you were Kylie.' At least she smiled; she was not yet deadly serious. It suddenly occurred to me, as if I heard an echo of the words, she had said: *When I succeed here* ...I could be middle-aged by then. 'We'd be happy together —'

'I know that. But —'

Selfishly I thought of what I'd be giving up in material terms. A guaranteed job at a hundred thousand a year, maybe more as my experience grew; a comfortable life in a comfortable country; a lower cost of living; a much, much better climate ... What would be my prospects here? Right now it was raining outside, which was one more reason we had come to bed instead of going sightseeing. I had experience, certainly, but it was limited; the sort of stories that reporters on provincial newspapers in this country would have covered dozens of times. I was presentable to look at, dressed well and I had good voice, the Australian accent and the rising inflection not particularly obvious. Australian newspapermen had made their mark in Fleet Street, and I don't mean Rupert Murdoch; but I was not a newspaperman. I was a Channel 15 reporter, a different breed, the voice-over never allowed an opinion, viewed with suspicion if it came up with a memorable phrase. There would be a long queue ahead of me at the BBC and ITN.

'You could give up reporting. Be a fulltime writer —'

'Darling heart —'

Her hair had fallen down over one side of her face, the way I liked it, the image of her that had sustained me in those empty months past, that would be with me in the empty months to come. I don't know what other lovers carry with them in absences; perhaps just a jigsaw because that's what love is. I had other images of Adele, erotic ones, but the dark hair down one side of her face, the half-smile, the depth of the eyes, were what I carried with me, as other lovers in other ages carried keepsakes.

'— I've written one script — sure, it's been taken and they're shooting it now. But I have a long way to go. The world is full of writers who wrote one book, one script, one play.' I was arguing, of course, for the secure job, the good pay, the (if you like) lack of ambition; but I wasn't going to put that as argument. 'Maybe in a year or two, when I've written something else —'

'What about your film script, the one you said you left in Hollywood?'

'I rang the agent yesterday, while you were out — where did you go anyway?'

'To put my name down with a model agency, just in case.' She said it almost as if she had put her name down with a brothel.

'Lingerie ads? Back to the Brazilian? I'm going home —'

She slapped me. 'Back to your man in Hollywood . . .'

'He said that right now producers don't know what they want. September Eleven —' It had become a day of infamy, marked on calendars in red, on memory and the tongue. '— September Eleven has thrown them. They're not even sure people will keep going to the movies —'

'Of course they will! Where else will they find escapism, except at the movies and theatre?'

'Sure, you're right. But what will they want to see? *Saving Private Ryan* or a remake of *Lassie, Come Home*? Forget Hollywood — for me, anyway. They're not busting a gut to hear from Jack Shakespeare. Give me time, darling —'

Which was what she had asked of me.

Perhaps she realised it, because when I pulled her towards me, kissed her, let my hand explore, she didn't struggle. While outside our window the rain came down like grey curtains on the future.

Next day, the day before I was to leave for home, we went out to Hammersmith, to the flat she was to share with Milly Brown. It was in a drab Victorian house in a drab street; none of it obscured but made to look even more depressing by the steady, mocking rain. When our taxi drew up I couldn't help but notice that Adele hesitated before getting out. Like Marie Antoinette hesitating before stepping out of the tumbrel.

I got out, paid the driver what looked like a down payment on purchase of the taxi, and followed Adele up the chipped steps to the uninviting front door.

Milly Brown saved the day; or part of it. She was about my age, nondescriptively pretty, but with a calm exuberance (is there such a thing?) that you knew would never be defeated by drab houses and drab weather.

'Directors remember me, but the public don't. I change the colour of my hair or the style and I play bit parts in "The Bill" and "Taggart" and a BBC costume drama and nobody recognises me. I'm always in work, like those studio players in old Hollywood movies. I'm the Glenda Farrell of the twenty-first century.'

Another late late movie fan. But I couldn't help myself, not looking at Adele: 'You don't want to be discovered, be a star?'

'Sure.' She had a lovely smile, her most attractive feature. 'Who doesn't, eh, Del?'

'All of us,' said Adele, marshalling battalions behind her.

'In the meantime ... Monday I'm taking you to my agent. I've told him you're a knockout for looks.'

Actors, I was learning, can talk to each other like this, as if sizing up commodities. I've never heard TV reporters compliment each other, except in obituaries, when it no longer matters.

Adele took the compliment as if it were a canapé. 'I hope he looks past my looks. Does he try to place you in the theatre as well as in TV?'

'He'd put you in a circus if the money was right.'

I was impressed by Milly's practicality, but Adele's smile was just bad acting.

The flat, a two-bedroomer, was as drab as the exterior of the house. Milly had tried to brighten it with back-home posters; Bondi Beach hung beside a large brown stain on one wall. The furniture looked as if it had been retrieved from a garbage dump; the pattern on the thin carpet was worn through to the underside. The only new item in the place looked to be the TV set and that was new, I guessed, only because it was rented. Adele's bedroom would have kept the libido at a low level; a teenage lover would have needed Viagra. I didn't see the kitchen, already depressed enough.

'When war breaks out, will you be covering it?' asked Milly.

'What war?' I felt Adele's hand tighten in mine.

'The tip is there will be war in Afghanistan, while they go after this guy, bin whatever-his-name-is. I go out with a guy from the BBC, a reporter like you.' I felt Adele's hand tighten again. 'He says they've been told to get ready.'

I felt a lift, a vision of new territories: not of war but of somewhere beyond the suburbs of Sydney.

'I think I'm safe,' I said, trying not sound like a draft dodger. 'Our channel never spends money if it can avoid it. CNN and ITN will cover it for us.'

I felt the hand in mine relax. 'I'm trying to talk Jack into coming over here and working,' Adele said.

Milly looked at me and said no more than, 'Good luck.' Like a girl who knew where the queues were.

We took Milly out to lunch, at a steakhouse where the steaks cost me what a whole steer would cost back home.

The wine was good, an Australian shiraz, but it was the only reasonable item on the bill. On top of everything I kept the British government in the black with a VAT of 17½ per cent.

'If ever your agent wants someone to play Scrooge,' Adele said to Milly, 'tell him Jack's available.'

'I like a man who's careful with money,' said Milly, 'on other people.'

When we left Milly I kissed her on the cheek and whispered, 'Look after her.' She nodded and I knew that, if Adele was to be in good hands in London, they would be Milly's.

Adele and I went back to the hotel and went to bed. We surfaced, showered, dressed and went down to dinner, where I went berserk, ordered a bottle of Krug and enjoyed the Last Supper. Then we went back upstairs and went to bed, where we made love all night, except for breathing breaks, like squirrels hoarding nuts (mine) for a long long winter.

In the morning we had breakfast in our room and said goodbye. I didn't want a public farewell at the airport; I wanted to hold her to me and weep if I felt like it. I didn't weep, holding her tightly to me in the bedroom, but the tears were there at the back of my eyes. She wept, holding nothing back, and I almost said, 'Come home with me.' But I didn't and I'll never know if I missed an opportunity.

'Write to me — phone me —' She was murmuring against my cheek, like a woman asking to be saved.

'All the time — never turn your mobile off —'

Before I left I gave her all my traveller's cheques. 'Just in case.'

She didn't refuse them. She looked at me frankly and said, 'You know it's going to be tough?'

'Yes. I'm just trying to keep you out of lingerie ads —'

With the final kiss I said, 'Good luck.'

She just nodded and closed the door on me.

3

I flew home, across the Middle East where the scabs of war were once more being peeled back, through Singapore, where, with what little money I had left, I bought presents for Lynne. Then on into the best climate in the world, blue sky stretching away to every horizon.

Lynne met me at the airport, hugged me as if I were her infant brother. 'God, you have no idea how I worried about you and Adele in New York! She's all right?'

'She doesn't talk about it —'

'What about Mum? How did she take it, all that horror?'

'I think Mum will be matter-of-fact about the end of the world. She and Dad are okay — they want to come home for the wedding. How's the front row forward?'

'Happy. So am I.' She took the Honda Civic out of the car park at full speed, snaking into the passing traffic as if she owned the road. 'Are you? Happy?'

'Yes,' I said. 'Now and again.'

She left it at that. She was a selfish driver, but not with her feelings.

I went back to the small, small world of Channel 15. I drove into the car park and sat for almost five minutes looking at it as a real estate developer might have. Was this what I wanted compared to living in England with Adele and trying to start another career? But when I got out of the MG I knew what I would settle for. I had to confess it: I was deeply in love, but not desperate.

Les Dibley welcomed me back with his version of open arms, a flap of the hand. 'Gird your loins, son. If war breaks out in Afghanistan, there is a rumour the board may spend some money and send a team there to cover it. I dunno whether Osama bin Laden has scared the shit out of them or whether they've had a burst of patriotic fervour, which sometimes happens if they've got nothing else to occupy them. Gird your loins, anyway. In the meantime I've got a *thrilling* assignment for you —'

The other commercial channels had had some success with so-called reality shows: Big Brother, Big Sister, Big Deal. Chockablock with no talent and some of the most unappealing personalities, if you could say they had personality, since the Stone Age.

Entwistle's two little darlings had persuaded Daddy to do a reality show called 'Little Sister'. He took the idea to an in-house producer and the program director and they, knowing on which side of their bread the butter could turn rancid, said it was a *fantastic* idea and couldn't understand why they hadn't though of it.

It was based on a weekend camp for twelve girls aged seven to ten. Jilly Goodluck, a one-time morning game show hostess, was persuaded to come out of unemployment, where she would have been better off, to be the matron. She was a blonde who had had more one-night stands than a free-call hooker. She had the proper worn look for the job.

'They've suggested you interview one of the little darlings as a promotion for the show,' she said. 'Which one do you want?'

'I don't want any of them.'

'You want to tell Mr Entwistle that?'

So I interviewed Sharynne-Jeanagh (I kid you not). She was a middle-aged eight year old, with knowing eyes and a tea-cosy of brown curls tipped with gold; her head looked as if it was about to burst into flame at any moment. All the other kids looked the same, except for the hairstyles. It was like being in a retirement home for midgets.

I had to start somewhere: 'What do you want to be when you grow up?'

'A singer and actoress like Jennifer Lopez.'

'Not a great dramatic actor — actress like Edith Evans?'

'Eh?'

Come home, dear Adele, come home.

They screened the pilot and that was it; its ratings were lower than the Sunday morning church broadcast. It suggested that only relatives and other masochists had looked in.

A week later Entwistle sent for me, made no mention of the fiasco. His opening remark was: 'You had a good holiday overseas?'

'Very good.'

'Liked that stuff you did on September Eleven.'

'One does one's best.'

'See anything of what'shername? Miss Ambar?'

Subtle as a Stone Age club; he should have been on one of the reality shows. I'd have to suggest it to the two little darlings. 'Oh, quite a lot of her. She was in the World Trade Center that morning, barely got out alive.'

'I didn't know that.' So Les Dibley had kept that between ourselves. 'You didn't interview her?'

'Too distressed. It was pretty shattering.' I changed the subject: 'You wanted to see me about something?'

'Yes, yes,' he said, suddenly brisk. He was in a purple shirt today, with white collar and cuffs, and purple braces. Behind him the model yacht looked to be on another tack, as if trying to veer away from him. 'The war's about to start in Afghanistan, looking for that bastard Osama bin Laden. It'll all be over in a couple of weeks, so we're sending a crew to cover it.' The channel's budget evidently would cover only a couple of weeks; extravagance could not be afforded. The Pentagon had better stick to schedule. 'You fancy yourself as a war correspondent?'

I'm not a coward, but I'm cautious. The thought of an overseas assignment, to a war zone, was exciting; but I didn't fancy the possibility of being killed. I had heard of the number of correspondents and cameramen who had been killed in Vietnam; some had died in Bosnia and other small wars. But the search for news was in my blood; I knew Dad would have jumped at the chance. I said, quietly but firmly, 'When do we leave?'

He actually looked proud of me. But I knew it was a sudden burst of pride, after virtually no gestation, that Channel 15, *his* channel, was moving on to something big,

out of bus smashes and school gang fights and murder in
the suburbs into what promised to be a *real* war. The
ratings suddenly began to look like a rainbow.

'We've engaged a military expert to brief you on what
to expect.'

I knew nothing about Afghanistan or war. Like most
Australians I knew Afghanistan was somewhere between
Pakistan and — what country? The library atlas, which
looked as if it had never been opened till I asked for it,
showed me it had Iran to the east and half a dozen post-
Soviet states to the north. The military expert, at two
hundred dollars an hour for two hours, gave us basic advice
on how to keep our heads down and said he thought the
war wouldn't last long; a prediction that suited Channel
15's budget. Rupe Hellinger, Jason Tully and I learned how
to put on our flak jackets, had a final briefing from an army
public relations major and we were ready for war.

Mum and Dad rang me, alerted by Lynne. Mum was
worried but in control: 'Don't try to be Bruce Willis —'

'Mum, I'm a natural-born coward.'

Dad came on the line: 'Don't try and play that record
when you're with the troops — they don't find it funny.
All the troops I met in Bosnia were shit-scared, but did
their job. You do yours. Good luck. Keep in touch. If you
meet a carpet-seller named Walid Hassan, give him my
regards. I met him in Kabul — that rug in the entrance
hall, I bought from him.' Over the line I felt him press my
shoulder, keeping everything under control. 'How does
Adele feel about you going?'

'Ah ...' I hesitated. 'I'm just about to tell her.'

'Good luck there,' said my mother, cutting in, and hung up.

I waited a while, then rang London. I had spoken to her each day since I'd got back, but it was only for each of us to tell how much we missed the other. This morning, midnight her time, was different. She got in with her news before I could get in with mine: 'Oh darling — the most wonderful news! I've got a job.'

'Already?'

'Milly's agent is a wonder! Twenty lines in "The Bill".'

'You're playing a cop? That's going to raise the heat around Sun Hill —'

'No, a hooker.'

Well, that was a start. I wondered if Chekhov had ever attempted to write *The Three Hookers*.

'That's great. But don't get the crew too excited.' I took my time, as if I were preparing to interview someone: 'Darling, I'm going to Afghanistan —'

'Where?'

Another one who had never looked at an atlas. 'Afghanistan. I leave on Thursday —'

'No!' She had placed the region in her mind, remembered headlines. I've said before: love is selfish. And it was good to hear. 'No, Jack, don't go!'

'Del, I have to — it's my biggest opportunity —'

'No, darling — *please*! I don't want to lose you — I'm a jinx —'

I hadn't expected this; and I tried to be patient. 'Darling heart, you're not a jinx — not as far as I'm concerned. I'll be okay, I'm not going to try for any heroics.'

'I don't care! Please, Jack — don't go.'

I wanted to say she had once asked why I had no ambition. Now, suddenly, I had been bitten by it. And I had thought she would understand.

'Jack?' I had been silent for an age; or so she thought. 'Jack — *please* —'

I took a deep breath. 'Del — I'm sorry. I'm going. I'll be careful, play it safe . . . I don't want to sound selfish. I love you —'

'I know that.' At least she wasn't sounding petulant. 'Will you call me every night?'

'Every night, I promise.' *To let you know I'm alive and you are not a jinx.*

'I love you,' she said and I knew it was the truth.

Chapter Seven

1

We flew out two days later for Islamabad. Rupe and Jason were as excited as I was; but you'd never have known it. Talk about casual Aussies ... You'd have thought we'd been going to wars since the Peloponnesian stoush, Spartans with cameras, mikes and flak jackets. The air hostesses hovered around us like vestal virgins and one of them offered me her temple phone number.

I had talked again last night with Adele and she had wept. But she hadn't mentioned the word *jinx* again, nor had she said *goodbye*. The curtain was still up, the candles still lit.

My ignorance of the region began with Islamabad. Till we arrived there I didn't know it was a modern city, younger than our own Canberra, built no more than fifty years ago. It had wide streets, not the bazaar alleys I had expected; there were buildings made ugly by their very size; and a mosque, the world's largest, that to me, not an admirer of large cathedrals, seemed to reduce prayer to a whisper. Somehow the whole city looked heartless, soulless, built only for administration.

We soon became aware that the war that had started across the border to the west was not popular with the masses. Crude effigies of President Bush were burnt every day; so was the American flag. Australia seemed to have escaped the hatred; but that was no reason to wave an Australian flag, no matter how small. We left Islamabad with relief, going in convoy up to Peshawar. The trip, in a taxi that looked and sounded as if it had carried Kipling around the same area, was expensive. War profiteers are not necessarily fat, cigar-smoking tycoons who make armaments. Our taxi driver was a skinny boy, younger than Jason, with a wide smile made ugly by the few teeth he had and a habit of passing wind every ten kilometres. I spent the journey looking away from him, staring out at the countryside where camels and ancient tractors worked side by side in the fields and where children stood amongst crops of stones and waved to us as if in farewell.

We came to Peshawar, a city that fitted its surroundings; it was what I had imagined was a reminder of an ancient past. It was ten miles east of the Khyber Pass, it had known history, seen Alexander the Great pass through, had saluted Nadir Shah, Zemaun Shah; and had known the British. I had done a rushed course in the region's history, skipping through books suggested by my father. But, as always, the real was different from the page.

We hired another taxi and were driven to the refugee camp outside the city; it, too, was a city, of tents, desolate, the end of the world. Rupe looked at me and shook his head.

'I don't want to shoot this. If you want it, here's the camera —'

'Nup. Les Dibley might run it, but Entwistle would can it.'

What we were looking at was not for the viewers of Channel 15, a poll of whom had shown they were not in favour of too many immigrants. Nor would Canberra, with whom the board of directors were arm-in-arm, want to see it. The government's policy of allowing only 4000 refugees a year into the country was a bitter joke beside what we were looking at: the thin end of a funnel that opened out to a mass of several hundred thousands. And, we had been told, there were millions more in Iran, Jordan and other countries. So we got back into the taxi and returned to Peshawar, to the hotel with its white tablecloths in the restaurant and the full menu and the waiters who knew when God was smiling on them. We sent nothing and our viewers back home had their stomachs spared from upset as they prepared for dinner. Les Dibley rang and asked why we hadn't filed anything and I said we had run into censorship but everything should be okay tomorrow.

'You're bullshitting me —'

'No, Les. Never.'

But I knew we had got off to a poor start by sacrificing a reporter's impartiality. We had become our own censors.

That night I rang Adele. 'I'm still safe. The war's quite a distance away yet —'

'Darling, do be careful, don't be brave.' Even a poor connection could not spoil the beauty of that voice.

'How'd the hooker role go? What sort of accent did you have? Were you an Aussie hooker?'

'No, a Russian, they're supposed to be the best. I was Olga from the Volga.' She laughed, a lovely sound. 'I'll pray for you, Jack.'

'Do that.' Though I wondered if God listened to a lapsed C of E. I wasn't sure He listened to a lapsed R C. But that night I started my night prayers again, just in case.

Next day we got under way: a convoy of three ramshackle trucks hired by us and several American correspondents. We climbed through the Khyber Pass, a winding road that, at times, offered unbelievable views: patches of green where crops grew, silvery snakes of water, and crumpled hills that rose into crumpled mountains. And above us American bombers wrote vapour trails on the blueboard of the sky, like a shorthand that everyone would soon come to know.

We passed traffic heading for the Pakistani border: in trucks, buses, cars and on foot, none of them taking any notice of us. Then we cut east, moving along rough dirt roads, passing through villages where the villagers came out to either stare at us or shout abuse. But nobody stoned us or shot at us and we went on. The hills around us looked as if they grew only rocks and I made notes, wondering how these people lived. My own past life, of comfort and security, now seemed a shameful mockery. I had been protected too long.

Jason must have been thinking the same thing: 'Jeez, it's a long way from Coogee and the surf.' He was a boardrider and all year round had a deep tan. It struck me only then that, in his fatigues and his flak jacket, he looked even younger than back home. 'Do these poor bastards ever dream of better things?'

'Who knows, Jay? I don't think I want to ask them.'

Then the war, out of nowhere, was with us. We were labouring up a steep incline between a cleft in a hill when a shot rang out and the front truck swerved to the side, its driver dead. Out of the rocks came the Taliban, a dozen on either side of the road: savage-looking bearded men, except for three beardless boys who couldn't have been more than fourteen or fifteen. We had been told that the Taliban recruited youngsters who grew old before their time, who might never actually reach old or even middle age. These three kids had blank faces, but there was no mistaking the look on the faces of the older men. We were the enemy, no matter who we were or where we came from.

The leader stepped forward, bearded, begrimed, dressed all in black with a black turban. He carried a Russian AK-47 and in a worn holster on his belt an American Smith & Wesson; he had no prejudice when it came to choice of weapons.

He pointed the rifle at us and motioned for all of us to get out of the trucks. We got down, fourteen of us, and for the first time in my life I felt I was a real foreigner. We stood there in a line, like reluctant recruits for the Taliban cause. I was nervous and so, it seemed, was everyone else in the line.

The leader moved down past us, taking his time, something like contempt in the brown face above the dark beard. He passed all the Americans, as if recognising them as the only enemy; then he came to me. All of us were dressed identically, in army fatigues with battle jackets, some of us with flak jackets over them. But he chose to speak to me. And he spoke in English with a slight American accent: 'Where do you think you're going?' His eyes had foyers, you didn't know what was behind them.

Somehow I managed to keep my voice steady. 'To Taloqan.'

'To join the Alliance? The enemy?'

'No. To report the war objectively.'

It was a stupid reply and I saw one of the Americans look at me as if I had cracked a joke; but nerves were taking hold of me. The Taliban leader shook his head, turned to his men, said something, and they all laughed; all except the boys, who probably didn't know the meaning of objectivity. Then he turned back to me.

'You go no further, you will turn back. You have food?'

'Yes.' We had been advised to take as much as we could with us.

'We want it.'

It was useless to argue. It was a beautiful day, the autumn air was clear as French glass; in the distance a shallow river occasionally semaphored silver flashes, like messages of hope. Behind us, beyond the hills through which we had been climbing, was the beginning of the Hindu Kush, its higher peaks mantled with snow. Everything was set for a peaceful retreat.

And then it happened. The two remaining drivers of the trucks, Pakistanis eager to prove their neutrality, were handing down the cardboard boxes of food we had been warned to carry with us. Then, for some reason, one of the drivers started to hand down Rupe's camera equipment.

It was Jason, standing nearest to it, who protested: 'Hey, leave that alone! That's ours —'

The leader turned on him and shot him. It was as callous an act as I hope never to see again. Jason looked at him in surprise: it was surprise rather than shock. His brow furrowed, his eyes blinked, and then he went down, holding his chest where the bullet had gone in.

Rupe dropped beside him, looked up at the leader and snarled, 'You bastard!'

The Taliban lifted his gun and for a moment it looked as if Rupe, too, was going to die. Then he lowered the gun and said almost casually, 'You stupid sonofabitch. Keep your fucking equipment.'

Then one of the Americans, a grizzled veteran of other wars, said, 'Are you an American?'

There were rumours that an American and an Australian had been picked up amongst the Taliban.

'No,' said the leader, and in the beard he seemed to be smiling. 'I went to —' He named an American college I had never heard of. 'They tried to teach me stupidity, but I managed to cheat them.'

There was no answer to that and I was glad no one attempted it. The American veteran looked at me and shook his head and that was the only comment.

The leader stepped back, stood on an embankment while his men loaded the food boxes onto the lead truck, the one that was still half-on, half-off the narrow road.

Occasionally he would look up and down the line of foreigners and there was no mistaking the look on his face: we were the despicable enemy. Infidels who didn't understand the medieval.

When the loading was done, one of the men climbed into the truck and, with some difficulty, got it back on the road. Then the leader stepped down from the embankment and paused in front of me.

'Go back where you came from and stay there! Learn the truth, there is no objectivity in war!'

I could only stare at him and wonder how this educated man had come home to fight for a medieval regime. Where women were of no account, cruelty was routine, books were burnt, public executions were weekly entertainment. I still have a long way to go to understand the dark depths of another man's soul.

The Taliban men crowded onto the truck and it went growling up the rise till it disappeared round the steep angle of the upper hillside. The last thing I saw was the three boys standing at the back of the truck, staring at us with faces bland as infants'.

'And to think,' said the veteran American, whose name was Coxon, 'that not so long ago we backed those bastards against the Russians.'

I had no answer to that because I had been only a teenager when that war had occurred.

Then Rupe, on his knees beside Jason, said, 'Come on, let's get him in the truck.'

I had seen dozens of dead bodies in disasters back home; this was the first time I had actually handled one.

We lifted Jason gently into the back of the truck, covered him with a groundsheet one of the Americans gave us.

We walked back down the road while the drivers warily backed the trucks down. Twice they almost went over the side, but at last they were on the flat and able to turn round. We climbed aboard and, in silence, drove back down the pass and to Peshawar.

2

I thought I was grown up, but I found I still had some things to learn. How to cope with the sudden, violent death of a workmate and friend; and to arrange the transport of his body back to his family in Sydney. I had been hit by the murder of Tom Barini, but more for Adele's sake; he was her friend.

Rupe Hellinger, to my surprise and despair, went to pieces. Jason had been his protégé and suddenly it was as if Rupe had lost one of his own sons, kids back home in the peace and security of Eastwood. He left everything to me and I did the best I could, always on the edge of breaking down as he had.

I rang Les Dibley and told him what had happened. He was shocked into silence, so much so that I thought he had gone off the line.

'Les?'

He came back, his voice thick. 'Send him home — the body. We'll tell his folks and arrange everything at this end. How are you and Rupe?'

'Shattered.'

'You want to stay on there?'

I hadn't really thought about it; he was offering escape. But I said, 'I want to stay, Les. I don't know about Rupe —'

But Rupe was seated beside me and he nodded. 'I'll stay. We'll find another sound guy.'

'Entwistle or the board may want to bring you home —'

'Stuff 'em. Rupe and I are staying. Send more money.'

'You're asking for the moon, son, but I'll try.'

'How are things back there?'

'Rotten to the core, but it makes great news. Another company went down the gurgler today, but the bosses walked away with humongous golden handshakes. The Taliban are in the wrong country.' Then his voice softened, the roughness gone: 'You're both okay? Really?'

I hesitated, looked at Rupe, who shook his head. 'No, Les, we're not okay. But we'll survive.'

'Keep your head down,' he said and hung up.

We had to find a soundman to take Jason's place. The manager of our hotel, a thin slab of a man with excellent false teeth that were always on display, as if he was not going to waste the expense of them, offered us a man. 'He is a Nuristani, very experienced.'

'He's a what?' said Rupe and looked at me. But I was just as ignorant as he was. The atlas of our education was gaining more and more pages.

'From across the border, in the Hindu Kush. They used to be called Kafiri. They've been there since only God knows how long. Nuristan is called The Country of Light.'

A light that hadn't shone as far south as Riverview College and Rupe's Epping High.

'The myth is that they are descended from deserters from Alexander the Great's army. Before them were the Aspasians, who were blond and God knows where they came from. They're very proud, the Nuristani.'

'Just what we want,' said Rupe. 'A proud soundman. Does this guy speak English?'

The manager nodded. 'Five languages. He has worked for the BBC, the Americans, the French —'

'Bring him in,' I said.

Abdul Samir might have been a wrestler before he became a multilingual soundman. He was shorter than I but almost twice as broad; his neck could have supported a roof let alone the bald head above it. He had a broad friendly face and blue eyes as old as time. We found he had no illusions and no politics and always knew someone who knew someone.

'We want to go to Kabul,' we said.

'No problem,' he said.

I waited for him to say *No worries, mate*, but he wasn't fluent in Australian.

The war was well under way and the Taliban were on the run. There were now enough media personnel to form our own corps; but we were fighting each other for permission and transport to get us to the scene of the action. Then one morning, courtesy of Abdul Samir, we were in a bus, one of four, headed again for the Khyber, but this time to go straight on to Kabul.

The night before we left I phoned Adele. She had not

heard of nor read of Jason's death; I didn't ask if she watched the BBC or any of the other channels or read the newspapers. If she wanted to remain ignorant, let her be. People are not unintelligent if they don't watch every minute of television or read every page of a newspaper. In a way I was glad she knew nothing of what had happened to Jason; I didn't want her worrying even more about me. We just talked as lovers.

'I'm missing you, darling heart —'

'Jack.' She turned my name into a love-note. 'You're being careful?'

'Couldn't be carefuller. You working?'

'A job tomorrow, modelling. Negligée, expensive stuff. No Brazilian necessary.'

'Put the most expensive negligée on lay-by. I'll pay for it.'

Lovers' talk may be pregnant (if that is the word), but it is mostly banal to the point of embarrassment if overheard by others. I don't know if Shakespeare (Will, that is) and Dryden and Byron and Shelley whispered sonnets when on the pillow beside their lovers, but chances are their words were as featherweight as Adele's and mine. The depth of love is in the look and the touch.

'You getting anything in the theatre?'

'I'm auditioning.' Which meant she was getting nothing. 'It's crowded —'

Come home, dear Adele, come home.

We left Peshawar by first light next morning. I had come to notice that the light in the northern hemisphere was different from that which had thrown shadows back home. It was almost as if one could measure it in terms of thickness, as if it were in sheets. The dawn coming up from the hills east of Peshawar had none of the challenge that came up out of the sea off our coast. Or so it seemed as I looked back.

The climb up the Khyber was slow, partly due to the age of the buses, partly because the road was a slow river of refugees. They were coming down the long snake of the road in their hundreds, heading for the border where they would be turned back and would then spread out looking for holes in the long frontier between the two countries. Some of them shouted at us, the kids running back to ask for coins, but most of them trudged on with that stunned look that refugees have worn since war became a habit of mankind.

'Jesus!' Rupe was sitting by a grimy window, looking out at the poor buggers slowly drifting by us. 'I'll never complain again about any bloody thing!'

'Yes, you will,' I said; I was acquiring wisdom by the day.

He looked sideways at me, then nodded. 'Yeah, you're right.'

Abdul Samir was in the seat in front of me. I asked him, 'Have you got a family?'

He turned back, nodded. 'A wife and three daughters.'

'Where are they?'

'A long way from this.' He jerked his head at the window. 'At my village, up in the Hindu Kush. Some day I'll bring my daughters out to let them see —' Then he shook his head and there was sudden pain in his eyes. 'But not yet . . .'

At last we were coming into Kabul. I don't know what I had expected. Perhaps more giants of history have passed through what used to be called Caubul than through any other city. Alexander, Genghis Khan, Tamberlaine had been greeted by its citizens, not always with flowers and cheers. It had, seemingly, been here forever. It had once been beautiful, I'd read; back in the nineteenth century, during the British occupation, the conquerors had enjoyed it to the full. There had been horse-racing, skating, cricket. The beautiful Afghan women, put in a queue behind their men's preference for the bums of boys, had slept with the British officers, who, putting behind them (if that is the position) the sins of their public schooldays, plunged wholeheartedly into what was offered them. All that had disappeared in the massacre by an Afghan army led by warlords; there had been a solitary survivor, a doctor who, like the hero in an old Western movie, had escaped and ridden the perilous miles to Jalalabad with the dreadful news. And now the warlords were back once again and, as we clambered down out of the buses, I looked at the neglect and destruction that the Taliban had wrought upon the city.

'Jesus,' said Rupe, looking around. 'Why bother?'

Abdul Samir raised an eyebrow. 'The Americans are not interested in Kabul. They are here only for Osama bin Laden and al-Qaeda.' He waved a hand around him. 'The chiefs will fight about this. Let them.'

The fighting here was over and the war had moved on towards the hills and mountains to the east. The reason for the war had escaped: no one knew where Osama bin Laden was. Six feet six, a long beard, magnetic eyes:

probably at the time the most displayed image in the world. And the troops couldn't find him. *They seek him here, they seek him there*: Baroness Orczy could have written volumes about him.

The city, with the Taliban gone, fleeing east or south to Kandahar, was now overrun with warlords, all eager for their share of what they hoped would be the spoils: the power and, most importantly, the aid that would soon be flowing in. I decided this was where our stories would be. In our hotel, a one-star job charging five-star prices, Rupe and Abdul Samir and I watched the nightly television news of the hunt for bin Laden and Omar Mullah in the mountains to the south-east and decided there was not much excitement in long shots of bombs bursting on tree-bare, rocky mountainsides.

So we set about finding a warlord to talk to. Here Abdul Samir again earned his wages. On our second day he came back to the hotel where Rupe and I were lunching on what could have been old goat or old shoe leather, washed down with Coca-Cola at Krug prices.

'This afternoon we meet Akbar Yaqub. He is from Taloqan.'

Where we had been heading when Jason was shot. 'An Alliance chief?'

Abdul shrugged. 'For now. Yesterday also ...' He shrugged again.

'How big a warlord is he?' I wasn't interested in interviewing a gang leader.

'Medium-sized. He is young for a warlord, but he is very ambitious.'

Where had I heard that before? 'Does he speak English?'

'No, only Dari.'

I had never heard of it; but then, like most Anglo-Australians, my knowledge of languages other than English was abysmal. There are a dozen nationalities on the staff of Channel 15 and I had done no better than pick up a word or two from their languages.

'You can speak it?'

'Of course,' said Abdul.

We met Akbar Yaqub in the garden of a house on what was known as Legation Hill; or had been in the British days. We sat on carpets under a thin-leafed lemon tree, with four bearded bodyguards seated around us like the corner-posts of a boxing ring. We were not made to feel welcome, just tolerated.

Akbar was younger than I had expected, no more than thirty at the most, a junior warlord. He was tall and handsome, his looks spoiled only by his thin straggly beard, like solidified dribble. He was dressed in a grey blouse, over it a green waistcoat, black baggy pantaloons and brand new tan boots that were obviously too small for him, since he kept moving his feet and wincing every so often. On his head, also brand new, was the rolled-up woollen *pakal* hat that so many of them wore. He fingered yellow worry-beads and an AK-47 lay on the carpet beside him, a contrast he evidently was unaware of.

I squatted down on the carpet with Abdul Samir beside me. Rupe moved around with his camera, eyed suspiciously by the bodyguards. I put my first question: 'Now the war is almost over, what are your plans?'

The translated answer was stilted: 'I shall become part of the government of the new Afghanistan.'

With umpteen warlords saying the same thing, government was going to be crowded and rowdy. 'The Taliban are finished?'

'Forever.' He slid his finger across his throat, smiled with broken teeth, and the four corner-posts laughed.

'Will you help find Osama bin Laden?'

He shrugged. 'He is the Americans' problem.'

The interview lasted another ten minutes and I knew I had nothing that was going to spark any interest back home, except to the perceptive. He posed, with vanity, for a couple of close-ups by Rupe; then he stood up, picking up the AK-47 as if it were just a walking-stick he had put down. Standing he was stiff with arrogance; or sore feet. He said something directly to me, then stalked out of the garden, followed by the four bodyguards. He walked awkwardly, as if the boots were killing him.

'What did he say?' I asked Abdul.

'Remember my name.'

'Will it be necessary?'

Abdul shook his head. 'He will be dead soon. The big men won't share power with the little men.'

Three weeks later, back home by then, I learned that Akbar Yaqub had been killed by another warlord, a big one.

Chapter Eight

1

We left Afghanistan for home a week after the interview with Akbar Yaqub. The war was getting nowhere in its main purpose; Osama bin Laden had disappeared into the smoke of American bombs. Entwistle and the board decided enough money had been spent on telling the viewers what they wanted to know, or didn't want to know, about the war. The ratings had gone neither up nor down with our coverage from Afghanistan. That could have been our fault, because I knew in my heart I had done nothing as a war correspondent. I had been not much more than a bystander.

I had seen one shot fired in anger (if, indeed, it had been in anger), the one that killed Jason. Of course each night in Kabul there were shots, but they were mostly celebration; if people died from them, we heard nothing the next morning. The warlords did not hold press conferences and the Americans were concerned only with the Big Picture. Each day, they had told us, they were closing in on bin Laden . . .

Rupe and I went to see Jason's parents and his fourteen-year-old sister. They lived in a small semi-detached in a back street of Coogee, with no sight of the surf or the sea.

Chilla Tully was a council worker, an Irish immigrant who had been here thirty years; Ombra Tully was, to my surprise, Greek. They embraced both me and Rupe, *hugging* us, both of them weeping. Andy, their daughter, stood off and watched us.

It was she who accompanied us to the front gate. 'They'll miss him forever. Mum has always wanted us both to be the best.'

'What do you want to be?'

'An actor.'

Oh Christ, more disappointment. 'Andy Tully — I'll look for your name.'

'No, Andromeda. Jason and Andromeda. Mum's a dreamer.'

'Are you a dreamer?'

'No.' She was dark-haired and black-eyed, more Greek than Irish, attractive but a long way from beautiful. Never the leading lady, always the leading lady's best friend. 'Neither is Dad. One dreamer in the family is enough.'

I had never asked Jason if he was a dreamer. I kissed her on the cheek, squeezed her shoulder. 'Good luck, Andromeda.'

'Jason thought a lot of you. He used to tell me about you.'

'Rupe and I thought a lot of him.'

I was close to tears, it was time to go.

As we drove away Rupe said, 'I heard what young Andy said. Her mother will never get over it. Dreamers never do.'

Suddenly I was sad for another dreamer on the other side of the world.

Les Dibley was sympathetic to what I thought of as my failure. 'Wars never go according to the script. Generals have known that for centuries — though they never learn from it. Forget it, Jack. Here's a nice juicy item for you, one that'll have the viewers slobbering. A girl kills her lover and his wife — it's usually the other way round.'

'I love your cynicism, Les. It's a tonic.'

'It's the only way to survive, mate, in a job like ours. Try and get a shot of the killer without a towel over her head. Especially if she's a good sort.'

'You're callous too, Les.'

'It helps.'

I settled back into the peace and security of Longueville. Lynne was relieved that I had come home safely. 'I said a prayer for you every night and I guess God was listening to me.'

She was another lapsed R C. 'Nick is glad, too, that you're home.'

Their marriage was planned for March. 'Where are you going to live?'

'We're still looking. Prices are bloody ridiculous. But relax — we're not going to move back in here with you. How's Adele?'

'Okay, I guess —'

'Still ambitious?'

'Still.'

I phoned Adele two and three times a week and wrote her my weekly *billet-doux* — 'Milly thinks they're so romantic. Only her mum writes her letters.'

'I'm old-fashioned.'

'And I love you for it.'

'Getting any work?'

'Not much, but enough. I'm auditioning everywhere. But —'

I waited for the silence to be broken; then broke it myself: 'But?'

'It's tough. Even Americans are coming over here looking for work. I'm getting by, darling, but it's all in television. Every time they want a good-looking hooker, I get a call.'

'Marry me and I'll get you out of that life of sin.'

It was the usual lovers' talk, banality going round in circles. I put down the phone each time with a feeling of emptiness.

One weekend I went out to Bulinga Creek. Kate and Luke greeted me as if I were already part of the family. We sat on the wide front verandah of the house, sipping drinks, and looked out past the avenue of poplars to the land turning gold under the late sun. Far out in the paddocks a willy-willy spun like the ghost of a whirling dervish, was there for half a minute at the most and then was gone. There was peace here that Afghanistan had looked as if it had never experienced.

They had asked me about Afghanistan, but only obliquely, and I had replied obliquely, skirting any talk of Jason's death. They sensed my reticence and didn't press the subject.

'I think we're in for another drought,' Luke now said. 'The met blokes say another bad El Niño is on the way.'

He seemed more subdued than when I had seen him last; and *older*? 'The world's going downhill.'

'The climate, you mean?' I had covered stories on it, but I was a city man and was partially blind and partially deaf to environment problems.

'No, everything. Terrorism, the climate, ethics — everything.' He sipped his beer. Kate and I were drinking white wine, but he had his good old-fashioned Aussie strong-as-you-can-take-it beer. He looked as if he might keep at it till he was drunk. Then, abruptly, he changed the subject: 'Adele's working, she tells us.'

'TV stuff. I don't think that's what she wants to do.'

'She needs the money,' said Kate. 'She can't be choosy.'

'Why don't you go over there, grab her and bring her home and marry her?' The beer was working on Luke.

Kate said coolly but firmly, 'Let him make his own decisions — and her, too. She'll come home in her own time, not with a gun at her head. Is she living comfortably, Jack?'

'I think so.' I wasn't going to describe how and where she was living. 'She has a great flatmate, Milly.'

'Another actress, isn't she?' Luke was beginning to look surly, something I had never expected of him. Suddenly he stood up, said, 'I need another beer,' and went inside.

Kate didn't look at me, but stared out across the paddocks now turning green-gold under the sun. I sat in silence, waiting for her to break it. Then, without looking at me, she said, 'He's worried stiff. Things are not going well.'

'Wool prices, that sort of thing?'

'No — though if the drought comes, that will affect prices. No, it's his investments.'

I had forgotten Tonetel, had had very little interest in it to begin with. 'I thought Tonetel was going to be the biggest thing since the invention of the telephone. It's always advertising, sponsoring this, sponsoring that. My boss, Entwistle, is on the board.'

'Have you seen its share price?'

I looked at only the shares I held; the rest of the stock exchange list in the morning papers was just a blur to be ignored. 'No.'

'The're twenty cents. He paid almost three dollars.'

That sounded like chickenfeed; but: 'I shouldn't ask this — but how much did he invest?'

Then Luke came back with another drink and Kate poured me some more wine, giving me a warning look as she did so. Luke had either sobered up; or quietened down. He flopped back in his squatter's chair, looked out at the fading landscape, then looked at me and said, almost gently, 'I love this place.'

'I can understand why,' I said; and did. 'I spoke to my dad last night in New York. He said that the more he lived overseas, the more he thought Australia was the Lucky Country. Even though it was originally meant as a satirical title. Donald Horne, wasn't it?'

Luke nodded. 'Let's hope it stays that way. Lucky.'

Sunday they took me to lunch at a neighbouring property owned by another of the old district families. There were a dozen or more people there, plus kids, and I couldn't help but contrast it with the family gatherings I had seen in Afghanistan, where food was short, peace was brittle and landmines grew in the fields as grain grew here.

I was the centre of interest because I had been to the latest of wars. But what could I tell them that television had not already told them? The world now was instant movies.

'This bloke bin Laden —' He was a nuggety man, all bone and sinew, dry as leather in complexion and voice. He had been introduced to me as Joe Someone-or-Other, who owned a property some fifty miles further west, out where the plains began. 'Do we have to be afraid of him?'

'I don't know,' I said, munching on a lamb chop held in the hand. 'The warlords in Kabul didn't seem to care a damn about him. As for us, I don't know if he knows we exist.'

'Well, let's hope he never finds out. I grow wheat, we export a lot of it to the Middle East. The last thing we bloody want is a war over there ... Luke tells me you're Adele's boyfriend, that right? Nice girl. My lad had his eye on her, but he never had a hope. How's she doing over there in London?'

'Okay.'

'You oughta go over there and bring her home.'

'Mind your own business,' said Kate, coming from the flank, giving him a smile that eased the bruising. It had struck me that half the men at the gathering were in love with her, but Luke had won the race and they respected that. She pressed my arm and smiled at me too, and I was half in love with her. 'She'll come home in her own time.'

I drove back to Sydney late that afternoon, climbing over the Blue Mountains, wearing a certain sadness that I couldn't explain to myself. I had never been one of those natives who loved the 'wide brown land' and thought those on the land were the salt of the earth. I had lived all my life on the coastal strip, where, I had always thought, the energy was and where the money was made. But now I was realising there was a backbone that had supported us for so long, that had kept going through decades, that now was crumbling. Country people were beginning to feel they no longer mattered, that those in the cities had forgotten them.

For Luke and Kate and their friends it was no longer the Lucky Country. The coin was spinning in the air and they didn't know which way it would land.

2

I didn't lead a hermitic life. I took Hilary Reingold to movies and to dinner. At her door she would play the mock seduction and once or twice I responded with an open-mouth kiss and a grinding of the pelvis. There would be a stiffening down below, but then I would start to think of Adele in the same situation and jealousy would tap me on the shoulder. Some salacious bastard in London, like a Hugh Grant character, was trying to seduce her. I would pull away from Hilary, pat her rump and depart, wallowing masochistically in my jealousy. When jealousy dies, love is in danger.

Then one morning Entwistle, all red-striped shirt, white collar and cuffs, red braces and bonhomie, sent for me. 'How'd you like to go to London?'

'With the PM?' The man was planning another of his overseas pilgrimages, either to London or Washington, never to New Delhi or Tokyo. The cynical joke now was that our politicians spent more time on planes than they did on parliamentary benches. Les Dibley, a one-eyed historian, said he had never known such cynicism about politics and politicians.

'No, a year's assignment.' He was enjoying himself, Big-Hearted Jared. 'We're setting up a London bureau.'

I sat on my excitement, though it was buckjumping like a rodeo bull. 'I'd like that. I think I need to broaden my horizons —' *Listen to me!* 'And the way things are going, terrorist threats and all that, we need our own voice —'

It is a characteristic of bullshit artists that they admire bullshit, even if, in my case, it was involuntary. 'Just what I told the board! Almost those words!'

He had just come back from London, where he had been with the program director buying local rights to cheap British productions. Our major money went on American sitcoms and movies, in which, the demographics said, our viewers' tastes lay. Viewers' tastes were treated as epicurean.

'We've rented office space just off Fleet Street and leased a flat in a converted warehouse on the river, just below Tower Bridge. You should be pretty comfortable, though the board has said not to go mad with the expenses.' Then, oh so casually, 'Is Miss Ambar still in New York?'

'No, she's in London actually.' Oh, so casually.

For a moment I thought he was going to cancel my posting. His face matched his shirt, but he recovered. 'You're still friendly with her?'

'Sort of.' It was none of his business, but I couldn't tell him so. Not if I wanted to get to London.

'She should come back here. We could give her plenty of work.'

'If I see her, I'll tell her. How's Mrs Entwistle?'

She had been featured in the Sunday gossip columns wearing a dress that made Liz Hurley's famous frontless job look like a nun's habit.

'Oh, busy, very busy. She loves charity work.'

Baring her boobs for the homeless. But I didn't say that.

'When do I leave?'

'The weekend too soon?'

Yesterday wouldn't have been too soon. 'I'll be ready.'

'Better luck than in Afghanistan.'

You bastard: the only reference he had made to me on Jason's death. 'I'll try.'

When I rang Adele to tell her, she screamed with delight. Edith Evans couldn't have been louder. 'Oh darling, I'll be at the airport! Come naked!'

'Won't immigration object to that?'

I left for London a month before Lynne and Nick were to be married. I bought them a wedding present in advance, a top-of-the-range TV set — 'So that you can watch me in full digital.'

They drove me to the airport on a day when the weather said, *Stay home, son, London will never be like this*. But Adele would be there in the English winter and that would be warmth enough.

I was warmed at the moment at the happiness of Lynne and Nick in each other. She had at last found the man she had been looking for. 'I'm sorry I'm going to miss the Big Day.'

'We'll send you a video.'

Lynne was driving at her usual breakneck speed and Nick was sitting beside her, seemingly unaware of the danger at every traffic light. He turned back to me: 'Good luck with your girl.'

He had never met Adele, but Lynne had obviously told him about her. 'I won't marry her over there. Too much competition.'

He looked puzzled and Lynne, taking her eyes off the road, enlightened him: 'She's in love with theatre. She wants to be Edith Thorndyke.'

'Evans,' I said.

Nick knew neither of them, Edith or Sybil. 'I once went out with an actress —'

Lynne brought the car to a shuddering halt and Nick and I pitched forward in our seat belts. She looked at us and smiled that smile that only women can wear: 'A red light.'

At the airport I kissed Lynne, holding her tight, then hugged Nick. 'Take care of her, you bastard, or I'll come back.'

'You'd play what? Inside-centre? Just my meat.' And he gave me an 800-pound gorilla hug in return. Never try to be too affectionate with a front-row forward.

The trip to London took longer than Captain Cook's voyage to Australia back in the eighteenth century. I tried to sleep, but Adele kept walking through my dreams. Two of the hostesses who knew me from on-camera hovered over me and the gay head steward stroked my hand a couple of times, but even awake I was dreaming.

We came into Heathrow through a mist of cold rain. All the ground staff were wrapped up as if going out into a storm and the wreck of the Hesperus. The grey sky looked as if it stretched from Siberia to the States. But everything was suddenly warmer inside the terminal.

She was there, while I waited in a line of 949 assorted Pakistanis, Afghans, Iraqis and other sad-looking immigrants hoping for a better life here in Britain. At last I was through Customs and Immigration and in her arms. She was as beautiful as I remembered; but a little strained-looking? It was five months since we had seen each other, held each other, and I don't care what other lovers say, it was an eternity for me. For us?

I don't know why I had doubts; I shouldn't have been unsettled. I was doubting her faithfulness and I was ashamed. But she had been here in temptation's way ... I was jealous, with no reason to be.

I held her tightly to me and she bit me as she kissed me. She was weeping and all at once the doubt was gone; and the jealousy went back into the blood where it hid like venom.

'Oh darling!' She pushed me away, looked at me. 'You haven't changed, thank God. Have you?'

'No. Have you?'

She shook her head, which was kept warm by a fur hat. She wore a thick camelhair coat, the habitual silk scarf round her throat, and her handbag, on a long strap from her shoulder, was a Vuitton. She was either still extravagant or she was making money somewhere.

But she had no car — 'Parking's too difficult.' So we took a taxi and we got into it and held hands and stuttered and stammered as we tried to bridge the months we had been apart. Teenagers couldn't have been less sophisticated.

The taxi driver, a Pakistani, stayed in his seat while Adele and I unloaded my laptop, three suitcases and briefcase. He looked at the tip I gave him as if it were counterfeit money and drove away with no more farewell than a sour look. I was going to have to adjust, a refugee in another country, though on expenses.

The exterior of the warehouse had been cleaned up, the brickwork looking as if it had been tuckpointed. The entrance lobby had palms in pots as if suggesting an oasis of welcome. An oasis in wintry London? Where better? The lift was new and worked smoothly and the flat turned out to be larger and more attractive than I had expected. The furniture was what I always thought of as *moderne*, with sofa backs too low and glass coffee tables that threatened to chop you off at the knees. But the view up-river through the large window set in one wall was — well, not as pleasant and peaceful as that from Longueville, but it too was better than I had expected. I could be happy here, if . . .

'Are you jet-lagged?'

'Not that much.'

We went to bed and it was just as it had ever been. Later, I lay looking at her and murmured, 'You're still beautiful.'

'*Still*? What did you expect — me to have become a hag?'

'No —'

'You men amuse me. You tell us we're beautiful and all you're after is the ugliest part of us.'

'How many guys have told you you're beautiful?'

'Two or three. But don't worry — they didn't get what they were after. I kept it for you. What about you and your urges? I know what they're like.'

'I took Hilary Reingold to dinner several times, but I never did more than shake hands with her.'

'I remember her. She had sex written all over her.'

'I must have missed it . . . Come here . . .'

Later, sitting at the dining room table, all glass and steel, drinking coffee, the only viand of any sort in the kitchen, all steel and granite, we looked out on the river. Tugs were going downstream, a cruise boat edged out from a wharf opposite us. I said as casually as I could, 'This is better than Hammersmith.'

'Yes,' she said and seemed to be waiting.

'Would you move in with me?'

She gave me a smile that split me in two. 'I thought you'd never ask.'

3

The weather, of course, was freezing. The wind blew in from Siberia, carrying, I imagined, the cries of *gulag* prisoners of long ago. Rain was always a threat, coming up like dark-clad Celts out of the valleys of the blue-black clouds. I bought myself a Burberry with a zip-in lining and a brown-and-white checked cap, became a *foreign correspondent.*

The office that had been rented, ever aware of Channel 15's budget obsession, was a cubbyhole in a press agency. I hired a secretary, Imogen, who had been educated at Roedean, could recite Keats and sing songs by Kravitz. She was an attractive blonde and she ran the office with all the competence of a naval commander.

I also hired a cameraman, Rhys Jones, from the Welsh Rhonda. He was black-haired and chunky and always morose at the decline of Welsh rugby. But he was impressed by me when I told him I had read Gwyn Thomas, recommended by my father: 'Oh, boyo, then you've read the best. A comic man, but a sad one.'

My soundman was Sacha Majid, a Pakistani Cockney, who read only Nick Hornby's music column and had a library of CDs. 'I could lend you some, Jack, I've got the best of all of them.'

'I'm not very musical, Sacha. But I can whistle "Waltzing Matilda" —'

The mixture of accents in our cubicle was a discordant music. I was surprised and pleased how quickly we became a team.

Milly Brown didn't mind Adele's moving out. It seemed that she had committed herself to the BBC guy and she was moving in with him. The actors were going up in the world, at least in accommodation.

We collected Adele's gear from her flat. Though the sun was shining thinly on the day, the street looked no more inviting than the first time I had seen it. Adele had attempted to brighten up the flat by buying a print of one of Lloyd Rees's Sydney Harbour scenes and we brought that back to the warehouse apartment and hung it on a wall opposite a dark John Piper print that was part of the rental. A week after we had moved in I went to the New South Wales government offices and bought a large bright print of beaches and hung that in the main bedroom.

Since she had left Kirribilli Adele had learned to cook and housekeep. She was a long way from gourmet standards; it is a myth that every country girl is born a cook. But she satisfied me with what she put on the table, because, as she told me, it was served 'with tender loving care.' We went shopping together at a nearby supermarket and she knew what she wanted, even to knowing what the bargain buy was for today. She had become everyday practical. But for ...

'I'm still trying.' It was a Sunday morning, my day off, and we were in the big living room. The Sunday papers were strewn around us, one of my newly discovered pleasures; back home Sunday was now owned by the tabloids. I had been reading the theatre reviews and, almost idly, had asked her if she was losing hope. 'It takes time, Jack. At least now most of the producers have *seen* me —'

But not offered jobs; but I didn't say that. I sometimes wondered, if we were actually married, whether there would be hesitation between us. This was the first time I had actually *lived* with a girl and I was still learning.

'Why don't you concentrate on TV? The quality stuff, I mean, not hookers in cop shows.'

'Darling, I want room to *move*. You can do that on stage, but in TV and films you're restricted by the camera.'

I had once seen a grainy photographed stage play starring Ellen Terry and, I think, Henry Irving or it might have been Beerbohm Tree. At the time, before I had met Adele, all three had been remote historical figures as far as I was concerned, back there with medieval minstrels and puppeteers. The actors had been all over the stage, covering it like soccer plays after scoring a goal, though not pulling their sweaters over their heads. There had been arms waving, heads jerking, certainly *movement*. Technique had improved since then, especially with the restrictions of theatre-in-the-round, otherwise audiences would have been ducking and weaving like the referee in a boxing ring. But Adele evidently admired the old school.

'If we could get you on the Michael Parkinson show — he likes beautiful women —'

'Not a hope. Be realistic, darling. He talks to *stars*.'

She was practical about publicity, but not ambition.

We went to the theatre twice a week, to the West End and the Fringe houses, and I began to tire of it. Fortunately she did not want to go nightclubbing or pub-crawling. But I was finding that living with a woman, in an imitation of marriage, was far different from dating and one-night stands. I had never thought of myself as weak-willed, but I began to feel — well, *dominated*. Or was I imagining it?

I had settled down to work, though it was not as easy as I had expected. Les Dibley rang me to tell me my first few stories were not what Channel 15's audience wanted; they were not interested in Tony Blair's problems nor the Brits' aversion to the *euro*. Then out in East Anglia, in a small village, a man murdered his wife, cut her up into manageable pieces, wrapped them in *News of the World* sheets and buried them in his vegetable allotment under a rhubarb patch.

'It's put me off rhubarb pie forever,' said Rhys.

'It's history repeating itself,' said Les Dibley when I had filed my final cover. 'America has more vicious crime and lots of it, but the Brits — well, no, the *English* — they go in for the bizarre. Before your time, son, there were Heath and Christie, then the Moors murders, then some bloke who murdered a dozen or more girls and buried 'em in his backyard —'

'Don't go on, Les.' I had been sickened by the story. What had come as a shock was that I had been sickened by the coverage; it had been almost a carnival, the tabloids trying to outdo each other, the TV crews acting like *paparazzi*, ourselves included.

'It's life, Jack. All the bastards are not terrorists. Have a good day —'

'It's 11 p.m., Les —'

'Enjoy the rest of it, then. When I called your flat yesterday, a girl answered. Have you got a maid and who's paying?'

'It was Miss Ambar, Les, and that's just between you and me and nobody else, okay?'

'Son, you know I'm not a gossip.'

I laughed, but I trusted him. 'Goodnight, Les. Give my love to your wife and the six brats.'

Then Adele got a call from her agent. A German film producer had seen her on TV and was coming to London to test her for a major film, a remake of *Wuthering Heights*.

. She was excited by the prospect; Edith Evans and the *expanse* of the stage had had a curtain lowered on them for the time being. 'He's testing me for Catherine — what a part!'

I had never read the book nor seen the old Hollywood movie with Laurence Olivier and Merle Oberon, nor a later British version; both of them had come and gone before I was born. 'I'll say a Hail Mary for you —'

'Don't joke, Jack.'

'I'm not joking — I'd really like you to get the part.' I was convincing myself I really would.

I had just come in from a dreary day in the rain, interviewing a horse trainer who had just bought a major interest in an Australian stud. Les Dibley's interest in asking for the story was that the trainer was married to a pop singer whose father was a dead Australian jockey. Channel 15's viewers never knew the lengths we went to to get a story.

I had had a shower, was in my pyjamas and dressing-gown, ready for dinner, hungry as any of the horses at the stud where we had been this afternoon. 'What's for dinner?'

'Oh God — I forgot! When I got the call, it was 5.30 —'

Our first row started from something as small as that. It went from a nasty remark by me to a sharp retort by her and the words exploded like fireworks. Talk about extravagant gestures; we both outdid Terry and Irving. It was bloody ridiculous, but I'll bet the ridiculous is in half the rows between lovers. It finished, for the moment, when she stormed, yes, *stormed* into the bedroom and slammed the door so hard I waited for it to fall off its hinges.

I slumped down in a chair, exhausted by the row and the dreary, chilly day. And I was bloody hungry, I suddenly realised. I got up and went into the kitchen, found some chicken *cacciatore* in the freezer, got it out and put it in the microwave. Have you ever noticed in all those commercials about frozen dinners that no one looks unhappy? I looked at myself in the mirror beside the wall-phone and I looked as miserable as it was possible to be. No advertisement at all for chicken *cacciatore* ...

Then behind me she said, 'Is there enough for me?'

I got out another serving of the chicken, put it in the microwave, then turned and took her in my arms. 'That's out of the way.'

'What?'

'Our first row.' I kissed her wet cheeks; she had been weeping. 'I'm sorry —'

She didn't say she was sorry, but I let it pass. We had dinner, then went to bed, where the love-making was gentler than we were used to, as if the argument had been a blood-letting.

Next day she went for the interview with the German producer. I had a good day. The rain had stopped, the wind had died and I caught Kylie Minogue, fully dressed, coming out of a recording studio and she gave me five minutes, as charming and articulate as my mother and what more could a TV reporter ask? Rhys and Sacha were equally charmed by her and we went back to file the story, beaming at each other as if we had scored the Interview of the Century.

I went home in a good mood, walking the distance because I felt so good and had missed the usual walk that morning. I had come to know the area in which we lived, got to know casually some of the neighbours and had come to acknowledge that the Brits were just like us Aussies, only different.

I let myself into the apartment and, while still at the open door, knew something was wrong. Adele was there, curled up in a chair. One look told me things had not gone well.

'The producer was a she, not a he, and she wants to make a big *porno* movie of *Wuthering Heights*!'

I wanted to laugh, but managed to choke it back. 'Heathcliff running around bollocky on — where? — the Yorkshire moors? That'll turn him into a hermaphrodite —'

'She wants to film it in *Norway*! Don't laugh or I'll kick you in the —'

'What would your part — Catherine? — be doing? Running around naked too? I don't want some slobbering actor running his hands over you —'

'Neither do I. I didn't bother to listen to her — I just walked out.'

'How did your agent get you into something like that?' I pulled up a chair, sat down opposite her, took her hand in mine. Without meaning to, I sounded like an analyst with his first client: 'Darling heart, I think you're going to have to sort yourself out —'

'Don't start lecturing me!' I didn't realise it then, but she was taking her frustration and anger out on me because there was nobody else.

'Shut up and listen!' I was still holding her hand, could feel her trembling. 'You're aiming for the top of the tree and you've got a ladder with no rungs in it.' I'd never get away with a speech like that on camera; Les Dibley would edit me dead. 'Okay, you gave the finger to the porno movie. But you're going to have to take bit parts, hookers, whatever comes up, and build a CV. You're too choosy —'

She clouted me with her free hand, but said nothing.

I should have clouted her in return, knocked some sense into her; but I'm not a belter of women and can't understand men who are. 'For Crissake, be sensible —'

'You've grown tired of keeping me, is that it?'

That was when I almost clouted her. Instead, I jumped to my feet, grabbed my Burberry and cap and slammed out of the apartment. It was dramatic; no, melodramatic, Henry Irving couldn't have done better. But going down in the lift, its slowness mocking me for my rashness, I knew we had reached that cliché, a crossroads. Two rows in two days. We were both going to have to tread carefully from now on.

I walked for an hour, not as an exercise but to clear my head. There was no wind, unless it was high up where the stars looked wind-burnished, as bright as the lighted windows across the river. A cruise boat went by, a party on board in full swing; they were singing some country-

and-western song, not 'Knees Up, Mother Brown', which someone had told me was the traditional river-boat song. Tradition was going down-river with the tide. I passed a couple having a knee-trembler in a doorway and silently wished them happiness, though I could think of a better place to have it. It was time to go home.

When I let myself in the door, wondering how I would be received, I could smell cooking. She was in the kitchen, hair pulled back, apron on, wooden spoon in hand. The dining table was set, two places, wine glasses at the ready.

As if nothing had happened: 'It's just pasta, but I'm making a sauce Mum taught me, a Bulinga Creek special.'

'Smells good.' I hesitated, then still in Burberry and cap, as if ready for another quick departure, I stepped behind her and kissed the back of her neck.

She turned her head, her face close against mine. 'No regrets, okay? No sorrys, okay?'

'Okay,' I said and took off my coat and cap, home again.

But from then on we both knew we were walking an alpine ledge. We went to bed, but there was no sex; we held each other as if roped together for safety. We were on a learning curve.

Back home Lynne and Nick were married and had moved into an apartment they had bought, with a river view. 'We paid the earth for it, but what's money for? But I shouldn't ask you that question, Shylock. How's Adele?'

'Fine. Getting some work, a bit of this, a bit of that.'

'How's yours? Work, I mean. You look as if you're floundering sometimes.'

She should have been a critic. 'It's not as easy as I though it would be. Channel 15 is on a different planet.'

My mother and father had gone home for the wedding, but were now back in New York, with Mum more homesick than ever for Sydney. I began to feel that way myself, but kept it to myself.

I talked to them once a week in New York and Mum's question was always loaded: 'How's Adele?' *When is she going to marry you?*

'Fine, Mum. How's Dad?'

'Busy as hell. The UN and the White House aren't exactly pals right now. Saddam Hussein is the argument now, Osama bin Laden seems to have been forgotten. Dad's running around, doing that old thing, spreading oil on troubled waters. Trouble is, he says, oil's part of the problem. I think he's ready for retirement. Give our love to Adele. How is she?'

'You've asked me that, Mum. Goodnight.'

Adele and I didn't live in isolation; we had a social life. Milly Brown and her man, Jeff, came to dinner; so did others, mostly actors whom Adele had come to know. Jeff and I, TV reporters, discussed the world, while the actors discussed their artificial world; there was no limit to our sense of superiority, but we kept it to ourselves. He was older than I, in his late thirties, and he had been all over the map.

'Latin America was the most interesting.' He was a small man, not much bigger than Milly, with dark curly hair, a moustache and a Scots accent that he had managed to sieve. 'Everybody was so bloody passionate — it was dead easy interviewing them. The women as well as the men —'

'You ever get to Brazil?'

'Twice. Great scenery.' The moustache spread across his face as he smiled. 'I didn't want to leave Rio.'

'How do you feel, living with an actor?' It had taken me quite a while to ask that question.

He looked at me shrewdly. 'They're another breed, aren't they?'

Again smug in our superiority we looked across at the other breed. There were our two women and four other couples, several of them well-known faces on television. But none of them was a star and their dreams hovered above their conversation like a miasma.

I said, 'When they play in a film or TV series based on a real event, I wonder how they feel? Playing a real-life hero or heroine?'

'I've never asked them.' Then he said, almost casually, 'Milly tells me you're a part-time writer.'

'Very part-time. I did a TV pilot and the series is running back home now, at the bottom of the ratings. They didn't manage to sell it anywhere, except Bangladesh and Patagonia. They haven't renewed it.' I didn't mention my film script, now somewhere on the Hollywood rubbish heap.

'I once interviewed a writer, an American.' He said nothing more, just sipped his drink.

'And —?'

'Nothing.'

Writers, American or otherwise, were obviously another breed, not as interesting as passionate Latin American revolutionaries. I was glad he had not attempted to interview me.

Adele came across to us. 'What are you two discussing?'

'Women,' I said and Jeff nodded in agreement.

'And what did you come up with?'

'You're another breed,' said Jeff. 'Isn't that what we said, Jack?'

'Absolutely. Another breed.' I raised my glass to her.

'You're liars, both of you.'

'Then we should be on the stage,' said Jeff, and I was glad he said it, not me. 'Where everything is make-believe.'

She looked at him; then at me. The second glance was longer, but I managed to look innocent. 'Milly has told me — Jeff's very cynical.'

'It's the Scots in me,' said Jeff, as if he sensed I needed a lifeline. 'The English have made us so. We were pure believers once.'

She gave us another long look, then stroked the cheek of each of us, said, 'Bollocks,' and went back to the actors.

'You and she don't agree about the theatre,' said Jeff, looking after her.

'Not the theatre. *Her*. She wants to be Edith Evans.'

'With those looks?' He shook his head. 'Ambition, ambition. I wanted to be Richard Dimbleby.' An icon from the fifties and sixties, for you late arrivals who think the Big Bang of Creation was in the seventies. 'The BBC said I didn't have the necessary magisterial look. I thought I was born with it, being a Presbyterian. You ambitious?'

'No,' I said, truthfully.

'You sound smug.'

'No. Safe.'

Across the room the actors were looking at us, an audience puzzled by the other breed. Us.

Chapter Nine

1

Then the weather changed. Summer came in early, or so it seemed. The sky every day was cloudless and a softer blue than back home. Londoners were suddenly a new race; the younger ones showed their navels, just like back home, and looked no more attractive. I've never been an admirer of navels, beringed or otherwise; I always think of it as the thumbprint God overlooked. On the fashion scene colour replaced drabness. I remembered an old fashion editor on a Channel 15 morning chat show remarking that the sixties had ruined the British colour sense when Mary Quant matched purple with yellow. But the colour this early summer was fine. Though I still couldn't get used to purple or green hair. I dared not think what colour scheme they had around the pubic area, Brazilian or otherwise.

I was still having trouble getting stories that suited Les Dibley; or the viewers of Channel 15. Then the Queen Mother died, and a little later, Princess Margaret. Though I was a lifelong republican by heritage and belief, I covered both stories with the necessary respect. The Queen Mum's funeral drew high ratings on Channel 15;

evidently republicans and monarchists joined forces in front of the screens. There is no doubt the Brits do ceremony better than anyone else and Royal funerals and weddings make great television. Rhys got some eye-catching images and even Entwistle sent us a message of congratulations.

We covered a terrorist scare at Heathrow and got some mileage out of that; armoured vehicles and gun-toting soldiers always suggest drama, even if there is none. Afghanistan had faded from the map, as it had so often; and Osama bin Laden was a ghost on the edge of the news. Washington was now talking of Saddam Hussein, a resurrected menace. Les Dibley told me people were looking up their atlases again, trying to get the Middle East sorted out. Kylie Minogue released a new album, the cover showing all bum, and Les asked for a story on that. There were devastating floods in China and a sniper was on the loose in the suburbs of Washington. But Britain, for *real* Channel 15 news, was as barren as the deserts of Iraq.

Then, almost out of the summer blue, Adele landed Queen Gertrude in *Hamlet* at a Fringe theatre. She came to the office for the first time, so excited she had to tell me immediately. She strode through the press agency's big office, already a queen, and VDTs stopped as if there had been a power breakdown. She came into our cubbyhole and Imogen, Rhys and Sacha were instant fans. Catherine Zeta-Jones couldn't have got a better reception.

'Where's he been keeping you?' said Imogen with unEnglish directness. 'We thought he went home to some sort of abbey with lots of monks.'

'So you're going to be Hamlet's mother?' said Rhys. 'I heard the other day that mums are getting younger.'

'You remind me of someone,' said Sacha. 'Someone I've seen in the last couple of days.'

'All right, you lot.' It was time for me to step in, to take formal, if clothed possession. 'We're going out to lunch. If the Queen abdicates, ask her to hold it till I get back.'

I was lightheaded. We walked through the outer office and the VDTs were still lifeless, as were some of the journalists. Adele gave them smiles, rapt in her own news, and the women in the room looked sourly at their dumb, sex-starved male co-workers. I felt like Antony walking Cleopatra down to her barge. Talk about Shakespearean, Jack of that ilk!

Out in the street we waited for her barge, a bus. She was holding my hand as we stood in the small queue and I could feel the excitement in her. The two men in the queue looked at her with sudden interest and the three women looked at the men, knowing them for what they were, lechers.

Then the bus drew up alongside us and there she was, stretched along its side in the briefest of lingerie, briefness that required a Brazilian cut.

'Oh no!'

The two men must have missed the poster: they clambered aboard to grab seats before the women; chivalry died out when buses were invented. But the three women paused, ran their eyes along the length of the bus, stood back as if at the Tate Gallery. Then they looked Adele up and down.

'You're showing a lot there, love,' said one of them, and the other two, stout ladies both whose lingerie would have covered a sofa, nodded in agreement. 'I'd watch out,' she said and gave me a look that said I already had my fly open.

'I'm her protector,' I said.

'Yeah,' said one of the stout ladies, 'and we're the Spice Girls.'

Then they clambered aboard and the bus moved on, taking Adele, all seven metres of her, up Fleet Street and all the way to Richmond, ogling queues all along the route.

'How the hell did that happen?'

I was feeling angry, but she was livid, all of her beauty suddenly gone as it does in anger: 'That bastard Maddux — he let them do that!'

'That's the *Vogue* stuff you did in Milan?'

'It was in *Vogue*, but it wasn't for them, it was a two-page ad. It was for an Italian designer — Indello.' She was so angry, she was spluttering, another deduction from her beauty.

'Maddux mightn't be responsible —'

'Of course he is! He did the deal!'

Then my mobile rang: it was Rhys: 'Jack, we've just had a call from Les Dibley — what is it, the middle of the night out there? He sounded worked up. They've got word another IT company, a London one, is going belly-up and it's linked with an Australian company. He wants us down the City pronto to interview these guys going down the toilet —'

'Rhys, can't it wait?'

Rhys gave me some Welsh sarcasm: 'Jack, I couldn't give a stuff about companies going broke, some of them deserve it. But Mr Dibley didn't seem too pleased about having to get out of bed in the middle of the night. He wanted to know why we hadn't got word of what was happening ... Perhaps you'd like to get him out of bed again?'

'Okay, pull your head in. I'm at the bus stop in Fleet Street — I'll be back in the office in a coupla minutes.' I clicked off. 'Darling, I've got to leave you —'

'You can't!'

'I have to.' I didn't think she meant to be selfish; she had been run over by a bus poster. 'I'll put you in a taxi — go home and I'll be there as soon's I get this job done.'

She didn't argue; suddenly all anger seemed to run out of her. I hailed a taxi, kissed her and put her in it, then went back to the office. As I did so, another bus went past. There she was: breasts, legs and rump in wide-screen. And that look that always got to me, the hair down over one eye, the smile that said sex was what she liked most of all. There for an army of guys to leer at. Even as I stopped to look after the bus, people were staring at it. A girl looked at me and sneered: I was obviously just another lecher.

Rhys, Sacha and I went down to the City, to the labyrinth of streets and lanes where money was dug out of mines twenty-storeys high, found the executives who refused to talk to us, found sacked workers who couldn't wait to talk to us. It was a story that had been good for the past six months, here, New York, Sydney. Executives walking away with fortunes and the mine-workers left with bugger-all. The story still had legs and we got some good stuff on tape from some very articulate workers, men and women, who sprayed four-letter words like dirt on a grave. Tomorrow's morning and evening news would be laced with *beeps*, but Channel 15 viewers were practised lip-readers. It was a good story and I didn't neglect it. But I was eager to get home as soon as possible to Adele.

'I remember now where I'd seen her —' said Sacha tentatively.

'Don't, Sacha.' I explained how it had all begun. 'It was supposed to be just in *Vogue*, that's all.'

'You could sue London Transport,' said Imogen.

'And have her spread across the front page of the *Mirror* and the *Sun*? No, thanks. All we can hope is that the graffiti kids go berserk with their cans, cover her up.'

Rhys laughed. 'They'll just add their own decorations. As they say, Jack, you'll just have to wear it.'

'She's not wearing much,' said Sacha; then grinned at me. 'Sorry, Jack.'

When I got back to the apartment Adele was pacing up and down, looked as if she had been for the past couple of hours. She was doing it almost automatically; I had to grab her arm to halt her. 'Del — slow down. Let's try and look at this calmly —'

'How can you be calm about it? And expect me to be? I want to shoot that shit Tod Maddux — he's the one who let this happen —'

'Wait till morning, Sydney time, then call him. Maybe he knows nothing about it —'

'Of course he bloody knows! I'll call him now! What time is it?'

'Back home? About three o'clock in the morning —'

'Good! I'll get him while he's half asleep!'

She found his number in her diary, called him. I picked up the extension and waited. A sleepy voice came on the line: 'Yeah? Who the fuck is this?'

'I'll tell you who the fuck it is — it's fucking Adele Ambar!' I'd never heard her swear, except in bed. I looked at her warningly: *Play it cool.* But I might as well have told a female gorilla to stop slamming her mate. 'What the hell were you up to, letting those Italians plaster me all over London buses? I've just seen a huge poster of me —'

'Adele darling . . .' He was wide awake now, smooth as cream. I wanted to squeeze down the line and throttle him. 'I had nothing to do with it. It was in your contract, you signed it —'

I looked at her and she frowned, shaking her head; but as if in doubt, not denial. How many of us ever read every line of a contract? I knew the worst at once.

Maddux was still talking: 'They've had the posters all over Europe for the past month. You're a sensation, you're bigger than Calvin Klein and his balls-bags —'

'Why didn't someone get in touch with me?' She was flustered now.

'I dunno, I only learned about it myself a week ago, I was as flabbergasted as you are —'

Bullshit, I said silently. If he had been round at the time, he'd have known everything about the Magna Carta before it was signed. He'd have been smooth-talking Simon de Montfort.

'I've been in touch with them and they're coming good with more money, they're so pleased with the reaction —'

'Tod, I'm not interested in the money.'

I went to shake my head at that, but thought better of it.

'Del, love, don't be stupid. You'll be able to name your own terms from now on — I'll put you right up there with Megan Gale in Italy, with Claudia What'shername in the rest of Europe —'

'Tod, I'm an actor, I don't want to be a model —'

'Del, it's 50,000 dollars, US —'

'That doesn't sound like much, for such wide display,' I said on the extension.

'Who's that?'

'Her financial adviser.'

'Well, mister, I don't think you could've done any better. I worked my arse off to get her that —'

'Shut up, Tod,' said Adele and hung up.

I put down the extension. 'You shouldn't have done that. We have no idea how far this is going to spread. The States, back home, South America —'

Suddenly the horror of it hit me, my girl being leched after by leering rapists all over the world.

'I'm going to be a laughing-stock.' She slumped down in a chair. 'God, some bloody lesbian thinking I was ideal for a porno movie, now this! Nobody will cast me in anything — I'll finish up as just another James Bond girl, if I'm lucky —'

'Wait a minute.' I pulled up a chair opposite her; we were in the same position as in our previous rows. 'Marilyn Monroe posed nude on a calendar when she first started out and that was years ago, when nudity was taboo. But she did all right later on.'

She looked at me, her anger rising again. 'You don't care I'm plastered half-naked all over the sides of buses — all over Europe, he said —'

'Of course I bloody care! But you should've read the contract —' I paused, took a breath. 'Don't let's fight, darling. It's done and I hate it as much as you — randy bastards perving at you —' I put my hand under her jawline, held her face close to mine. 'It's done and you have to turn your back on it —'

Then, God bless her, she started to laugh. 'That'll only give them a better look at my bum, like Kylie Minogue's!'

I wonder if laughter has ever stopped a potential war? We hugged each other and, God help us, Edith Evans was back on the boards. We went to bed, what the French with their usual flair in the matter of love, or what passes for it, call *cinq à sept*. Anger, disappointment, embarrassment, everything was forgotten. At *sept* we got out of bed, showered and dressed and went out to dinner. It was a small, quiet restaurant one block from the river that served Australian wines and we drank to us with a Hunter shiraz; she, as usual, started with champagne; she was back to normal. No one amongst the other diners recognised her. Or if they did, they, with old-style English manners, made no show of it.

Then, back at the apartment, getting ready for bed, the

phone rang. It was her mother: 'Del, we've just looked at the early morning news. You're on it! Or rather, you're on the side of a bus!'

'Oh God, Mum! What'll the neighbours think?' But, still in good humour, she was laughing.

She had gestured for me to take up the extension. Now her father came on the line: 'We've already had six calls. A daughter of mine, exposing herself like that —' But he, too, was laughing. 'How'd it happen?'

'Dad, it's too long a story.' She had sobered for the moment. 'I'm not happy about it. Neither is Jack.'

'No, I guess not,' said Kate. 'Is he there?'

She and Luke knew we were living together and Kate, on a call to me when Adele was out, had confided that they were pleased. *Maybe now she'll come to her senses*, she had said.

'I'm here, Kate. No, I'm not happy. But there's nothing we can do about it. Just let's hope we don't get these posters back in Australia. How are things with you?'

There was silence for a long moment, then Luke said, 'Could be better The drought's getting worse. We've had bugger-all rain in months.'

'We'll get by,' said Kate. 'Look after yourselves.'

They hung up and Adele said, 'They're worried.'

'Droughts are cyclical, aren't they? They've weathered them before.'

'Yes. I can remember two ... But Mum's never been as — as abrupt as that.' She crawled into bed. Now, with the warmer weather, we were both sleeping naked, but tonight the libido had abruptly cooled for both of us. The call from

Bulinga Creek was worrying her and, seeing that, it worried me. 'I don't know, I feel I'm deserting them —'

I put my arm under her head. 'Darling heart, you've got your own worries. You're Hamlet's mother, Queen Gert, what more could you worry about? When's the first reading?'

'Thursday.' She kissed me. 'What would I do without you?'

'Who am I? Rosencrantz or Guildenstern?'

2

The theatre was an old converted factory in North London. Efforts had been made to decorate it with coloured hessian drapes, but it was still pretty drab. Everything about the place suggested a shoestring budget. Including the fact that it was staging *Hamlet* in modern dress.

Queen Gertrude looked as if she was on her way to a cocktail party. *Drinks at six on the battlements of Elsinore.* King Claudius looked like the manager of a small firm on the edge of bankruptcy. His suit suggested it hadn't been pressed since he had bought it; Sketchley evidently had no dry-cleaning shops in Denmark. Polonius looked like the ailing firm's accountant; when Hamlet ran him through behind the curtain, a man in front of me said, 'Well, he's redundant.' Rosencrantz and Guildenstern were a couple of salesmen with no orders in their books. And Hamlet? There could never have been a weedier melancholy Dane than this guy. He looked like the last of a long line of royalty in which the human sperm had finally been reduced to piss. Ophelia would have done better in a nunnery.

It was a disaster from the opening scene. Yet the packed audience sat up with approval every time Gertrude, the poster queen of underwear, came on stage. I guessed half the audience had never before seen a Shakespeare play, but the theatre management must have welcomed them with theatrically opened arms. The play ran for a week with full houses every night. Autograph-hunters waited at the stage door for Adele, ignoring all the other players. I waited for her too, knowing masochism was not my thing. I did arrive each night just in time to take her home in the second-hand Morgan I had bought, now that summer was on us.

The first night she got into the car, sat staring straight ahead for a moment, then said, 'It wasn't very good, was it?'

'You were.' She had been; just. 'But the others ... Hamlet sounded as if he had been castrated when he began, *To be or not to be* ... Where'd they dig him up?'

'He's the director's boyfriend.' She was silent again as I headed the car for home; then after a mile or so, she said, 'I'm not having much luck, am I?'

'No-o.' I drove carefully because I was having to answer carefully. 'Luck's part of the game unless you're in the public service.'

All over the world I heard bureaucrats rise up when they heard me.

'That bloody poster! The girls as well as the guys were slobbering over me tonight, asking me how I'd got my gorgeous figure! God, I felt like a strip-tease queen!'

'That might've lightened up Hamlet ... Diana Rigg had a gorgeous figure. At least she did when she was in "The Avengers."' The series had been before my time, but I had seen reruns of it on pay-TV.

'She was always in black leather, never in her undies. She may still have a gorgeous figure, but she's in her sixties now and she wouldn't let anyone plaster her all over the side of a bus, not even in black leather.'

There was no point in arguing, because I felt the same as she did, but for different reasons. She was protecting her ambition, I was protecting my possession.

Over the next few weeks she got no theatre or TV offers, but several model agencies rang her, promising work. She was polite but firm: 'No, thank you. No, especially lingerie.'

I, too, was finding it hard to get work; or work that interested Channel 15. The economic slump in Europe didn't interest the battlers back home; a billion-dollar collapse in Germany was no more than a flatulence sound on the other side of the world. I tried to resurrect Afghanistan and, almost in desperation, suggested to Les Dibley I should make a quick trip to Kabul and see how things were going as the warlords tried to work out what democracy was. But:

'Jack, son, our viewers couldn't care less about the Afghans. Since our SAS troops — whom we were never allowed to name or show their faces — since they've come home, forget Afghanistan. The Americans have turned their backs on it and now they're whirling their lassoos for Saddam Hussein in Iraq —'

'How about a quick trip to Baghdad?'

'I'll put it to God' — I could see him blessing himself at the other end of the line — 'but I don't think he'll go for it, unless you pay your own way and take the time out of your leave quota. In the meantime, someone showed me a wire item that says Jennifer Lopez is secretly in Stratford, rehearsing to play the lead in *Othello* — or anyway, the female lead, Iago or someone —'

'Iago was the villain.'

'She'd be good at that,' he said and hung up.

I hadn't heard even a rumour of Ms Lopez and Stratford, but if it meant a trip to the birthplace of my namesake, against office costs, I'd be in it. Adele and I drove up in the Morgan, a lovely little car, and Rhys and Sacha followed in Rhys's Rover.

'I wonder why they haven't broadcast it?' asked Adele. 'Unless she wants to see how she goes first —'

'You sound jealous.'

'Wouldn't you be? These Hollywood film stars coming over to grab plum roles.'

'Ask *The Times* if you can do the review.'

We got to the theatres, asked questions and were laughed at. We went out to Ann Hathaway's cottage and when I asked if they had a visitors' book so that I could inscribe my name and make them look up, they said someone named Marlowe had swiped it.

So we went to the Othello restaurant and nightclub where the theatre folk, laughing like drains, had directed us. There Senorita Geneva Lopez, a Spanish flamenco dancer, was featured nightly. We dined, applauded Geneva Lopez, and, when diners were invited to join her on the floor, we all four got up and clacked our heels and clicked our fingers and had a high old time. Adele kissed Geneva and Geneva kissed Adele and it looked like something out of an Almodovar film. Then in the early hours of a cool summer morning we drove back to London and the search for another story, any story.

I had begun to doubt my honesty as a TV reporter. My dad, who had always been a newspaperman, had told me more than once that the image had more impact than the word. He had cited instances from the Vietnam war: the small naked girl fleeing from the napalm bomb, the police chief about to fire his pistol into the head of a Viet Cong. No amount of words nor front-page photographs could equal the truth and the impact of the newsreel shots of the collapse of the World Trade Center. A survey had shown that 65 per cent of the Australian population never read a newspaper; one of the commercial channels back home boasted that its viewers got more news from their telecasts than from any other source. Yet I didn't want to be anywhere but on television.

Adele, for all her self-delusion, was honest in her ambition to be nothing less than a dramatic actor.

Then in August two little girls disappeared in an eastern county village. A caravan of carrion birds headed out of London, ourselves amongst them. You remember it: our screens back home, all channels, even the ABC, lapped it up. Then the accused kidnappers and murderers, a school caretaker and his girlfriend, residents of the village but outsiders, were arrested. I was disgusted at how we feasted on the whole scene.

'Jesus,' I said, 'do we have to chase every bloody angle on this?'

'Jack, it happens and we cover it,' said Rhys. 'Let the editors worry about the moral aspect.'

'How do you feel, Sacha?'

He shrugged. 'My grandfather told me stories about what happened back in 1947, when India and Pakistan were separated. If we'd had TV in those days, we'd have been there. He said it was just slaughter, people killing each other when they met on the roads, some going east, some going west. You've led a sheltered life in Australia, Jack.'

Indeed I had.

Summer passed slowly and Adele and I, at weekends, went into the country in the Morgan, both of us getting back some of our home tan under the sun and with the breeze in our faces. I had read a lot about the English countryside, but it was getting harder to find it; England seemed to be well on the way to having as many motorways as Los Angeles. But we found pockets of what the tourist board advertised and stayed in thatched-roofed pubs and ate at small restaurants on quiet riverbanks. My mother had told me horrendous tales of English cooking in her days in London, when the vegetables were like bath sponges and sauce came out of a bottle. But Adele and I had no complaints. The 537 chefs on television had had their influence.

The Indello posters had disappeared from the sides of buses, replaced by beer posters; already drunk on lechery, the men in bus queues were invited to add to the foam around their lips. Adele, to my and her relief, was once more anonymous; or almost. Her looks still attracted attention and some of the sharper-eyed recognised her. But they didn't pester her and she was once more amiable and easy to live with. Never marry a model, fellers, not one who can be stretched almost-naked along the side of a bus.

'Jack, darling —'

We were sitting outside a pub on the bank of a small stream in Shropshire. Across the narrow strip of water a cricket match was in progress on a village green. What looked like white bedsheets were hung between poles at either end of the ground as sightscreens. Out in the middle a mix of two portly men, several younger ones and a small teenager were the fielding team. At the wicket were a partnership of one batsman with a bushy grey beard and a young man in a multi-coloured cap. I remembered books thrust on me by my dad, a cricket lover: by Robertson Glasgow, Arlott and the classic comic novel, *England, Their England*. It was all so bucolic it looked staged, put on for the benefit of the tourists seated outside the pub across the river. Peace, remote from the world, was perfect.

'— you're not happy, are you?'

I gave my attention back to her. She was in a royal blue shirt and white slacks, dark glasses pushed back on her head, the habitual silk scarf tied to her handbag, and elegant loafers. She looked absolutely gorgeous. And worried. 'Is it me or your job or what?'

I hadn't thought it was so obvious. 'My job.'

'Why?'

I took my time, because I was talking to myself as much as to her. 'Trying to find stories for viewers who aren't interested in what happens here. They aren't interested in the Royals any more, not since Diana died. They couldn't care less about British politics and they're the same way when it comes to Britain's immigration problems. They're even bored these days by English scandal, they think it's old hat. The IRA no longer makes trouble, so they don't make news. I suggested to Les Dibley that I might go looking for stories on the Continent, but he said to leave that to SBS.' The national multicultural channel back in Sydney. 'I *am* worried, Del. I'm afraid they'll call me home.'

'Oh no!' She reached for my hand. Drinkers at other tables looked at us, the men with what I thought was envy, the women with curiosity. 'They can't!'

'You could come home with me ...' It was the wrong place to say it, but it was out before I could shut my mouth. Over on the village green there was a loud shout of *Howzat*! And the greybeard was walking away from his wicket. The other drinkers looked away for a moment at the cricket, then back at us. Discreetly, of course, being English.

Her hand tightened on mine, as if clutching at me for safety. But then it loosened, though she still held my hand. 'Darling, I can't.'

I had the sense not to say, *Why not?* If I was to argue with her, this was not the place. But the problem had to be faced soon. I was in danger of being recalled to Sydney at any moment; Les Dibley's voice had been full of warning for the past month. My chances of being wooed by any of the British broadcasters were virtually nil; Australians were no longer the favourites they had once been back in my father's day. I could resign, stay on in London and take my chances as a scriptwriter; but I had no confidence in that prospect and I was not *dying* to be a writer. Not as Adele was *dying* to be a dramatic actress. It was again the same old thing: ambition. Or lack of it.

'I promised myself I'd give it two years,' said Adele. 'I can't give up because of a few setbacks.'

Over on the green a new batsman had come to the crease. He was in what looked like brand-new whites, had brand-new pads and a brand-new bat and was, for God's sake, wearing what looked like a brand-new helmet with faceguard. Wearing a helmet for a village cricket match? I waited for him to be bowled first ball. The bowler, a medium pacer, ran up; all he had to do was bowl a quick yorker. Instead of which he bowled short. The batsman stepped inside it, swung his bat in a beautiful curve and the ball soared into the air. It seemed to hang there for five minutes, then it came down with a splash in the stream just below us.

'See that?' Adele exclaimed. 'That's what I want to do! Hit them for six!'

It was time to go home. I paid the bill and walked to the car, eyes following us like security cameras. For once I felt no thrill being beside Adele; the eyes, the male eyes, were stripping her, voyeurs from another bus stop. I had better get used to it. And so had she.

Over the next week neither of us found anything of use to us: no news for me, no roles for her. The anniversary of September Eleven came and went and she looked at none of the horror shots that were revived on television. We didn't speak of it and I respected her silence. Rupe Hellinger and I had never revived memories of horrors we had covered. Not even Jason's murder. It was not cowardice, but a Band-Aid against nightmares.

Then she got a call to read for a revival of *The Three Sisters* at another Fringe theatre. Her agent had told the producers that she had played the role back in Sydney; I'm also sure the producers knew she had played a role on the side of a bus. Whatever were her own thoughts, she didn't let me know them. She went for the reading and got the role of Masha, the part she had played back home.

'Darling, this is the beginning.' She was all excitement, like an academy graduate who had just landed her first role.

'I hope so,' I said and kissed her.

She pushed me away, looked hard at me. 'You don't mean that.'

I had talked to Les Dibley that morning. He had hinted that the writing was on the wall, the graffiti of recall. 'I do mean it, darling. I *want* you to get the parts that are going to get you noticed.'

'You really do?'

'Really.' I was becoming a practised liar. Which, I guess, is part of keeping love alive. The French, who claim to have invented romantic love, have always followed that philosophy.

The theatre was out beyond Hampstead, where Chekhov would get more response than in Brixton or Battersea. It was comfortably furnished, had a proscenium stage and was, in effect, a West End house that had somehow escaped its moorings. I cast an eye over the audience and there didn't appear to be more than the usual quota of lechers. Adele looked safe.

It was a good production and I thought she did well. There was her usual lack of nuance, but she said her lines clearly and, generally, with the right emphasis, and she moved, as usual, with grace. When she first appeared I noticed that heads in the audience leaned together and there were whispers, but no one seemed to be licking his lips. Of course, I was looking only at the back of their heads.

When the curtain went down there was a good applause. The cast took their bows together, no one starred, and from my seat in the fourth row I could see Adele's face glowing with pleasure. I was pleased for her, but, with her up there above me, I felt like I was farewelling her on some departing liner. Maybe the *Titanic*.

We went home to bed and had a wonderful night, she with celebration, I almost with desperation. In the morning came the cold light of the reviews.

The papers had sent their third-string critics; aspirants, like Adele, for lead roles. The *Daily Telegraph* was polite, but it read like an obituary. *The Guardian* wondered, if with the Moscow mix these days of crime and capitalism, Chekhov was still relevant. Neither of them mentioned Adele. *The Times* did, in passing: 'Masha was played by Adele Ambar, who is a part-time model and has played Russian prostitutes on television. She gave a certain carnal *elan* to Chekhov that I hadn't noticed before ... '

'Oh, what a shit!' She hurled that paper from her. '*Carnal*. God, I couldn't have been more ... more virginal!'

That hadn't struck me; but I wasn't going to argue. 'Darling heart, critics are like actors — they have to make their name. Forget him.'

'You thought I was good, didn't you?'

'I did.' Which was the truth; but being just good wasn't enough. 'You looked a bit nervous at first —'

'I was. Terribly. My legs were wobbling.'

'No one would have noticed. Look, just get better. It's a two-week run and if your agent is any good, he'll have other producers come and look at you.'

'Oh, you're so supportive — I don't know what I'd do without you!' She hugged me, almost took my lips off with the fierceness of her kiss. 'Let's go back to bed and be carnal!'

I had to say no, I was already late for the office. When I got there Rhys, Sacha and Imogen were waiting for me, faces stiff with concern.

'What's the matter?'

'Haven't you heard?' said Rhys. 'It's on the morning news —'

'What, for Crissake?' Adele and I had been only concerned with her reviews; we hadn't turned on either the radio or the television. 'What?'

'A terrorist bombing in Bali. A coupla hundred killed, many of them Australians —'

Almost on cue, Les Dibley called. Imogen answered it, then handed it to me.

'Les, we've just got the news about Bali —'

'It's a horror story, son. We've sent a crew up there — Rupe's on camera, he'll know what we want. We're now on the terrorist list, Jack — it's time to come home, we've got our own stories to cover. This is official, Jack, but we'll put it on paper. We're closing you down and you're to come home immediately.'

'How immediately?' Though I had been expecting this call, I still suddenly felt empty.

'I'll give you forty-eight hours, you'll have things to clear up. Tell your crew I'm sorry. Pay 'em up to the end of the week. I'll talk to you in the morning, our time.' He hung up abruptly.

I put the phone down. 'It's all over. They're closing the office.'

Rhys and Sacha took it well; they were in a game where permanency was never to be trusted. Rhys said, 'We did our best, Jack. It's just a pity you buggers are at the other end of the earth.'

'Except for terrorists,' said Sacha. 'They're all over.'

Imogen didn't take it well. She burst into tears and for the first time in my life I found myself acting as a boss, one who had to comfort a girl who had just lost a job she loved and, as I found out as the day wore on, needed.

'My boyfriend has kicked me out.' She'd never mentioned him before; I had always imagined she lived with her parents, though she had never mentioned them either. 'I'm broke, Jack.'

'What about your parents?' I felt suddenly ashamed. I was supposed to be in charge of the office, but I hadn't bothered to learn much about those who worked for me. My education was still uncompleted. 'Can't you move back with them?'

'There's only my mother and she lives in Devon —'

I had been really self-centred. All I had been concerned with had been *my* job and *my* girl. And I still had to go home and tell her the bad news.

'Imogen —' It is not a name that rolls easily off the tongue, especially when the tongue is having trouble with what it is going to say. 'How much money is in the office account?'

She told me: more than enough for what I had in mind: 'Draw a month's salary, for each of you. Let's reverse what Enron and all those other gangs of executives have been doing, and look after the workers first.'

'Hooray,' she said and raised her fist in a Roedean socialist left gesture.

'They'll bellow back home, but I'll say you were going to sue us and let all Fleet Street know. I don't have time to go recommending you to someone else — I wish I did.' I kissed her, on the cheek. Bosses' privileges go just so far. 'I'm sorry, love. But as Les Dibley keeps telling us, that's the way the world turns.'

'You're a lovely man, Jack.'

'I'll tell my girl you told me that.' I kissed her again. 'Good luck.'

Then I went home to tell Adele the bad news. But she had already left for the theatre and I had to wait till she came home again. I could have called her during the day from the office, but that would have been unfair.

Les Dibley rang again just as I was putting some fish fingers and chips in the microwave.

'We want you to stop off in Singapore and go to Bali —'

'No, Les.' It took me no time to refuse him. 'I appreciate what you're trying to do, but you've already got someone there, right? I'll come home and start interviewing the relatives and friends right away, but I'm not going to Bali to cut in on — who's doing it?'

'Mike Kostas.'

He and I had never been rivals and I was not going to start a match now. 'None better. Les, I'm not feeling the best at the moment. I've just sacked three good people and I'm home now waiting to tell my girl the bad news —'

'Jack, you're a working reporter —'

'Don't give me any of that, Les. There must've been times when you wished you weren't on a job.'

His sigh was like wind down the line. 'Okay, come straight home. You fixed up the others?'

'Yes, I gave 'em a month's pay in lieu of —'

'You *what*?'

But I had hung up. I spent the rest of the evening waiting for Adele. I checked what had to be done. I was twenty-seven years old, a top reporter on a hundred thousand a year plus expenses, and this was the first time in my life I'd had to sit down and sort out ordinary things that have to be done when your life takes a wrong turning.

The rent on the apartment was paid for two months, so that would give Adele time to find another place to live. Unless, of course, Entwistle charged her for the accommodation, just to spite me. I would give her the Morgan, which I knew she drove with as much pleasure as I did. She would not need money: the $50,000 for the poster job had arrived, less his commission, from Tod Maddux. All that would be missing would be me.

She arrived home, glowing. 'Oh darling, the audience loved it tonight! And my agent has got me another reading next week — in a new play by David Hare!'

'Darling heart — sit down. I've got some bad news.' And I gave it to her as gently as I could.

I had expected her to be stunned, but she wasn't. 'You've been hinting at it —'

'The Bali bombing has brought it to a head. I dunno whether they expect terrorists to come to the mainland, but it's on the cards. Bush is threatening Iraq and Howard is falling in behind him ... Del, I've got to go back. It's not just that they've recalled me, but that's where my stories are going to be.'

'When do you leave?'

'Tomorrow night.'

That shocked her. She flung herself at me, weeping. Later, in bed, just before we went to sleep, she said, 'What happens to us?'

It was as if we were estranged, were talking divorce. I was shocked at the matter-of-factness in her voice. She was in my arms, but she might as well have been on the other side of the bed. 'What do you mean?'

'Darling ...' Her voice softened. 'I may never come home.'

You will. But I couldn't tell her that. 'Don't you love me?'

She kneed me, not as a joke but viciously. 'Of course I do! You know that — Jesus, you make me wild at times! You're the one who's running off, not me. You're the one who thinks more of his job —'

'Listen to who's talking.' I rolled away from her, massaged my sore crotch. 'Chasing bloody dreams —'

Then, as sometimes happened, her mood changed. She lay on her back and stared at the dark ceiling, said, just as matter-of-factly, 'You're right. But there's nothing I can do about it, Jack. That's the way I am, have been since I was a teenager. Even when I was studying farm management, for Dad's sake, I dreamed of being on the stage. Your trouble is, you've never been a dreamer.'

I was still sore, in the crotch and in the mind. 'It's a bit late to start now.' I sat up in bed, switched on a bedside lamp. 'Del, I love you, that'll never change. But I'm not going to latch myself to your dream. I could stay here, marry you, and twenty years down the track we'd still be waiting for what you dream of. And I'd be bloody miserable and, for all we know, struggling to make a crust. I may be selfish and, I dunno, *cruel* to you, but I'd never be happy here, not if I couldn't match you, job for job. And I don't think I could make it here, not as good as I've got back home.'

'All you think about are material things —'

'Cut it out — you're not exactly . . .' I had to think of a word . . . '*ascetic*. You still buy cashmere —'

'One has to dress to be noticed.'

'Bullshit. You buy it because you've been used to it all your life. Your mum and dad indulged you —'

'Leave them out of it!' She turned towards me, was suddenly angry.

'Okay, okay, I'm sorry. I shouldn't have mentioned them, this is just between you and me —'

It was an argument that was going to get us nowhere and she recognised it before I did. She sat up, swung her legs over the side of the bed. 'I'll sleep in the other room —'

'No!' I reached across and grabbed her by the shoulder. 'No, Del, *please*.'

She turned her head, the hair fell down over her eye; it was the bloody look that melted me. 'Jack . . . Not if we're going to fight . . .'

I just shook my head and said miserably, 'I love you.'

She lay back, looked up at me. 'Forget the future.'

I just nodded and took formal possession of the moment.

3

I flew out of London the following night. We said our farewell just before she left for the theatre. I was holding her tightly when I said, 'About the Morgan. Check the oil and water each week —'

'Stop it! For God's sake, I grew up on tractors and an old ute. Will you write me your *billet-doux*?'

'Every week and twice a week in a leap year.'

'That's two years away. I may be home by then —'

I drew my face away from hers, frowned.

'I'm not promising. But ...' She kissed me. 'Let's see how things pan out.'

That was our farewell. We parted almost theatrically, arms held out to each other, fingers reluctant to let go. Then she was gone and I waited for Rhys, Sacha and Imogen to pick me up in Rhys's old Rover.

He had brought his wife with him. I had never met her before, indeed couldn't remember his mentioning her much, and I was surprised to find she was black, a West Indian girl from Cardiff. I sat between her and Imogen in the back seat, while Rhys and Sacha rode up front. Sacha and Imogen sang sad songs by ancient groups, Pink Floyd and Credence Clearwater Revival, and Rhys's wife, Carlotta, held my hand as if she had known me for years. Then Rhys sang 'Come Back To The Valleys' and Carlotta sang with him in a lovely clear voice and I almost wept.

In the airport hall, after I had checked in my luggage, Rhys and Sacha shook hands with me. 'Good luck, boyo,' said Rhys and his voice was suddenly more Welsh than usual. 'Come back some time and we'll find a lovely story to tell. No murders, no rapes.'

Sacha hugged me. 'It's been great, Jack. I didn't think an Aussie could be such a gentleman.'

'We're learning, mate.'

Carlotta hugged me, then kissed me on both cheeks. 'We should've met sooner, Jack.'

Then it was Imogen's turn. 'Kiss me properly, Jack, none of this on-the-cheek stuff. I'll stand in for Adele.'

I got the open-mouth, tongue-down-the-throat treatment and she finished with the old pelvic howdy-do, like Hilary Reingold. 'There, that's for Adele. Only don't tell her.'

'I thought you gels from Roedean only played hockey?'

They were all crying, even Carlotta, when I left and walked, blinded by tears, through the departure gate. I was closing a chapter in my life that I hadn't appreciated till the pages were turned over.

Chapter Ten

1

I flew home, my misery heavier than my luggage. The hostess welcomed me with a big smile: 'Welcome aboard, Mr Shakespeare. Have you been on holiday?'

Don't ever kid yourself that the voters back home have missed you.

I came back to a country that, though not scared, was suddenly very sober. Terrorism was on the doorstep and there was no guarantee that our guard-dogs were enough protection. It had been a constant drumbeat of my dad's that Australians, from top to bottom, never took the long view. And now we were wondering when and where the bombers would strike next.

Lynne and Nick met me at the airport. They both hugged me, Nick like a brother; he was now part of the family. I held Lynne away from me and said, 'You've put on weight.'

'I'm four months pregnant. You're going to be an uncle.'

Here, I thought, is an uncomplicated partnership. 'A boy or a girl?'

'We haven't tested. We'll take whatever comes.'

I looked at Nick, a hundred and ten kilos of solid rock.

'If it's a girl, will she play front row?'

'Over my dead body,' said Lynne and Nick, a man deeply in love, just smiled.

They had been living in the house at Longueville while the apartment development they had bought into was finished. Now they had been a week in the apartment and they took me there. It was on the Parramatta River, a seagull's flight across the narrow end of the harbour to the family home on the Lane Cover River. We were a family who like our water views, which were now approaching the price of a Rembrandt.

Nick was with a merchant bank, where, I could only guess, a Masters in Philosophy was a help, especially in today's climate. Lynne still had her marketing job and they looked comfortably fixed. The apartment had only two bedrooms, but it was large and the view was stunning. Everything was perfect for them and I felt a certain envy.

'How's Adele?' Lynne hadn't mentioned her up till now.

'I thought you'd never ask . . .'

'You didn't mention her. I was wondering — is it all off?'

'Anything but. Except . . .'

'The same old thing? She wants to be Edith Whoever?'

I nodded, looked at Nick. 'You're lucky, married to a girl with no ambition.'

'Oh, I had it once,' said Lynne. 'Nick has it. He's going to make his fortune — *our* fortune,' she smiled as she corrected herself. 'Then he's going into politics. He's a Green.'

'A merchant banker a Greenie? You're joking!'

He grinned, but not self-consciously. 'It takes all sorts to make a world. I thought you knew that.'

Indeed I did, recognising individual by individual. The education of Shakespeare, J.

'Is Adele still on the sides of London buses?' asked Lynne, mixing a salad.

'That was something else I thought you'd never ask. No, she's not. That's something we don't talk about — she was lumbered into it —'

'Was she paid?' asked the merchant banker, notes rustling in his voice.

'Oh yes, quite a lot. But it bruised her modesty.'

'I didn't know models or actresses had any.' Then Lynne smiled. 'Sorry. You're no closer to marrying her?'

I looked at Nick. 'Does she grill you like this all the time?'

'All the time. She's got a file on every girl in my office.' But he kissed her.

They took me home to Longueville. Lynne had thought of everything. The kitchen was stocked, I could live for a month by microwave. My bed had been made and turned down. The clothes I had left behind had been taken out of mothballs and hung in my closet.

'I've arranged for a woman to come in three days a week and keep you in order. Mrs Golightly —'

'You're joking again. Holly Golightly's daughter?' Lynne had always been a fan of Audrey Hepburn.

'No, she's for real. The same size as Nick and you do what she tells you. You'll love her.'

I thanked them both and they went back to their bliss.

Our house was large. Three double bedrooms, a study, two bathrooms, dining room, living room, kitchen; built in the 1920s, another century, another way of living. Dad had bought it just over thirty years ago, mortgaged to the roof-beam; it was now worth probably close to two million, clear of any debt. We were middle-class fortunates, which, I guess, is the most comfortable class to belong to. We had neither the fears of the rich nor the despair of the poor; all that had to be avoided was smugness. All that spoiled it was that I had no one to share it with.

I called Adele and she was as lonely as I was. 'I wander around the flat *looking* for you ... How's Sydney?'

'Still in the same place, still looking as good as ever. You sound homesick,' I said hopefully.

'Not yet, Jack —' I could see her smiling at the other end of the line.

We told each other how much we missed each other; then hung up. I was dead-tired, sleep hung on my face like Glad-Wrap. I fell into bed, reached for her, half-asleep; but she wasn't there. I slept for twelve hours and was woken by the phone. It was Les Dibley, welcoming me back with an open arm: single. He was probably just as effusive at the birth of each of his kids.

'Rupe is back from Bali and he'll be waiting for you this afternoon. Two o'clock, an interview with the parents of a kid who died in the bombing there.'

'Les, for Crissake, let me get my breath —'

'Just breathe deep, son. Two o'clock. Rupe will pick you up. You've got a new sound guy, nice kid named Suzy.'

'Suzy?'

'It's God's new rule. The gender barrier is down. Two o'clock.' And he hung up.

Then I was aware of someone standing in the bedroom door. It was Mrs Golightly, all ninety kilos of her. But she had a smile as wide as a football field.

'Call me Sally. I'm easy to get on with, so long's you do what I tell you.'

A joker, when you're jet-lagged and only half-awake.

I showered and dressed and when I went out into the kitchen she had cereal ready, banana cut up on it, and bacon and eggs to follow. 'You married, Sally?'

'Yep. He does what he's told too.' Again the fifty-metre smile. She was going to take a bit of time to get used to.

I was waiting out by the front gate when Rupe drew up in the Channel 15 van. With him was Suzy Wadsworth, a six-foot blonde who looked as if she could carry not only the mike but a pop group's entire sound system. Her friendliness was oversized and I waited for her to slap me on the back. Sydney had been taken over by Amazons while I had been away. Fortunately she just shook hands with me, though that was like getting friendly with a vice. I wasn't in the best of humour.

'What's the matter with you? You sound like you've got shit on the liver.' Rupe was in the back seat with me as we drove away. Channel 15 never wasted money on a driver and the sound guy, male or female, was expected to be chauffeur.

'I'm jet-lagged, disoriented, buggered — why the hell was I called out my first day back?'

'Jack, you haven't heard the bad news . . . They're laying off staff. Advertising is off, things are tight. They asked me if I'd take a pay cut and I said no. They backed down, but that's the way they're thinking. They may suggest it to you. Tell 'em to get stuffed.'

That woke me up; even the jet-lag sloughed off. 'Where are we heading now?'

'Paradise Valley.'

It was a Housing Commission development leftover from the 1950s, one of those pockets that time and government have forgotten. Mostly weatherboard houses, one or two fibro, a few brick. Some of them had gardens in front, but there was still an air of neglect: not by those who lived there, but by those who had sent them there. The streets were narrow, with few trees; there was no community or shopping centre. It was not a slum, nothing like those I had seen in Pakistan, but it was not what it should have been. And some kid had left here for a holiday in an exotic location and been blown to smithereens by strangers.

His parents were middle-aged in years, elderly by experience. They looked even more aged now, grief deepening the lines in their faces. Brian, the father, shook his head, thinly thatched, in despair: 'He was only nineteen. His first ever holiday. He was an apprentice panel-beater, been saving for the holiday all year — Jesus!' He shook his head again and began to weep.

His wife, Dot, thin and weary, put her arm round him. 'Why do you want to talk to us?'

People had come out of the other houses, stood at a distance as if crime scene tapes held them back. A baby in a woman's arms began to cry and she tried to hush it.

'Why us?' Dot repeated.

I had to snatch at a reason: 'Because they may show this on TV back in Indonesia and the people who killed your son will get a wider view of what they've done to ordinary people like you . . . '

It was feeble and Brian saw it: 'And you think the bastards will care?'

'I don't know, Brian. But it may get to their police and the authorities and they'll go flat out to catch whoever let off the bombs.'

I was aware of Suzy standing just out of camera-range, blinking as if trying to hold back tears. Rupe, behind his camera, was impassive. He had learned long ago that emotion behind the camera only spoiled the image. Brian and Dot were the messengers.

Both of them suddenly turned and held each other, faces buried in each other's shoulder. There was a stir amongst the spectators, but they didn't move forward. I said nothing, Rupe ran the camera a few more moments, then it was over. It was The Image, as Dad would have described it, but all I felt was embarrassment and shame.

We thanked them for their help and left them, going back to our van. The woman with the baby on her hip sneered at us: 'You oughta be ashamed of yourself!'

'Nah,' said a teenage girl, all scraggly hair and loose T-shirt, 'we'll still all watch it on TV tonight.'

We left them, driving away down the street with its three or four spindly trees, past the houses that looked as forgotten as the people inside them, back to the world that we thought was the real one.

I was sitting up front with Suzy. 'That got to you, didn't it? What was your job before this?'

'I was an assistant on —' She named a soap opera. 'I used to think that was real.'

'No,' said Rupe from the back seat. 'What we saw today is real.'

'But things must get better for people like them.' Suzy, I was to discover, was an incurable optimist; if she had been a taxi driver she would have looked for fares in the Harbour Tunnel. 'That dead boy probably had hopes, prospects —'

'Yeah,' said Rupe. '*Had*. Not any more.'

Back at Channel 15 the first thing I noticed was that several desks in the newsroom were vacant: no papers on them, the computers blank. The staff still in the room, and even they seemed fewer, waved to me and welcomed me back.

Les Dibley greeted me as if I'd never been away: 'How'd it go?'

'How did what go?'

'This afternoon's piece.'

'Les, I've been away — what? — almost a year and that's all the welcome back I get? How'd this afternoon go?'

'Son, I'm an old-time Aussie — laconic as they come, nothing fantastic.' But then he grinned, an expression that didn't improve him. 'Okay, how was London? How's your girl?'

'Both are fine. It's another country, Les, but occasionally we fitted in.'

'How's she fitting in? We saw those posters — geez, what wouldn't I give for a display like that!'

'You'd make a horrible sight, Les. Your wife and the six kids would run you out of the house.' I got up from my chair, leaned across and kissed him on both cheeks. The others in the newsroom clapped and whistled. 'I'm home, Les.'

He wiped his cheeks. 'I have some good news for you, some you don't deserve. They're not going to cut your salary.'

'I thought they might increase it —'

'Balls.'

Then Hilary Reingold was tickling the back of my neck. 'Welcome back, honey. You still celibate?'

'Just started.'

'Mr Entwistle wants to see you. How was London?'

I told her while she escorted me across the courtyard to the administration building, where the money was. 'You'd have the time of your life there, Hil.'

'I was there six, seven years ago. Yeah, I had the time of my life. He went off and married a duchess or someone. How's your girl?'

'She's okay.' I looked at Hilary and saw something I had not seen before: an air of disappointment, of resignation. 'You still holding your job?'

'Just.'

'How's your love life?' I said, a little cautiously.

'Just,' she said and left me. The good times for the good-time girl, it seemed, were fading.

Entwistle was in blue-and-white checked shirt, white collar and cuffs, checked braces; I felt I'd suddenly developed astigmatism. But he was all bonhomie and behind him the yacht sailed nowhere on an even keel. 'So you're back! How was London?'

I told him, a record that was now starting to sound scratchy. But then I spread the butter: 'But it's good to be back in Sydney ...'

'Best city in the world,' he said, though he spent all his holidays as far away from it as he could get. 'It's full of stories at the moment, as Les has no doubt told you. The Bali bombing ...' He shook his head. 'Bloody terrible. The drought ...' Shook his head again 'Bloody terrible.'

'I hear things are tight in our game?' I couldn't have been more off-hand.

Shook his head again. 'Advertising's down to hell. Things are tight, Jack. You're not thinking of asking for a raise?'

'Nothing's further from my mind. How are Mrs Entwistle and the girls?'

'Couldn't be better. How's —' As if he was struggling to remember her name. 'Miss Ambar?'

'Fine. She's looking after the London flat till the agent gets a new tenant. Otherwise we'd be charged with breaking the lease.'

He had to show some authority: 'Did you authorise that?'

'No. I just thought it good policy for her to stay there. With no one in it, squatters could move in and we'd be responsible till the lease runs out.' I was developing into a glib liar; I should go into politics with Nick. 'London's full of squatters.'

'Yeah,' he said and I could read his miserable mind: *There is one named Miss Ambar squatting there now.* 'Well, welcome back. There's plenty for you to do ...'

So that was it: welcome back to work straightaway. No thanks for what I'd done while away, watch your step or your pay will be cut. Why did I expect a civic reception when I wasn't a sports star?

I went home to the oh-so-fortunate comfort of Longueville, didn't turn on the television to watch Brian and Dot clinging to each other on their brown-grassed lawn. I don't know what else was on the news that evening; I didn't care. Mrs Golightly had prepared a dinner for me, with a note: *Five minutes in the microwave. I've cleaned all your shoes. When did you last clean them?* I was being taken over.

Later I called the Ambars at Bulinga Creek. 'It's Jack —'

'We know your voice by now,' said Kate. 'Del called to say you were coming home. Glad to be back?'

'No, I miss her.'

'Join the club. How is she? Luke's on the extension ...'

Was she warning me of something?

'She's fine, great health, plenty of spirit —'

'But?' That was Luke, coming in from left field.

I hesitated, then said, 'Still dreaming, Luke. It's tough going, over there. She gets parts, but they're more like teasers, to keep her trying. How are things with you?'

'Tough. This is just about the worst drought I can remember. The country further out looks like a dust bowl. You ever read Steinbeck's *The Grapes of Wrath*?' Dad had told me that country people read much more than city folk; it was probably true. 'I saw the old movie the other night. Some thoughtless bastard ran it on pay-TV and, like a bloody masochist, I watched it. Old Model-T Fords coming out of dust storms, loaded with everything they owned. I keep waiting for it to happen here. Not *here*, but out further west.'

I couldn't believe he sounded so miserable. My silence was broken by Kate: 'When are you coming up to see us?'

'This weekend okay?'

'See you Saturday morning,' she said and hung up.

I sat a while, sorting my thoughts like a fossicker looking for a flicker of gold. Then I rang Adele: 'I've just been talking to your parents.'

'How did they sound?'

'Not happy. The drought —'

'I'm worried for them, Jack. I've never heard Dad sound the way he does at the moment ... Do you think I should come home?'

Yes. But all I said was, 'Wait a while, see how things go. How was the reading for the Hare play?'

'No good.'

She didn't elaborate, so I didn't press it. 'I think I'm going to find it hard to settle down out here ... I'm missing you.'

'Same here. Darling, why couldn't we have been just two ordinary people, battlers —'

I had seen two of them today, had pitied them not envied them. 'Neither of us would have liked it. Luck has spoiled us. Have you started looking for a place to move to?'

'Tomorrow. I *loved* this apartment —'

'That was because it was rent-free and I came with it.'

'That was what I was going to say.'

Banality again, but it sustained us. *If music be the food of love, play on* ... That other Shakespeare sometimes got carried away.

Next afternoon, after we had come back from covering a water shortage in the city's dams, a result of the drought, I had a call from the police. It was Sergeant Killick.

'Jack, I'd like to see you. Don't mention to anyone that I've called you. Can you meet me at Milsons Point, down under the Bridge?'

'Phil, what is this?'

'I know it sounds like cloak-and-dagger stuff. But ... How about 6.30 this evening? I'll be there on that walk around the harbour's edge. And remember — no word to anyone.'

I had rented a car while I made up my mind what was going to replace the MG and the Morgan. I had fallen into a new role: a male who suddenly didn't have everything laid on. Forty-eight hours back in the house at Longueville and I was beginning to appreciate how, unobtrusively, Lynne had looked after me. I needed a wife or a live-in partner — if only to remind me of what not to take for granted. I was putty in Mrs Golightly's massive hands.

I drove the rented Civic, one like Lynne's, back to the city and down to Milsons Point. It was daylight-saving season and there was still plenty of light in the sky. Thin clouds, not rain clouds, were just beginning to tinge with gold along their edges. A flight of currawongs were a wavering black line as they went up-harbour. Ferries and river craft were coming and going, peak-hour traffic on the water. I parked the car under the Bridge and walked down to the edge of the harbour. Phil Killick was there, leaning on the iron railing that bordered the walkway. He straightened up as I approached.

'Sorry about the cloak-and-dagger stuff,' he repeated. 'But you're news and you could be spotted —'

'I'm not news, I'm a news reporter.'

'Same difference, Jack. They see you every night … It's about Tom Barini.'

'You've got the guy who killed him?' I wasn't sure what I felt, but it wasn't satisfaction. And I didn't know why.

'Yeah. But …' He leaned back on the railing and looked out at the low-slung river-cat going up the harbour. 'Yeah, we've got him and he's owned up.' He turned back to me. 'But he's dying of AIDS, Jack. He'll be gone in three months at the outside. He's confessed to the murder and it's an open-and-shut case. But what's the point?'

I was slow on the uptake: 'The point of what?'

'Charging him. It could take nine months, a year, before we could bring him into court — he'll be long dead by then. It just opens up something that maybe Tom Barini's family and Tom's friend, Miss Ambar, would rather forget. I mean, having it all out in the open in court. A gay murder. Some papers still make a meal of that sort of stuff.'

'Some families want revenge. I've seen it, you've seen it.'

'Sure. While the killer is still alive. But this guy won't be.'

'So what do you do?'

The everyday surrounded us. Two joggers went by, sweating, breathing heavily, maybe their joints creaking. Ferries cruised by, suddenly wary as a large container ship, ugly as a brick wall, came downstream. Above us trains rumbled across the Bridge and there was the whirr of tyres like a humming of a wire with no music to it.

'We just close the file. We'll have the West Australian police tell his family what we've done and why. If they insist it all comes out, then we'll have to go along. There's also Miss Ambar. She shared the flat with him. Will she want it to come out in the open?'

'I don't know. She's never talked about it.'

'Do you want to talk to her about it?'

I took my time. 'No-o. No, I don't think I want to talk to her. Have you told anyone else about this?'

'No. And with everything else that's happened since — the pressure on Iraq, the Bali bombing — I don't think anyone remembers it, Jack. One thing George Rainone and I have learned: murder is soon forgotten. Except by those who are hurt by it.'

I took my time again; then said, 'Close the file. If ever she asks, maybe some time down the track, I'll tell her. But I don't think she'd ever want me reporting it on the news.'

'Good. Let's keep it between ourselves,' said Killick. 'We haven't seen you lately. You been away?'

2

Friday, after work, I bought another car, a two-year-old manual gear Alfa-Romeo convertible. It had had, the sales guy told me with transparent insincerity, only one owner, an elderly lady who drove it once a week to her bridge club. It had 28,000 ks on the clock, so her bridge club was in either Perth or Darwin. But it ran sweetly, the paintwork was unchipped and the interior looked almost new. And the price was right (mind your own business).

Saturday morning Mrs Golightly did not come in. I got my own breakfast, ran a cloth lightly over my shoes and packed my carry-all. I left the house and drove up to the local shopping centre. I bought a bottle of whisky and a bottle of French champagne; I had remembered that at dinner at Jasper's, Kate, like Adele, had started with a glass of champagne. I am, so the family say, tight with a dollar, but I can loosen up with people I respect and have affection for.

I drove out of the city for Bulinga Creek and the western slopes. It was a beautiful sunny day, just the day for a hood-down, sporty drive. I took the car up into the mountains, revelling in the gear changes and toeing-and-levelling the clutch as I overtook other cars, Flash Jack in his element. Then I heard the siren and saw the flashing red-and-blue lights in my rear-view mirror.

I pulled over and stopped. He was a young policeman, sober-faced but polite. 'The speed cameras timed you at 122 ks an hour, sir. The limit on this stretch is 100.'

'Sorry. I got carried away.'

'Yes, we all do that, sir. Even us, when we're chasing speedsters like you. Euphoria is catching. Your licence?'

I gave it to him, he wrote out a ticket and handed it to me.

'Thank you, Mr Shakespeare. Written any good plays lately?'

There are too many educated cops on the roads these days.

I drove on, more sedately. Once, far away on a ridge, I saw a bushfire getting under way, smoke rising like clouds being born in the trees. Then I was going down the western slopes, through Bathurst and Orange and out along the highway to Bulinga Creek, the land growing browner by the mile.

I turned into the avenue that led up to the homestead. Though it was spring the poplars looked as if they were waiting for winter; you could see through them; they needed Grandma Ambar there with her watering-can. The paddocks had grass in them, but it was just stubble, thin as the latest hairstyle among certain males back in Sydney. The cattle in the paddocks were thin and listless, their hides hanging on them as if on racks. Along the fence beside the avenue was a mob of sheep looking for what shade they could get from the poplars. They seemed to be leaning on each other, wool knitting itself together for strength.

I swung in before the house, got out of the car, took out my carry-all and my gifts. I sneaked a quick look at the garden; it looked as if it hadn't been watered in weeks. Then I went up the steps to Kate, who, gladdening my heart, didn't look as if she needed watering.

She kissed me. 'Welcome back. London looks as if it agreed with you.'

'I had good company. You look well.' I gave her the bottle of champagne and the bottle of whisky.

She kissed me again for the gifts, then led me into the house.

'I try to keep up appearances. Vanity, if you like . . . Luke's over at the Balgownies'. There's a stock sale on next week.'

'How are things?' The question was tentative; I was putting my foot into a pool that was drying up.

'Lousy, Jack. Terrible. But you didn't come up here to listen to our troubles . . . How's our girl?'

'Still dreaming. But I think she's losing heart. I was telling her the other night the advantages of Kirribilli —'

'We've sold that.' We were in the kitchen and she was making coffee. There was a plate of what looked like homemade cake on the table, something I hadn't seen since my mother had gone to New York. I would have to ask Mrs Golightly if she could bake a cake; she seemed capable of everything else. 'We haven't told Del.'

I said very carefully, 'Things are as bad as that?'

'Yes.' She poured the coffee, sat down at the big table across from me. This was the sort of kitchen you no longer saw, at least not in cities. Old-fashioned wooden cupboards and benches, not a square inch of Formica or granite anywhere; a big black oven-and-stove under a chimney: it had vases and decorated plates on it and obviously was no longer used; an electric stove-and-oven that somehow didn't look out of place; a sink and draining board that looked as if they had been there since the poplars out front had been mere sprigs. It was a statement of history and heritage and I found myself bending my knee to it. 'We're in danger of losing Bulinga Creek. Everything.'

'Shit,' I said.

She smiled, wryly. 'Indeed. But don't talk about it when Luke comes back. Tell us cheerful stories of London and our girl.'

'What happened? I mean, outside of the drought?' I was less careful now, wanting to *know*.

She pushed the cake towards me. 'I made it this morning. Coffee-and-cream — that's pure cream in the middle, none of your mock stuff squeezed out of a can ... What happened? Well, there's been the drought, that's stuffed everyone. Our friends, further out west, they're in real trouble, especially the grain farmers. Us? Luke lost a fortune with that company, Tonetel.'

'How'd he get into a gamble like that?' I should have asked Entwistle how he was handling his lost investment. Unless, of course, like all the wise directors in today's morality plays, he had got out well and truly paid. Shareholders were at last beginning to chant a war cry, Suckers of the World Unite! But many of them were too late. 'The IT game was always a bubble —'

'Jack, you're being wise after the event.'

'No, I was always — well, not *wise*. Sceptical. And I'm tight with the dollar, so I'm told. Are the banks breathing down your neck?'

'They're closer than that.' The slice of cake on her own plate was untouched, as if the cream in it had suddenly turned sour. 'They've got a noose round our necks.'

Suddenly she put her hand to her eyes and began to weep.

I got up, stumbling as I pushed my chair back, went round the table and held her in my arms. Then Luke walked in the back door.

He stopped, hung his hat on a row of hooks on the wall, then came and sat down on a chair next to Kate and took her hand. I let go of her, moved back to my own chair. I wanted to walk out of the room, out of the house, out of their lives. But that would be cowardice; and cruel. I wanted to marry their daughter, be part of them.

'She's told you?' Luke looked at me.

I nodded.

Then he gave his attention back to Kate. 'You all right, love?'

She dried her eyes, looked at me. 'Sorry, Jack. I'm not the teary sort —'

'I see a lot of tears in my game, Kate. I'm never embarrassed by them.' Made uncomfortable sometimes, but I was not going to tell her that.

Luke stood up. 'Jack and I are going for a walk. He can tell me about Del.'

So he and I went for a walk, down the long avenue of poplars that whispered in the slight breeze like gossiping neighbours. The paddocks stretched away on either side of us. A long line of kangaroos bounced gracefully along in the distance, like a moving frieze under a faded tapestry.

Luke said, almost as if talking to himself, 'I've seen more 'roos in the past three months than I've seen in the last three years. They're coming in, looking for something to eat. Thank Christ they're not carnivorous or they'd be at the stock. We want to shoot 'em all, but the animal-lovers down in the city are up in arms. No, that's the wrong word. They don't believe in arms against animals.'

The old city-versus-country issues; they went on all over the world. Except, of course, in countries where merely staying alive was the main issue. 'What happened, Luke? I mean, the Tonetel business —'

'I did a packet.' He was not as garrulous as usual; he, too, had dried up as the country had.

The breeze had freshened. Out in the paddocks dust rose in patches of brown mist, djinns waiting to pounce. The poplars stirred above us, bending a little at the tops. We walked in silence for almost a hundred metres, then Luke went on, 'I guess I got greedy. I kept reading about the money that was being made down in Sydney and Melbourne, kids who were millionaires at your age —'

I put on the mask of a grin: 'Not me, Luke. I'm comfortable, but no millionaire.'

He, too, managed a grin, patted my arm. 'No offence, Jack. Yeah, I fell for — what? The illusion? I guess that was it. I was going to make enough money to guarantee all this —' He waved an arm. 'All this forever. Now ...'

I had to ask: 'My boss, Entwistle, did he lose anything? Or did he get out before everything went belly-up?'

'I dunno, Jack. Maybe he did, maybe he didn't. There's going to be a class action, but we'll get bugger-all out of that.' We turned at the front gates, began to walk back. 'How's my girl? Our girl?'

'She's okay.'

'Don't tell her how things are with us.'

'Luke — when *are* you going to tell her? When the bailiffs come in, or whoever they send in these days? When everything's gone?'

'She's got her own problems.'

'No, Luke, she's got her dreams. Maybe they are the problem — well, yes, they are. But she'll never forgive you if you don't tell her the truth. I know her that well, Luke. I'm not as close to her as you are to Kate, but I *know* her. She's a dreamer, but she's not selfish.'

He walked in silence for a while, then he said, 'Okay, but not yet.'

We had lunch, just sandwiches and more cake. Then they left me to myself while Kate began cooking for dinner — 'We're having some friends over, you've met them' — and Luke went into his office to do his weekly books, where, I guessed, the red ink ran like blood. I didn't mind. I was part of the family, I could look after myself. I retreated to the verandah, settled myself into a chair and read the Saturday papers, our equivalent of London's Sunday papers.

I wandered into the kitchen late in the afternoon for scones (scones! How old-fashioned can you get?), homemade strawberry jam and tea (shades of summer afternoons in England). Kate was making soup — 'chilled dill and tomato. Luke's grandmother taught me this one, she was a great one for soups. She once heard that the Duchess of Windsor sneered at soup as *boring*. She instantly put the duchess in the same category as her stupid husband.'

'What else is on tonight?'

'Roast beef, three vegies. And key lime pie.'

'You must've known I was coming. My mother used to make that. Still does, in New York.'

'Did Adele feed you well?'

'Let's say she isn't in your or my mother's class. She did once make Bulinga Creek pasta sauce, said you'd taught her how.'

'What was it like?'

'The Italians are suing her.'

'I wish she'd come home,' said Kate and went back to cooking her tomatoes.

Dinner that night was a pleasure. I had met the three other couples on my previous visit; I kissed the women and shook hands with the men as if I belonged. There was no airy-fairy, smart-arse talk at the table; there was humour but not cocktail stuff. They talked of the 'dumb bastards' of both political parties, down in Sydney and Canberra; and that other 'dumb bastard' in the White House. I could not remember politicians, anywhere and at any level, ever being held in such low regard. They talked of the Bali bombing and the possibility of war in Iraq and the possible whereabouts of 'that other bastard bin Laden.' They did not talk about the drought. That was The Plague, to be avoided at a dinner party.

The weekend was, in a way, a homecoming. When I left on Sunday afternoon, I knew I would always be welcome here. If *here* survived . . .

'We'll be talking to Del tonight,' said Kate. 'We'll tell her how well you fit in here. She might get the message.'

'I hope so.'

She kissed me. 'Thanks for the champagne. I didn't open it at dinner. I'm going to take it to bed with me and get tipsy.'

'Don't fall asleep before I come in,' said Luke, and looked for the moment in good spirits.

Kate blew me another kiss, turned and went inside, hand to her eyes, and Luke walked me to my car. 'It's tough on her. I feel like a real bastard.'

'I'm sure she doesn't think that.'

He shrugged, then looked at the Alfa. 'Nice car.' Then he looked at me and said, 'Do you know how lucky you are, Jack?'

'I've started to realise it, yes.' I looked out and around us. The sun was still high in the sky; a small cloud drifted beneath it, like a mockery. Out in the far paddocks the mob of kangaroos had grown; cattle stood in a tight group watching them. Out on the highway an ambulance sped along, siren screaming, headlong towards another disaster. I turned back to Luke: 'How much longer can you hold on?'

He shrugged again, almost as if his shoulders were taking over from his tongue; all over the weekend he had been less, much less, voluble than before. 'The bank never asks that sort of question. The local manager is sympathetic, but his bosses down in Sydney ...' He spat into the dry earth of his garden: more bastards. 'Look after your money, Jack.'

'It's in jam jars under the bed,' I said, got into the Alfa and drove away. In the rear-vision mirror I saw him still standing in the driveway, growing smaller and smaller.

I climbed up into the mountains, drove sedately along the winding highway. The bushfire I had seen yesterday on a distant ridge had spread; there was a storm-bank of smoke that towered towards the sun. I passed the police car that had chased me yesterday and the young cop behind the wheel waved, approving my decorous speed. All the way back I was thinking ...

I called Adele as soon as I got home. She was still in bed, she said, the Sunday papers spread around her. 'Oh Jack, I wish you were here! This bed's so *big* —'

'Del, I've just come back from Bulinga Creek. I think you should come home.' I hadn't rehearsed being so blunt, it just came out.

She wasn't dumb; or maybe she had been thinking the same thing. 'It's as bad as that?'

'I think so. I couldn't get into the nitty-gritty with them, but I think they are broke, darling. Skint, stony broke. They're afraid of losing Bulinga Creek.'

She was silent a while, but I didn't press it; then she said, 'I'll leave as soon as I can. I'll call you.'

'Del, don't tell 'em I said anything. Let 'em think you'd already decided to come back.'

'Darling, I'm not dumb. I'm the prodigal daughter —'

I hung up, sat there in my bedroom in the solid house, every brick paid for, and wondered at my luck. She was coming home ...

3

I am reconstructing this from what Adele told me:

She hung up the phone, stared out the bedroom window at the river. She had come to love the Thames, a river of history. Its tides had carried great events, heroes and villains, playwrights and petty criminals. She loved London and England, where six weeks without rain was classed as a drought. And she loved what she was going to miss most, the theatre. But, sitting there on the bed, she decided she would not say goodbye to it all. She would come back. Maybe . . .

Thursday she had been to the reading of the David Hare play. She had done her best, thought she had been good enough to be called again. But as soon as the director and the producer had said, 'Thank you, Miss Ambar,' she had known she was off the list. Actors, practised in speech, know how to read other voices.

She had gone straight from the reading to the model agency that had called the day before. There were half a dozen other girls in the reception lobby: two young hopefuls with their portfolios, four girls with experience. But she was the star, if she wanted to be . . .

'It's lingerie, love,' said the agency manager. She was a woman who had started as a plain girl and manufactured herself into a fashion plate. 'It's Indello again, the outfit you did that fantastically wonderful spread for, you know, on the sides of buses.'

As if Adele needed reminding. But the other girls in the lobby sat up, especially the tyros. On the sides of buses! Fantastic!

'They want *you* — only you, they said — the money's fabulous, love —'

'Is it just a magazine spread?'

'No, darling, no! It'll be the magazines, yes, of course — *Vogue, Harper's Bazaar* — yes. But it'll be like that other campaign — on buses, billboards —'

'No.'

There was a sudden silence, as if Adele had passed wind, something models, of course, don't do.

'No? No what?'

'Just no,' said Adele and walked out with all the dramatic effect (she later told me) of Edith Evans exiting from *Hamlet*. The two young hopefuls looked after her with mouths and eyes wide open: oh, to be so much in demand one could pick and choose. The four experienced models just shook their heads and wondered why no one asked *them* to pose in lingerie, on the sides of buses or wherever.

Adele walked all the way home, in high heels, staggered into the apartment on feet that felt as if they had walked over two miles of hot coals. She fell onto the couch, lay there and wept: out of disappointment, frustration and loneliness. She had never felt so lonely.

Friday she moped about the apartment, her feet still sore. She called me, but I wasn't home and she didn't have the number of my new mobile. She knew she should be out looking for new accommodation, but that was beyond her the way she felt. She loved the apartment, taking its semi-luxury for granted after the first month in it. She sat on the tiny balcony, wrapped in a blanket against the chill of the autumn night, and watched a cruise boat slide by, all bright lights and cheery singing, revellers headed downstream, past the Tower of London where Anne

Boleyn had had her head chopped off, lucky girl, ending *her* frustration and disappointment. She was weeping again when she went inside, cursing herself for being so self-pitying. She still had that objectivity about herself in some regards. It just didn't extend to her dream.

Saturday she went out to see Milly Brown and Jeff. They lived in a flat in an old house in Swiss Cottage, an improvement on the flat in West Hammersmith. They had just come back from two weeks in Italy and were tanned and lazy and happy. She almost wept with envy; she was becoming very weepy and decided she had to put a stop to it. She kissed them and, for the day, loved them like a sister and brother.

They treated her to lunch at a restaurant in Hampstead and she got further down in the dumps. Judi Dench was at a far table, a Dame who, laughing and relaxed, was not playing the *grande dame*. Ian McKellen came in, was told he should have booked, and left without demur, a knight without a table, round or otherwise. In the far future, when *she* was a Dame, she would act with the same grace.

'— it's not the end of the world,' said Milly.

'What?'

'Being asked to pose nude. Well semi-nude. Nobody ever asks me to do that.'

'I do,' said Jeff and leered like a twelve year old.

Milly kicked him under the table. 'Del, you've got to start being practical. You can get plenty of work in TV. A producer guy was asking me about you the other day — where you've been hiding —'

'I haven't been *hiding*. No one's come looking for me.'

'Listen to her,' Milly said to Jeff, but her voice wasn't smug; she was showing the honesty of a real friend and Adele knew it. 'No one's come looking for her! Whoever comes looking for me?'

'I do,' said Jeff.

'Oh, for Crissakes, stop being such a — such a —'

Then Adele laughed and pressed the hand of each of them. 'I love you two. And I love you being in love.'

'She's missing Shakespeare,' Milly told Jeff. 'The one that's available.'

'I remember him,' said Jeff, face screwed up as if racking his memory. 'Nice bloke.'

'Don't rub it in,' said Adele and in the far corner Dame Judi Dench laughed as if she had heard.

Then on Sunday morning, her time, I rang her.

Monday she booked a flight to Sydney, leaving Thursday. She put the Morgan up for sale on the Internet and got a response that afternoon. He was a middle-aged Lothario, she said, trying to revive his youth, looking for the dolly birds of long ago. She gave him the sidelong glances, the purring voice and he fell for it and paid her what I had paid for it. He asked her out to dinner, but she told him she was going into a convent for a retreat and he gave up.

She relinquished the apartment, after making sure that the agents had a tenant wanting to move in. She transferred her money, plus the Morgan money, to her bank in Orange. She was, to her own surprise, rediscovering how practical she could be. She said goodbye to Milly and Jeff and her other friends. Then said goodbye to her agent: 'I don't know when I'll be back, Louise.'

Louise, whom I had met just once, was a tall angular woman with a face like a stretch of bad road and the disposition of someone who had driven over it. She had been handling actors for thirty years and had no time for stroking them nor consoling them. She told them when she took them on that acting was a mug's game, but there was no other game in the world if you had the acting bug. She was not unkind, just experienced.

'Take your time, love. If I got you work now, you'd have only half your mind on it. Some of my clients act that way anyway. But you have looks and a glimmer of talent —'

'A glimmer? That's all?'

'Adele, you think even the great ones began with anything more? Come back, love, and we'll start all over again. But cover up your arse if you want to be Edith Evans.' Then she smiled, the bad stretch of road almost smooth. 'But you looked great on the sides of those buses —'

'Up yours,' said Adele, ladylike, and kissed her goodbye.

She flew out Thursday night, farewelled by no one. She travelled business class, maybe her last extravagance she told herself. England fell away below her: a ribbon of light on a motorway, fields of darkness, a dream fading.

4

'Les,' I said, 'I'm taking a sickie Friday.'

'A sickie? You're healthier than Ian Thorpe.'

'I know that. But I've added it up and I have two weeks' sick leave due to me. So I'm taking a day of it. My girl's coming home —'

'Who fills in for you? We're short-staffed —'

'You can, Les. It's time we got a homely face in front of the camera, instead of handsome guys like me. I'm taking the day off, Les, regardless.'

He sat back in his chair, looking suddenly tired. He had been at the game forty years, seen and reported more crises than our political leaders had ever known or experienced.

'I could do with a year's sick leave. If you want to look at masochists of the world, son, look at editors.' He gestured at his desk and his computer screen. 'The shit of the world passes through us. And you want a sickie to see your girl?'

'Yes, Les, I do.'

He nodded, gave me a flicker of a smile and the day off. He promoted one of the girl trainees to take my place with Rupe and Suzy. I had seen them about, but so far since my return I had met none of them. If staff were being downsized, I wondered how long the trainees would survive.

Then Kate called me on my mobile: 'Will you meet her, Jack? We're having a problem up here.'

'What sort of problem?' Had the bank moved in, were the bailiffs gathering like vultures? Oh, how we had come to hate banks!

But she didn't elaborate. 'Meet her, Jack. Bring her up Saturday?'

'How's Luke?'

But she had hung up. I clicked off my mobile, sat back at my desk, stared at my computer. No message there, no daily homily. No *Today will be a better day*. No *Scorpio is in the ascendancy*. I would probably find more hope in a Chinese cracker. Then I looked up at the pretty blonde girl who stood beside me. 'Yes?'

'Jack, I'm Cressida Hartney.' I looked blank and she went on, stumbling a little: 'I'm to take your place — I mean I'm to stand in for you tomorrow. I understand you're not feeling well —'

'Sick as a dog. Sit down, Cressida.'

She did so, rather awkwardly. She was a looker, all right, but out of the current mould: long blonde hair, regular features, good figure, dress just right. Her voice was too light, but that was not a criterion at Channel 15. Looks were what we sold.

'You'll find Rupe and Suzy good to work with. When did you join us?'

'A month, no, six weeks ago. I've always dreamed of being on camera as a reporter, ever since I was in year seven at school and saw Kate Adie, you know, from the BBC or ITN, I forget which —'

Another dreamer; and I had to fly the flag: 'There have been some good Aussie girls on TV.'

'Oh, yes, I know.' She wasn't going to be branded unAustralian, the latest badge of shame. 'But you have to go overseas to really make it, don't you think? You've been there. I saw what you did in Afghanistan and New York, that September Eleven thing, and then London —'

She should be writing my reviews; so far I'd had none, except Les Dibley's. 'Dream on, Cressida. How'd you come by that name?'

'My mother loved Shakespeare.'

Time to go.

That night Dad rang from New York. 'I'm as busy as a blue-arsed fly. This Iraq business — you fellers interested in it?'

'Channel 15 or the nation?'

'That answers my question. I think you may be covering a war pretty soon, Jack. The White House lot are getting impatient. And Ten Downing Street, which surprises a lot of people here — Tony Blair is beginning to sound like Baroness Thatcher. The French, as usual, are being very French, the Russians are being Russian and the Germans are being German. Which seems to be surprising the Americans.' He laughed, like a cracked bell. 'Jack, when I come home —'

'When *are* you coming home?'

'When all this kerfuffle is over — and Christ knows when that will be. A coupla years — who knows? But when I do, I want to find a nice cushy job with no politics.' There was a faint sound down the line that I took to be a sigh. 'I'm tired, Jack.'

Parents, it seemed, were falling apart. Then Mum came on: 'Take no notice of him, he's enjoying every minute of it. I'm the one who's tired — lunches and dinners every day. I do more entertaining than Mrs Bush and all she has to prepare is hominy grits. Talk about screwing someone's arm — he's at it every day and loving it.'

'Women!' said Dad on the extension. 'I wonder what it would have been like working for Boadicea or Catherine the Great?'

'Catherine was nymphomaniacal —'

'I don't like the way this is going,' said my mother. 'Let's change the subject. How's Adele?'

'She's coming home tomorrow.'

A silence for a moment, then: 'She's given up?'

'I don't really know, Mum. The main reason she's coming back is that things aren't too good at Bulinga Creek. The bank is closing in. The drought and other things —'

'What other things?' asked Dad, still the investigative reporter. I wondered if he asked the French and the Russians and the Germans such blunt questions when they came to lunch or dinner. And knew that he would, blunt but oiled.

'Her father got into some IT stock —'

'Oh, tell him to come over here. The Land of the Free and Easy. Another stockbroker went to jail this week —'

'Give our love to Adele,' said my mother and hung up.

I could see her turning to Dad and either taking him in her arms or clouting him over the ear. Either way, it would be a love gesture.

Chapter Eleven

1

I went out to the airport on Friday with a mixture of feeling: anticipation, excitement, trepidation. Would this be just a temporary return, a gesture of concern for her parents? Would I be just the post to lean on while she was here, Jack the Reliable? Rosencrantz or Guildenstern?

She came through the arrivals gate looking like a queen. No denim jeans for her, no trainers on the feet, no looking as if she had just come from the dole office. Not at all: camel-hair coat, trouser-suit, shirt, the obligatory silk scarf: they don't travel like that no more, no more. People stared at her, wondering why they didn't recognise her.

I took her in my arms, feeling for the moment like the guy who had just won the lottery. 'Rosencrantz at your service.'

'Bullshit,' she said and kissed me, hard. 'Oh God!'

Oh God; but she said no more. Just linked her arm in mine as I wheeled her luggage out to the parking lot, to the Alfa. Several people looked at us, but, God help me, they were recognising me, not her. I gave them a smile as a tip.

She stood back to look at the car. 'Yours? A new car?'

'Pre-loved by a little old bridge-playing lady. Did you sell the Morgan?'

'For what you paid for it. The guy said I should've been up the Euston Road selling cars.'

We got into the car and then I took stock. I said carefully, 'Are you home for good?'

She said just as carefully, 'I'm not home yet.'

'Yes, you are. As soon as you came through that gate, you were home.'

Cars were pulling away from us on either side, full of welcome home, welcome home! A girl about to get into a car turned towards us, a bright smile lighting up her face, including us in her delight to be back where she belonged. The sun shone on us, another welcome.

'Jack, can't we wait till I see Mum and Dad? You haven't told me what the real situation is up there —'

I started up the car. The hood was down and she tied the scarf round her head. I put on my checked cap. We looked, I guessed, a debonair pair without a care in the world.

'I'm not sure, myself. But it's grim, darling. Very grim.'

She was silent for several kilometres, staring straight ahead, not looking around her. The trip in from the airport to the city is not exciting: small factories, warehouses, some drab houses amongst them like relics of another time. And, I noticed if she didn't, too many For Sale or For Lease signs.

Going over the Harbour Bridge she showed some excitement. 'Let's swing off here, go over to Kirribilli! I've still got my key —'

'Darling … Kirribilli is gone. They had to sell it.'

She was wearing dark glasses, but the frown above them was as plain as a new scar. 'Sold it? The flat?'

I nodded. 'I think Bulinga Creek may be the next one on the market.'

Bad news, tragic news, should never be delivered while driving. I felt my attention waver as she clutched my arm; I had to concentrate as if I had just had a nervous spasm. I didn't look at her, but *felt* her sudden silence.

We must have travelled another couple of kilometres before she said, 'They never let me know.'

'I don't know what's happening up there now. They asked me to bring you up tomorrow. Tomorrow, not today. As if they are — I *hope* as if they are planning a pleasant surprise. Maybe the bank is listening to them after all —'

'I hope so.'

We arrived at Longueville and I took her and her luggage inside. I dropped the luggage and hugged her. It was as if we had been apart for a year, instead of little more than a week. Maybe the distance between us had something to do with it. It's hard to feel physical at 10,000 kilometres or whatever it is between here and there.

When we came up for breath she looked around. 'The last time I was here was the night Tom —'

'Don't talk about it. I'll make some coffee.'

We went into the kitchen. There was a note from Mrs Golightly on the table: *I don't think you want me here today. I've cleaned your shoes. Again.*

'Who's Mrs Golightly?'

'A ninety-kilo treasure.'

She sat down and said, 'Have they found Tom's murderer yet?'

I busied myself with cups and saucers, got sugar out of a cupboard, found some store-bought cake that Lynne had put away in the biscuit tin. 'It's only instant —'

'Jack,' she said very deliberately, 'have they found Tom's murderer yet?'

Behind me the electric kettle was boiling. 'Yes ...' Then I told her what Sergeant Killick had told me. 'You don't want to go into court, do you?'

'Why didn't you tell me? You weren't going to, were you?'

I poured hot water into the cups, put them on the table, sat down. All very deliberate, taking my time. 'Del, do you feel any better, now you know they've caught the guy? The murder is history — but no one remembers it. Yeah, I feel better, knowing they've caught the guy. But I won't feel any better if it all becomes public. And neither will you.'

She stirred her coffee. 'I take milk, remember?'

I had forgotten. I got up, got milk from the fridge. For the past hour or so we had been fencing with each other. I felt uncertain with her, as if she were between planes, coming and going.

'Jack, what are you protecting me from?'

I took my time, stirring my own coffee. 'I don't know. You've had a lot of disappointment —'

She reached for my hand. 'Darling, I'm not *weak*. Dense sometimes, maybe stupid. But I'm not weak.'

I lifted her hand and kissed it, which was the only answer I could give without breaking down.

Then she said, 'I'd like to call them, Mum and Dad.'

'Go into my bedroom, there's a phone there.'

I didn't want to be privy to what she said to them. She was on the phone for ten minutes, then she came out to the kitchen again. 'They're okay. I spoke to Mum — Dad's out on the run somewhere. Can we leave first thing in the morning? Early?'

'Sure. Early as you like.'

She kissed me. 'Let's go to bed.'

Later I got out of bed, left her sleeping, and went out to the kitchen, pulling on a tracksuit and a pair of trainers. I had a glass of orange juice, left a note on the kitchen table, let myself out the back door and went down the side passage into the street. It was another beautiful day; out on the water a lone sculler went downstream, elegant to watch.

I walked for half an hour, sorting out the jumble-box that was my mind. She was back — but for how long? She had come back because of her parents, not because of me. I was bound to her in a way that only that other Shakespeare could describe.

To die upon a kiss . . . I knew then that if she went back to London, I would follow. Chasing my own dream . . .

She was in the kitchen, in a dressing-gown, when I got back. Her hair was loose and untidy, she wore no make-up; a woman in a dressing-gown, first thing in the morning, is not the most seductive sight. But I looked at her and she was the Queen of Sheba.

'Let's spend the rest of the day here,' she said. 'Maybe we'll go for a walk, so I can stretch my legs. I'll cook something for dinner ... Let's stay in and just be *us*.'

Then at six o'clock that evening the phone rang. I went into my bedroom, expecting it to be Les Dibley, telling me there was an emergency to be covered. But it was Kate.

'Can you come up now? Luke hasn't come home —'

'Kate, what are you saying?' I could hear the distress in her voice.

'He's been gone all day. He's not answering his mobile — I've called everyone — no one has seen him —'

'We'll leave right away.'

I hung up, stood for almost a minute, the mind jumbled again. Then I went back into the living room where Adele, seated on the couch, feet drawn up under her, was watching the Channel 7 news. She saw the concern on my face and clicked off the remote control.

'What is it?'

'I think we'd better head for Bulinga Creek.'

2

It took us ages to get out of the city sprawl. There was a pile-up on the major road out and it was almost dark, despite daylight saving, before we were on the motorway heading west. We climbed into the mountains as the light died; on a distant ridge, as last weekend, a bushfire blazed like a warning of disaster to come. We hardly spoke, just sat there beside each other as we headed — for what? The suicide of her father?

I dared not think of that, pushing it away each time it crept into my mind. Luke Ambar, I'd have said, was not the suicidal type; it would have been against his nature and his pride. And yet I had covered cases of men, and women, who had committed suicide out of pride or the ruining of it.

As we went along the crest of the mountains lightning flashed down to the south-east: another portent. 'Let's hope that brings rain,' I said for something to break our silence.

'What?' She had been a long way from me; but she recovered. 'Let's hope so. I remember as a kid I used to stand out in a paddock waiting to be struck.'

'Why, for Crissake?'

'I used to think it would be so dramatic, to die from lightning. Better than dull old measles or mumps.'

'Jesus, you must have been a pain — Edith Evans at six and a half!'

But then we were laughing and the mood had lightened and we went down the slopes and out through the towns to Bulinga Creek, hope rising, if only inch by inch.

All the lights in the big house were on as we drove up between the poplars. Kate must have been waiting for the approach of our headlights, for she was standing on the front verandah, came running down the steps to us as we pulled up. She had always struck me as a woman who took her time, would never hurry, but she was in full flight as she came to us. Adele struggled out of the car and the two of them hugged each other, Kate clutching at Adele as if she were drowning. I got out of the car, but stood on my own side of it till they had separated. They were both crying.

'Is he back?' I said.

Kate shook her head, dried her eyes. 'No. He went out first thing this morning — he took the ute, not the Range Rover. The police have been out all afternoon, but they've called off the search till dawn tomorrow. Come in. The Ellwoods are here, and Mum and Dad. Everyone's been so supportive. It's just not like Luke ...'

The Ellwoods had been at the dinner last weekend. They were country born and bred, a handsome couple in their forties. Kate's parents, Joe and Mollie Verard, were older and heavier, but in Mollie one could see where Kate's and Adele's beauty had come from. Joe was a retired stock-and-station agent and they lived in town, in Orange.

I was introduced to them and Mollie looked me up and down as her husband had once looked cattle and sheep up and down. Then she nodded to Adele: 'He'll do.'

Dave Ellwood and Joe Verard took me out to the kitchen for a beer.

'Leave the women alone for a while. They cry more freely when we're not around.' Joe gave me a beer. It was evidently taken for granted that real men, even a TV reporter, drank beer. 'It's a bugger, all this. I just can't believe Luke has gone off and caused all this bloody misery. His old man would've shot him. No, I shouldn't have said that.' I knew that Luke's parents were dead. 'He wants a kick in the arse when he comes back. He's in trouble, deep shit, but so are a lot of other people. I'm just glad I got out when I did.'

'He's done a packet in an investment down in Sydney,' I said for something to say. I was feeling my way here, an immigrant in my own land.

'More fool him,' said Dave Ellwood. I knew he was a grain farmer, that his crops this year had been not much more than stubble. 'I wouldn't trust those corporate bastards with a raffle ticket.'

But I sensed that, though they were criticising Luke, wanted to kick him in the arse, they were genuinely concerned for him, wanted him back in one living piece.

Then Rose Ellwood and Mollie Verard came into the kitchen. 'Adele tells us you haven't eaten. We'll get something —'

'Anything,' I said to be polite. 'Pop something in the microwave.'

Mollie looked affronted and Rose, a good-looking brunette, laughed. 'You've just insulted her. She's old-style Country Women's Association. If it's not cooked on a proper stove, it ain't cooked.'

Mollie shook her grey curly head. 'Progress is killing this country.' But she laughed as she said it, then waved her hands. 'Go on, get out of the kitchen.'

The four of them left an hour later, promising to be back first thing in the morning. Kate, Adele and I washed up the dinner things, then went into the living room. Only then did I notice that pillows and blankets had been brought into the room.

'Del and I aren't going to bed,' said Kate. 'We'll doss down here. Just in case Luke comes back during the night.'

'I can sleep in a chair —'

'No,' said Adele and took my arm and led me into a bedroom. 'Let me and Mum —'

'Keep watch?'

She nodded. 'I want to be with her, Jack. You understand?'

I kissed her. 'I think when he comes back he'll probably weep, seeing the two of you together waiting for him.'

She kissed me back, said softly, 'I love you,' and went out to keep vigil with her mother.

I went to bed, glad to crawl into it. Before I turned out the light I looked about the room. It, like the rest of the house, was old-fashioned: wardrobe, chest of drawers, a (so help me) rocking chair. On the walls were three faded sepia photos: Bulinga Creek of the past. One was a shot of the avenue, the poplars no taller then than a man. I turned out the light.

I was tired, but I slept fitfully, one ear awake for the male voice coming into the house. But it didn't come and when I woke at seven, Adele and Kate were already up and out in the kitchen. They were at breakfast when I stood in the doorway in my pyjamas, part of the family.

I raised my eyebrows, somehow afraid to voice the question, and they both shook their heads. Worry and the night had worn them out; their faces were strained, their eyes dull. Am I wrong, or does beauty fade quicker than plainness?

I left them, found a bathroom, showered, dressed and when I came out to the kitchen again a police officer was there with them. It was Inspector Hardman, the man I had worked with on the terrible smash out on the Mitchell Highway. He nodded to me as if it was natural I should be there.

'They've found Luke's ute about seven miles from here,' said Kate. She sounded in control, but I could see it was an effort. 'A helicopter sighted it.'

'And Luke?'

'No sign of him,' said Hardman.

'His gun is missing from the cabin,' said Adele. 'He always had it in a rack behind the seat.'

On that Kate abruptly walked out of the kitchen. I hesitated, then followed her, down the long central hallway and out onto the front verandah. She didn't look at me, just stood staring down the long avenue of poplars as if expecting him to be coming up towards her.

'He'll be back,' she said, as if talking to herself.

There was a police car in the driveway, a young uniformed officer standing beside it. He looked up at Kate, waved a tentative hand, and, almost automatically, she waved back.

'Kate, you've got to believe that —'

'I am believing it,' she said fiercely; then looked at me. 'Jack, I'll die without him —'

I took her hand as Adele came out with Inspector Hardman. 'Jack, drive me out to the ute. I'll bring it back. Stay here, Mum, in case he comes back while we're gone . . .'

'Of course,' said Kate, as if she had thought of nothing else.

'I'll come with you,' said Hardman and went down to the police car as a Landcruiser came up the avenue. It was the Ellwoods, come again to lend support.

'Good luck,' said Dave Ellwood. 'You'll find him, Del.'

She nodded and settled in beside me in the Alfa. We went down between the poplars, following the police car out along the road heading north-east. This was open country, parched from the drought, and some timbered slopes. A helicopter flew over us, hovered for a moment or two, then flew on ahead. There was no sign of any media trucks or cars and I was glad of that; this was personal, to be kept in the family. Neither of us spoke: words had lost their value, even as comfort. Then the police car was slowing, turning in through another gate opened for them by another cop.

We followed, pulled up as Hardman got out of the police car and came back to us. 'It's up there, Del, under those trees. I'll have one of my guys take it back.'

She was looking around her, frowning. 'Dad used to bring me out here when I was a kid —'

'Did he take you to a favourite spot or anything?'

I had listened to this sort of questioning a dozen times, listened to strangers answering.

'Not here. But yes — over near Ophir —' She was trying to recapture childhood, not as easy as one thinks, even for those of us only a decade or two out of it. We are too deep in the present. 'He would take me to see the diggings where my great —' She stumbled for a moment, losing count of the generations. 'Where the first gold strikes were made, where the Ambar money started.'

'How'd you get there?'

'We'd walk — up over that hill ...'

Hardman looked back up at the tree-covered hill. 'Christ, all that way? It must be five or six ks to the diggings.'

'He used to tell me that Grandpa Luke — he's named after him — he walked it, all the way from town.'

'Okay, you stay here, we'll do the walk, use the chopper. Stay here with her, Jack. You got a mobile?'

I held it up.

'No,' said Adele, clambering out of the car. I noticed she was wearing flat-heeled shoes, as if she had been expecting to take a walk. 'I'm coming with you, Inspector. Come with me, Jack.'

I was dressed for walking, as if for back home: tracksuit, trainers. I had put it all on without thinking, a morning habit that now proved useful. I got out of the car, stuck my mobile in the top of my pants, and we began to walk up the hill to — what would we find? I dared not think about that.

There were other police, half a dozen of them, and the helicopter kept circling overhead. I had learned, through experience, not to knock the police. Sure, there are bad apples in the bin and some of them are heavy-handed and maybe racist, but they do jobs that the rest of us are never called upon to undertake. Like finding suicides ...

The going was rough and the heat was growing. We passed through the shade of the trees and came out on open slopes. Hardman stopped every so often to get his breath and wipe his face. He was in uniform shirt and trousers and wore a hat instead of a cap; the armpits and the back of his shirt were dark with sweat. Adele was feeling it too, but there was no complaint. All my walking around Longueville was paying off. Several times magpies, nesting, came out of the trees at us, black-and-white dive bombers, till one of the cops took out his pistol and fired it. The birds went back to the trees, sat on the branches and eyed us like — like the Taliban in Afghanistan. Flies came back from wherever they go in winter and hovered around us, tasting our sweat.

After the shot, we all stopped, listening. But if Luke had heard it, he didn't fire off one in reply. The silence only seemed to increase. We walked on.

Adele walked steadily, sometimes taking my hand as we clambered up a steep rise. Sometimes she stopped to get her breath, and once she flinched as if she had pulled a muscle. But there was no hint of her giving up; we were going to find her father.

Then at last we came upon the first of the old diggings. We were not within sight of the small town of Ophir; that was somewhere over the hills ahead of us. We stopped as Adele held up a hand and looked around us.

My first impression was that we had come upon an old battlefield. There were short trenches dug into the hillside; overgrown openings that looked like dugouts. Yet a hundred and fifty years ago these hills had been overrun with fortune-hunters, the first Luke Ambar amongst them. There had probably been fights, fierce ones, but no wars.

Out of holes in the ground like these had come fortunes and history.

'We used to come here ...' Adele was reviving memories. 'Grandpa Luke's digging was somewhere up there.'

She pointed up a dry creek bed that ran down from the right. I nodded to Hardman. 'Let's go up there, Gerry. No, you stay here, Del. We'll find him.'

Alive, I hoped. She didn't argue, sat down on a rock and one of the young officers handed her a water bottle. She drank from it, then looked up at me. 'Find him, Jack —'

I pressed her shoulder and went on after Hardman, who, accompanied by a young officer, had already begun to climb up the creek bed. The helicopter hovered overhead till Hardman stopped and waved it away. It swung away immediately and almost at once silence fell on us again, almost tangible. We climbed on without talking; in the creek bed the heat seemed to be concentrated. We passed a cave, rotted timbers framing a tunnel dark as lost dreams.

Then, five minutes further up the creek, we found him. He was sitting on the ground in the entrance to another opening, leaning back against a wooden post, his rifle on the ground beside him. We pulled up and stood there without a word, Hardman, the young cop and myself; like a jury, I thought, but we passed no judgement. The cawing of a crow somewhere out of sight only highlighted our silence.

He looked up at us, silent too for a long moment. Then he said, 'G'day. I've really buggered things, haven't I?'

3

I carried his gun as we walked him back down the creek. It was fully loaded and I wondered how many times he had lifted it to his head while he had been slumped there at the doorway to where all the Ambar fortunes had begun. He was walking ahead of me, between Hardman and the young officer, his head bent and shoulders slumped. Once he stumbled and almost fell, but the young cop grabbed his arm and held him up.

Then we were coming out of the creek bed and Adele was rising from the rock she had been sitting on. I thought I heard her cry out, but I couldn't be sure; another crow cawed at the same time and somewhere a magpie carolled. Then Luke was stumbling towards her and they clashed in an embrace.

Hardman, the young officer and I turned away. I looked back up the creek bed, history run dry. I unhitched my mobile from my trouser-band and called Kate.

'He's safe.'

Chapter Twelve

1

Adele and Luke were in the back of the Alfa, I behind the wheel, the family chauffeur. They held hands and hardly spoke as we followed the police cars down the long road to the entrance to Bulinga Creek. There, Gerry Hardman, not getting out of the lead car, waved to us. Then the five cars went on back to town and I turned the Alfa into the avenue of poplars.

'I won't know what to say to her,' said Luke.

'Don't say anything,' said Adele. 'Let her do all the talking.'

In the rear-vision mirror I saw Luke, for once without words, nod and smile wryly.

Kate and the Ellwoods and the Verards were waiting for us on the verandah. I pulled the car in before the steps and Kate ran down them. Adele and I sat while Luke got out. The Ellwoods and Verards stood on the top step. We were an audience, a reluctant one.

Luke and Kate hugged each other, both weeping. Other people's emotion is contagious. The Ellwoods and the Verards came down the steps, patted Luke on the back and went across to their vehicles. They got into them and drove away. I noticed that both Rose Ellwood and Mollie Verard were weeping.

Then as Kate and Luke, arms round each other, seemingly oblivious of us, went up into the house, Adele said to me, 'Let's go for a walk.'

'You must be buggered —'

'I am. But I want to leave them alone ...' She got out of the car. 'Come on. I'll show you where I used to stand waiting for the lightning to strike me.'

'Jesus,' I said, but followed her.

We walked round the side of the house, out through the yards, past the sheds and down through a long paddock to an earth-dam now just a large puddle. At the end of the paddock cattle stood in the shade of a few trees, watching half a dozen kangaroos loping towards a distant fence, going over it in a long graceful bound, looking for pasture, anything to eat, further out. High in the cloudless sky an eaglehawk planed just as gracefully, silent music in the air.

'The dam was always full in those days,' said Adele, not remembering other droughts; or putting them out of her mind. 'I'd stand here and wait for the lightning to strike me, then I'd fall into the dam and they'd find me drowned.'

'You must've been a happy little Vegemite. If I'd known you then, I'd have smacked your arse. What did your mum and dad think?'

'They never knew.' She looked around her, at the paddocks stretching away to distant ridges, at what, if it all could be saved, would belong to her. 'Jack, I'm going to try and save as much of this as I can. It may be hopeless, but I'm going to try . . .'

'If I can help —' I tried not to make it sound like an empty gesture.

'Maybe just a little. I transferred money to my account in town, from London. I've still got three-quarters of that Indello money. I don't know what it is in Aussie dollars, but it must be six figures.'

'You can add the Morgan money to it.' And more, I added silently. But even as I said it, I could feel the debt around us, like a sea of dust.

'I don't know how big a hole Dad has dug, but maybe we can scrape enough to hold things off for a while — till the drought breaks —'

She was whistling into the wind, but I wasn't going to tell her that. Not out there, beside the empty dam where she had once waited for lightning to strike. 'Let's go back, see how they are.'

Hand in hand, we went back up to the house. Kate and Luke, composed now, were waiting for us. I felt a sudden belonging with them.

'Jack and I will get lunch,' said Adele. She kissed her father. 'You must be starving.'

'He just devoured me,' said Kate and laughed, happy as a new bride.

Over lunch, at the coffee and cake stage, Adele said, 'Dad, how much do you owe the bank?'

He shook his head. 'Too much, so don't let's spoil things by discussing it.'

'No.' I don't think I had ever seen her as firm as this. 'If we pay whatever interest is due, maybe we can stave them off.'

'For how long?' Even Kate looked resigned.

'Till we can organise our own sale of whatever has to go. We don't want a fire sale, which is what'll happen if the bank kicks us out. Dad, I've got money in the bank in town. We'll go in Monday and talk to the bank. Pay the interest, buy time —'

Luke looked at me. 'Did you teach her all this?'

'No, he didn't!' Adele snapped. 'I did two years of farm management, remember? I remember a few things they taught me. I earned fifty thousand US dollars for having myself spread half-naked along the sides of London buses. I hated it — the display, even the money. But now I'm going to use it. For farm management!'

Kate looked at her daughter, then at Luke and me. 'I think she means it.'

'Bloody oath I do!' said Adele in a vulgar but effective way that Edith Evans would never have achieved.

Later, when Kate and Luke had gone for a walk, Adele and I were in the kitchen washing up. She was at the sink, washing the plates, and I was wielding the tea-towel. I don't know why we hadn't put everything in the dishwasher; it was as if, standing there beside the sink and the draining board, we were a couple. She stopped for a moment and looked out through the window, at the yards and, beyond them, Kate and Luke in the distance.

'Jack . . .' She turned to me, rubber-gloved, soapy dish in her hand, hair down over one eye. 'Will you marry me?'

2

That was four months ago.

We were married a month after she proposed. Dad couldn't get away from the UN, but Mum came home for the wedding. It was held at Bulinga Creek, the local priest agreeing to marry us in the homestead. Adele didn't argue about what service we should have; she was quite happy for R C rites. Lynne, stout with pregnancy, and Nick, who was my best man, drove Mum up for the occasion.

'I'm glad it's happened,' Mum told me. 'I had begun to think she would never —'

'I was never in doubt,' I said, lying like a politician.

'Liar,' she said, recognising one.

Friends came from around the district. Even Les Dibley and his wife drove up from Sydney for the day.

'It's about time, son,' he said. 'You couldn't have made a better choice.'

'Actually, she chose me. How long do I get for my honeymoon?'

'A week, Jack, no more. You're on standby. If Bush and Howard and Blair go into Iraq, you're headed that way. I've talked God and the board into sending our own team to Baghdad or wherever. There are already rumours that, if and when it happens, the media guys will be embedded with the army units. Have you ever heard such bullshit? *Embedded.* But that's where you'll be, son. Embedded with some unit and, whether you like it or not, you'll be their PR man. You'll never dare criticise them. The good old days are gone, Jack. I was just a boy reporter in

Vietnam, but we told the truth out there. General Westmoreland hated our guts — the Five O'Clock Follies, the press conferences, were a joke. But we got away with the truth. Try for that, son, as much as you can.'

So Rupe Hellinger and I are on standby, waiting for the pre-emptive strike: lovely phrase. I have no time for Saddam Hussein, but, like Dad, I feel the UN should be given more time. Osama bin Laden has disappeared, gone like a character written out of the drama. Afghanistan is almost a forgotten war now, just another in its long litany of wars, only the warlords keeping echoes alive by warring amongst themselves. What keeps it alive for Rupe and me is the memory of Jason's death.

Bulinga Creek has been saved, but only just. Farm management expert Adele Ambar staved off the bank and, with the help of her grandfather Joe Verard, organised the selling-off of most of the acreage. Buyers came up from the city, men who had made their money there, and outbid the locals, who had little to spend anyway. The drought is still with us, stretching away hundreds of miles to the west, the worst in a century. Prayers for rain fall on the deaf ears of God. Not Entwistle.

While I've waited for the posting to Iraq, news-gathering has gone on. I have interviewed a middle-aged idiot who is speed-reading the sixteen volumes of *Remembrance Of Things Past* — he was glassy-eyed and talked at two-hundred words a minute; and Les Dibley, swearing at the same speed, canned it. I have reported on bushfires all around Sydney and down around Canberra. I did stories on unrest in the refugee detention camps. I have covered traffic carnage, murders and suicides. Sometimes I have struggled for words, but the images have gone out, punching the eye.

Kate and Luke are still at Bulinga Creek, still in the homestead, still with the avenue of poplars leading up to it. They now have only 300 hectares; enough, if and when the drought breaks, to keep them comfortable. History, family history, has been preserved.

Adele and I live at Longueville, will stay there till my parents come home at the end of the year. She is doing some part-time modelling, but mostly she is content to be a housewife. We go to the theatre and movies and went to see another play by Chekhov, another man on the edge of tides.

Sometimes, when she is unaware that I am watching her, she puts down the magazine or book she is reading and stares into the distance. Into the past ...

Once she looked at me and said softly, 'I'm sorry, Jack.'

'Sorry for what?'

'That I took so long to wake up. Wasting so much time dreaming ...'

I took her in my arms. 'No regrets, understand? No regrets.'

Time regretted is time wasted. But I know there will always be dreams in her, like a cancer in remission, and I shall have to guard her and myself against them.

Wish me luck ...

The Sundowners

JON CLEARY

The Sundowners tells the story of outback family the Carmodys as they travel around Australia, shearing, droving, trying to make ends meet and find that one special place they can settle down in. Along the way, Paddy, his wife Ida, and their son Sean meet some of the most memorable characters in modern fiction.

First published in the UK in 1951, the novel went on to be translated into several foreign languages and adapted into a highly successful feature film. It has now sold over three million copies worldwide. It is a book filled with kindness and happiness as well as toughness and danger, and is set against the magnificent backdrop of the wild, harsh and beautiful Australian landscape. Superbly written and deeply moving, it showcases one of Australia's most talented authors.

AVAILABLE AT ALL
GOOD BOOKSTORES

Degrees of Connection

JON CLEARY

Scobie Malone is back, with a new promotion and a new and bewildering murder to unravel.

No one particularly likes Natalie Shipwood, head of the supremely successful Orlando development company. But when her private secretary, Marilyn Hyx, is found murdered in her own home, it seems someone might be trying to tell Natalie something ... especially when it turns out that Orlando's success isn't quite what it's cracked up to be.

Through the murky world of rumour, leaked documents, creative accounting, sinister connections and Security Commission investigations, Malone and Clements track the killer.

And then another murder occurs, one that touches Scobie's family, and tests his loyalties to the very limit.

'A born writer ... Cleary is a grand entertainer.'
Weekend Australian

AVAILABLE AT ALL
GOOD BOOKSTORES